The
Bromance
Book Club

The *Bromance* Book Club

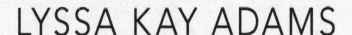

LYSSA KAY ADAMS

JOVE

New York

A JOVE BOOK
Published by Berkley
An imprint of Penguin Random House LLC
penguinrandomhouse.com

Copyright © 2019 by Lyssa Kay Adams

Library of Congress Cataloging-in-Publication Data

Names: Adams, Lyssa Kay, author.
Title: The bromance book club / Lyssa Kay Adams.
Description: First edition. | New York : Jove, 2019. |
Series: The bromance book club ; 1
Identifiers: LCCN 2019006240 | ISBN 9781984806093 (pbk.) |
ISBN 9781984806109 (ebook)
Subjects: | BISAC: FICTION / Romance / Romantic Comedy. |
FICTION / Romance / Sports. | FICTION / Women. | GSAFD: Love stories.
Classification: LCC PS3601.D385 B76 2019 | DDC 813/.6—dc23
LC record available at https://lccn.loc.gov/2019006240

First Edition: November 2019

Printed in the United States of America
1 3 5 7 9 10 8 6 4 2

Cover art by Jess Cruickshank
Cover design by Colleen Reinhart
Book design by Elke Sigal

To Grandma

*I definitely crapped a worm with
a bell on it this time, didn't I?*

ACKNOWLEDGMENTS

Writing and publishing a novel is a team effort. I wouldn't be living this dream without the help and support of so many people who deserve thanks.

First, thank you to my family, who has encouraged and supported me every day of my life. Mom, you have never let me forget what my dreams are or let me doubt that I can make them happen. To my husband: It was a scary leap of faith when I decided to write full time. You've been there every step of the way to make sure I could live this crazy dream. And Dad, my break-glass-in-case-of-emergency, thanks for always being the calm captain at the helm of the ship.

Huge thanks to my agent, Tara Gelsomino. You plucked me out of a Twitter pitch-fest and made all of this happen. Thank you for your guidance, your sense of humor, and your belief in my Bromance boys! And, of course, an equally huge thank-you to my wise, enthusiastic, and wickedly funny editor, Kristine E. Swartz, who fought hard to bring *The Bromance Book Club* to readers.

ACKNOWLEDGMENTS

My writing tribe, who has kept me sane (or some approximation of it): Meika Usher, Christina Mitchell, Alyssa Alexander, Victoria Solomon, Tamara Lush, and all the women of the Binderhaus. I love you all! Special shout-out to Anna Bradley for encouraging me to turn my little idea into a full-blown book!

For keeping me caffeinated as I wrote and edited, I have to thank the best baristas in the world: Joey, Walls, Brandon, Allie, and Alexa from the Okemos Biggby. No one mochas like you.

Finally, thank you to my daughter. You're the reason I do everything. Thank you for the big hugs, for the supportive messages on my whiteboard, and for the days of eating cereal when I was on deadline. Never forget you're the heroine of your own story. Write yourself a good one!

CHAPTER ONE

There was a reason Gavin Scott rarely drank.

He was bad at it.

As in, *face-planted on the carpet while reaching for the bottle* bad. And *too drunk to see in the dark so might as well stay down* bad.

Which is why he didn't get up when his best friend and Nashville Legends teammate, Delray Hicks, pounded on the door to his hotel room, a fourth-floor state of depression that reminded him every minute that he could at least screw up like a champion.

"Izz open," Gavin slurred.

The door swung wide. Del flipped on a blinding overhead light and immediately swore. "Shit. Man down." He turned and spoke to someone else. "Help me."

Del and another giant human lumbered toward him until their four massive hands grabbed his shoulders. In an instant, he was upright and leaning against the shitty couch that had come with the room. The ceiling spun, and his head fell back against the cushions.

"Come on." Del smacked his cheek. "Look alive."

Gavin sucked in air and managed to lift his head. He blinked twice but then ground the heels of his hands into his eye sockets. "I'm drunk."

"No shit," Del said. "What have you been drinking?"

Gavin lifted his hand to point at the bottle of craft bourbon on the coffee table. It had been a gift from a local distillery to every member of the team at the end of their season a few weeks ago. Del swore again. "Shit, man. Why not just pour grain alcohol down your throat?"

"Didn't have any."

"I'll get some water," said the other guy, whose blurry face sort of resembled Braden Mack, owner of several Nashville nightclubs, but that made zero sense. Why would he be there? They'd only met once at a charity golf thing. Since when were he and Del friends?

A third man suddenly walked in, and this time Gavin recognized him. It was one of his teammates, Yan Feliciano. *"Como es el?"*

How is he? Gavin understood that. Holy shit, he could speak Spanish when he was drunk.

Del shook his head. "He's about one shot away from listening to Ed Sheeran."

Gavin hiccupped. *"No me gusta* Ed Sheeran."

"Shut up," Del said.

"I don't stutter when I'm Spanish." Gavin hiccupped again. Something sour came up with it this time. "When 'm drunk."

Yan swore. *"Que pasó?"*

"Thea asked for a divorce," Del said.

Yan made a sound of disbelief. "My wife said there was a rumor about them having trouble, but I didn't believe it."

"Bleeveve it." Gavin groaned, dropping his head against the couch. A *divorce*. His wife of three years, the mother of his twin daughters, the woman who made him realize there really was a thing called love at first sight, was done with him. And it was his own fucking fault.

"Drink this," Del said, handing Gavin a bottle of water. And then, speaking to Yan again, said, "He's been staying here for the past two weeks."

"She kicked me out," Gavin said, dropping the unopened water.

"Because you've been acting like a douchebag."

"I know."

Del shook his head. "I warned you, man."

"I know."

"I told you she'd get sick of your ass if you didn't get your head out of it."

"I know." Gavin growled it this time, lifting his head. Too fast. He did it too fast. A wave of nausea warned that the bourbon was making a run for the nearest exit. Gavin swallowed and drew in a deep breath, but, oh shit . . . sweat dampened his forehead and his armpits.

"Oh fuck, he's turning green!" Might-Be-Braden-Mack yelled.

Massive hands grabbed him again and hauled him to his feet. They barely touched the floor as Del and Pretty-Sure-It-Was-Mack dragged him to the bathroom. Gavin stumbled to the toilet just as something the color of bad decisions exploded from his mouth. Mack swore with a gag and bolted. Del stayed, even when Gavin grunted like a tennis player in her backswing and heaved several more times.

"You never could handle the hard stuff," Del said.

"I'm dying." Gavin groaned again, falling to one knee.

"You're not dying."

"Then put me out of my mishery."

"Trust me. I'm tempted."

Gavin fell onto his ass and leaned against the beige bathroom wall. His knee collided with the beige tub hidden by a plastic, beige shower curtain. He made $15 million a year and was stuck in a shittier hotel room than his days as a minor leaguer. He could afford way better, but this was punishment. Self-imposed. He'd let his pride ruin the best thing that ever happened to him.

Del flushed the toilet and closed it. He walked out and returned a moment later with the water. "Drink. I mean it this time."

Gavin opened the bottle and sucked down half. After a few minutes, the room was no longer spinning. "What are they doing here?"

"You'll find out." Del sat down on the lid of the toilet and leaned forward, elbows on knees. "You all right?"

"No." Gavin's throat convulsed. *Shit.* He was going to lose it in front of Del. He squeezed his eyes shut and pressed the pad of his thumb into the space between his eyebrows.

"You go ahead and cry, man," Del said, tapping Gavin's foot with the toe of his sneaker. "No shame in that."

Gavin propped his head against the wall again as twin tears rolled down his cheeks. "I can't believe I lost her."

"You're not going to lose her."

"She w-w-wants a divorce, asshole."

Del didn't react to his stutter. No one on the team did anymore, mostly because Gavin had stopped trying to fight it around them. Which was one more in a long list of things he had Thea to thank for. Before he met her, he was self-conscious, hesitant to speak even in front of people he knew. But Thea was completely unfazed the first time he stuttered in front of her. She didn't try to finish his sentence, didn't look away in discomfort. She just waited until he got the words out. No one else besides his family had ever made him feel like he was more than just an awkward, stammering jock.

Which made it that much more of a betrayal when he'd discovered her lie a month ago. And that's what it felt like. A lie.

His wife had been faking it in bed their entire marriage.

"Did she say that?" Del asked. "Or did she say she thinks it's time to think about divorce?"

"What's the fucking difference?"

"One means she's definitely done with you. The other means you might still have a chance."

Gavin rolled his head against the wall in sloppy disagreement. "There's no chance. You didn't hear her voice. It was like talking to a stranger."

Del stood and towered over him. "Do you want to fight for your marriage?"

"Yes." Jesus, yes. More than anything. And shit, now his throat was closing again.

"What are you willing to do?"

"Anything."

"Do you mean that?"

"W-w-what the fuck? Of course I mean it."

"Good." Del offered his hand. "Then come on."

Gavin let Del pull him to his feet and then followed him back into the main room. His body felt as though it weighed a thousand pounds as he stumbled toward the couch and collapsed onto the cushions.

"Nice place you got here, Scott," Mack said, emerging from the kitchenette area. He polished a green apple on his shoulder and then took a large, loud bite.

"That's mine," Gavin grumbled.

"You weren't eating it."

"I was going to eat it."

"Sure. Right after you reached the bottom of that bottle."

Gavin flipped him off.

"Knock it off," Del ordered Mack. "We've all been where he is."

Wait. What? What the hell did that mean?

Yan claimed the seat on the opposite end of the couch and clunked his cowboy boots onto the coffee table. Mack leaned against the wall.

Del looked at them both. "What do you guys think?"

Mack took another bite and spoke with his mouth full. "I don't know. You really think he can handle it?"

Gavin dragged his hand down his face. He felt like he'd walked into the middle of a movie. A crappy one. "Can someone please explain to me wh-what's going on?"

Del crossed his arms. "We're going to save your marriage."

Gavin snorted, but the three pairs of eyes looking back at him were serious. He groaned. "I'm screwed."

"You said you were willing to do anything to get Thea back," Del said.

"Yes," Gavin mumbled.

"Then I need you to be honest."

Gavin tensed. Del lowered himself onto the coffee table. It protested under his six-four frame.

"Tell us what happened."

"I told you. She said—"

"I don't mean tonight. What *happened*?"

Gavin darted a glance at all three men. Even if Yan and Eating-His-Apple-Mack weren't there, Gavin wouldn't talk about that. It was too humiliating. It would be bad enough to admit that he couldn't satisfy his own wife in bed, but to also have to own up to the special kind of dumbfuckery that made him freak out, move into the guest room, punish his wife with the silent treatment, and refuse to hear her explanations because his ego was too fucking fragile to handle it? Yeah, no. He'd keep that to himself, thank you very much.

"I can't tell you," he finally mumbled.

"Why not?"

"It's personal."

"We're talking about your marriage. Of course it's personal," Del said.

"But this is too—"

Mack cut him off with a frustrated noise. "He's asking if you cheated on her, slapnuts."

Gavin swiveled his head to glare at Del. "Is that what you think? You actually think I would cheat on her?" Just the thought made him want to bend over the toilet again and evacuate what remained of his liquid dinner.

"No," Del said. "But we have to ask. It's a rule. We don't help cheaters."

"Who the hell is *we*? What the fuck is going on?"

"You said she seemed like a stranger last night," Del said. "Did it ever occur to you that maybe she is a stranger?"

Gavin shot him a *what the fuck* look.

"All spouses become strangers to each other at some point in a marriage," Del said. "All human beings are a work in progress, and we don't all change at the same pace. Who knows how many people have gotten divorced simply because they failed to recognize that what they thought were insurmountable problems were actually just temporary phases?" Del spread his hands wide. "But hell, you two? It's a wonder you two ever got to know each other at all."

"Is this supposed to be making me feel b-b-better?"

"You guys dated, what, four months before she got pregnant?"

"Three."

Mack coughed into his hand. It sounded like the word *shotgun*.

"Right," Del continued. "And the next thing you knew, you were getting married on a whim in a courthouse, and before the twins were even born you got called up to the bigs? Hell, Gavin, you've been on the road most of your marriage while she's been raising those girls practically on her own in a strange city. You think she's going to be the same person after all that?"

No, but dammit, that wasn't the problem with him and Thea. Sure, she had changed. So had he. But they were good parents, and they were happy. At least, he *thought* they were happy.

Del shrugged casually and sat up straight. "Look, all I'm saying is that our careers are hard enough on couples who date for years and know exactly what they're in for before getting married. But you two jumped into the deep end of the pool with

8

no life jackets. No marriage can survive that, even in the best circumstances. Not without some help."

"It's a little late for counsheling."

"No, it's not. But that's not what I'm talking about, anyway."

"What the fuck *are* you talking about?"

Del ignored him and instead eyed Yan and Mack again. "Well?"

"I say yes," Yan said. "He'll be useless to us next season if we don't get them back together."

Mack shrugged. "I'm good, if only to get him out of here. Because goddamn, dude." He gestured widely at the room.

Gavin slumped toward Yan. "How do I say *fuck off* in Spanish?"

Mack took a final bite of the apple and tossed the core over his shoulder. It landed perfectly in the sink. Gavin hated him more than anyone else in the entire world. "My daughters gave me that apple."

"Oops," Mack said.

"Listen up," Del said. "Sleep this off tonight. Tomorrow night, you'll meet us for your first official meeting."

"First official meeting of *what*?"

"The solution to all your problems."

They stared at him as if that explained everything. "That's it?"

"One more thing," Del said. "Under no circumstances are you to go see your wife."

CHAPTER TWO

Nothing on Earth is as strong as a woman who's good and fed up.

Of all the bits of folksy wisdom her Gran Gran had imparted over the years, Thea Scott hoped at least that one was true because, holy crap, this sledgehammer weighed a ton. Four attempts to hit her mark had only resulted in a minor dent in the wall and a major pulled muscle in her back. But dammit, Thea was not giving up. Three years they'd lived in this house, and for three years she'd been fantasizing about knocking down this wall.

Seeing how her marriage had officially come crumbling down yesterday, it only seemed fair that today it should be the wall's turn.

Besides, Thea really, *really* needed to hit something.

She swung the sledgehammer one more time with a grunt. Finally, the heavy end connected with a satisfying thud and left a gaping hole. With a whoop of victory, Thea yanked the hammer free and poked her face into her handiwork. She could almost feel the light from the other side just waiting to burst free from its sensibly beige prison. Who the hell would put a wall there, anyway? What architect in their right mind would separate the living room from the dining room and block all that glorious light from flowing through the downstairs?

Thea swung again, and a second hole joined the first. A chunk of drywall dropped to her feet as dust swirled into the air and coated her arms. Holy crap, that felt good.

Panting from exertion, Thea let the hammer fall to the plastic tarp she'd bought to protect the hardwood floor. Massaging her shoulder with one hand, she turned and surveyed the living room. Yes. Right there. Right by the French doors to the backyard. This was the perfect spot for her easel and paints. Someday, after finishing her degree, maybe she'd have her own art studio. But for now, she'd be satisfied just to paint again. She hadn't touched a blank canvas since the girls were born. Her greatest creative accomplishment these days was dyeing her white T-shirts to make the stains seem intentional.

She'd tried to make it work, the wall. She'd hung family photos in quirky patterns. Framed the girls' handprints and artwork. Displayed Gavin's favorite bat from high school. All with the idea that someday she'd fix it. Someday she would paint it a more vibrant color. Or maybe add built-ins. Or someday just knock down the entire damn thing and start over.

Thea knew *someday* had arrived the instant she woke up this morning, her eyes still swollen from a weak moment in the middle of the night when she'd cried in the bathroom with a fist pressed against her mouth to smother the sound.

Tears were pointless. Regrets wouldn't help her start over. There was only one way to move forward, and that was to come out swinging.

Literally.

So after breakfast, Thea sent the girls off to dance class with her sister, Liv, who'd been living with her since Gavin left. And then Thea dug out her old paint overalls, drove to the local hardware, and bought the sledgehammer.

"You know how to use this?" *the man at the counter asked.* *His arched eyebrow screamed "mansplainer."*

Thea curled her lips into a semblance of a smile. "Yep."

"Make sure your strongest hand is at the butt of the handle."

"Yep. I got it." Thea shoved the change in her pocket.

The man tugged on his suspenders. "Whatcha knockin' down?"

"Patriarchal power structures."

He blinked.

"A wall."

"Make sure it's not load-bearing first."

The need to hit something surged again like a bad case of Twitter rage. Thea hoisted the sledgehammer onto her shoulder, but just as she started to swing, the front door flew open. The girls ran inside, their tutus bouncing over little pink tights and their blonde pigtails swinging in unison. Their golden retriever, Butter Ball, patiently followed behind like a K9 nanny. Her sister, Liv, brought up the rear, holding Butter's leash.

"Mommy, what are you doing?" Amelia asked, screeching to a halt, a combination of awe and trepidation in her tiny voice. Thea didn't blame her. Mommy probably didn't look like Mommy right now.

"I'm knocking down a wall," Thea said, keeping her voice light.

"Aw, yeah," Liv said, rubbing her hands together. "I'm getting in on this action." Dropping Butter's leash, she crossed the room and reached for the sledgehammer. "Can I pretend it's his face?"

"Liv," Thea warned quietly. She knew her sister wouldn't intentionally say anything bad about Gavin in front of the girls. They'd both learned the hard way that the only people who suffer when one parent bad-mouths the other are the children. But Liv's mouth had a way of acting on its own sometimes. Like now.

"Whose face, Aunt Livvie?" Amelia asked.

Thea shot an *I told you so* look at her sister.

"My boss," Liv answered quickly. Liv worked for a notoriously tyrannical celebrity chef at a famous Nashville restaurant. Liv complained about him enough that the girls didn't question whether Liv was telling the truth or not.

"Can we hit the wall too?" Amelia asked.

"This is dangerous grown-up work," Thea said. "But you can watch."

Liv swung hard with a Tarzan cry and knocked another chunk of drywall to the floor. The girls cheered and jumped up and down. Ava let out a whoop and karate kicked the air. Amelia attempted a cartwheel. It was officially *on* in the living room.

"Damn, that felt good," Liv said, handing the sledgehammer back to Thea. "We need music for this."

As Thea took possession of the tool once again, Liv dug out her cell phone, swiped the screen a few times, and then the Bluetooth speakers throughout the house blared with the voice of Aretha Franklin demanding R-E-S-P-E-C-T.

Liv grabbed Gavin's bat from the floor, held it like a microphone, and started belting out the lyrics. She extended her hand to Thea, so Thea joined in for the girls' benefit, who laughed as if the impromptu concert was the funniest thing they'd ever seen.

And just like that, she and Liv were teenagers again, singing at the top of their lungs in the stuffy bedroom they shared at Gran Gran's house. It was there, while their mother was off finding herself in a haze of anger and alimony and their father was too busy cheating on wife number two to pay attention to his daughters, that they memorized P!nk songs and promised to never trust a man, to never be as weak as their mother or as selfish as their father, and to always protect each other.

It was them against the world. Always.

And now again. Only this time, Thea didn't just have a little sister to protect. She had to protect the girls. And she would. No matter what it took. She would make sure they never knew what it was like to grow up surrounded by tension or as the pawn between two warring parents.

A swell of sudden emotion stung the corners of Thea's eyes as an ache spread through her chest. Her voice caught on the lyrics as her throat convulsed. Spinning away from the girls, she swiped at her face.

Liv casually covered for her. "Hey, girls. Run upstairs and change your clothes, OK? First one to the stairs gets to pick the movie tonight."

The promise of competition sent the girls scrambling toward the stairs. Seconds later, the song quieted.

"You OK?" Liv asked.

A painful lump blocked Thea's voice. "What if I've already hurt them?"

"You haven't," Liv said sharply. "You are the best mom I have ever known."

"All I wanted, have ever wanted, was to give them a life that we never had. To give them safety and security and—"

Liv grabbed Thea's shoulders and turned her around. "He's the one who moved out."

"Yes, because I told him to go." She hadn't been able to take one more minute of the cold shoulder after nearly a month of him refusing to talk about anything and pouting in the guest room. Two toddlers in the household were her limit.

"And he couldn't go fast enough," Liv said.

True. Still, guilt gnawed at Thea's edges. There were things Liv didn't know. Gavin was wrong to react the way he did when he discovered Thea had been faking it in bed, but Thea shouldn't have let him find out that way. "It takes two people to ruin a relationship."

Liv tilted her head. "Sure, but I'm your sister, which means I'm biologically predisposed to only take your side."

They stared at each other, silently thanking God once again that they had at least one person they could always count on.

Thea once thought Gavin was that person too.

Damn him! Thea retrieved the sledgehammer. It was time to stand on her own two feet. To pick up where she left off when she gave up everything for him and his career. Time to start living up to the promises she and Liv made all those years ago.

Thea swung, and another hole broke the wall.

Liv laughed. "I'm not the only one picturing his face now, am I?"

"No," Thea growled, swinging again.

"Good. Get it out. You're a badass who doesn't need a man."

The speakers blared an angry Taylor Swift song about burning pictures.

Liv grabbed Gavin's bat from the floor again. "Watch out. I'm coming in."

"Wait! That's his favorite bat!"

"If he wanted it, he should've taken it with him," Liv said.

Thea ducked as Liv swung. There was a loud bang as it connected with the drywall.

Thea dropped the sledgehammer and wrenched the bat from Liv's hands. "We can't break that."

"It's just a bat."

"He won the state high school championship with it."

Liv rolled her eyes. "Men and their wood."

"It's important to him," Thea said.

"Isn't that the problem?" Liv snapped. "Baseball was always more important than you."

"No, it wasn't." The sudden deep timbre of Gavin's voice sent them both whipping around.

He stood ten feet away, as if their conversation had summoned him out of thin air. Butter barked and jogged toward him traitorously with a happy wag.

A tremor shook Thea from the inside out as she watched Gavin drop a hand on Butter's head for a distracted ear scratch. He wore a pair of faded jeans and a plain gray T-shirt. His damp hair stood askew, as if he'd raced through a shower and simply rubbed a towel over his head. His hazel eyes were bloodshot and rimmed with dark circles. At least two days' worth of brownish blonde stubble darkened his jaw.

But he still somehow managed to look irresistibly, unfairly sexy.

Liv turned down the music and crossed her arms. "What do you want, asshole?"

"Liv," Thea warned again. Then to Gavin, she said, "You don't live here anymore, Gavin. You can't just walk in."

He motioned to the door behind him. "I tried knocking." His eyes darted between the broken wall and the sledgehammer on the floor. "What—what are you doing?"

"Tearing down the wall."

"I see that," Gavin said slowly. "Why exactly?"

"Because I hate this wall."

Gavin's brows pulled together. "Is that my bat?"

Something hot and petty burned a path through her common sense. "Yep. Works great." Thea turned and slammed the bat into the wall.

Gavin ducked instinctively.

"I'm going to set up my easel here," Thea said. She slammed the bat again. "This stupid wall blocks all the good light."

"Maybe we should talk about this before you—" Gavin winced as Thea swung the bat a third time.

"Maybe we should have talked about a lot of things," Thea snapped, stepping away from the wall. She wiped a bead of sweat from her forehead.

A sudden squeal from the stairs interrupted them. "Daddy!" Amelia leapt from the bottom stair and raced toward Gavin. She threw her arms around his legs. "Mommy is breaking the wall!" She laughed, raising her hands to be picked up.

Gavin, still staring warily at Thea, hoisted her in his arms. Amelia instantly cocked her head. "Are you sick, Daddy?"

"Uh, no, honey," Gavin said. "I just didn't sleep very well last night." He kissed her cheek. "You smell like syrup. Did Mommy make special Saturday pancakes for breakfast?"

"Yeah, with chocolate chips!" It came out *chocate thips*.

Gavin met Thea's eyes, and for a moment they stopped being combatants and just became parents. Amelia had been showing signs of a lisp the past several months, and Gavin feared it was the beginning of a permanent speech problem like his. Thea offered a soft smile. "It's just a lisp," she said quietly.

Gavin reached his other arm toward Ava, who had shuffled slowly behind her sister. "Hey, squirt."

Ava wouldn't go near him and instead came to stand next to Thea. It was an act of instinctive protectiveness that broke Thea's heart, even more so when Ava lifted her chin in a bold tilt and declared, "Mommy cried."

Oh, no. Ava had been climbing into bed with her in the middle of the night ever since Gavin left. Had she heard Thea sneak into the bathroom last night? She didn't want the girls to *ever* hear her cry.

Gavin swallowed slowly. His eyes moved across Thea's face as if he'd never seen her before, stopping on freckles and blemishes she hadn't bothered to cover with makeup before he met her eyes again. Thea flushed under the weight of his stare. Why the hell was he looking at her like that?

"Can we take Butter for a walk?" Amelia said. That was their thing—taking the dog for a walk around the neighborhood. Or, at least, it used to be when Gavin still lived there.

"Another time, sweetie," Gavin said. "I need to talk to Mommy."

Amelia made a pouty face—a new, devastatingly effective technique she'd recently discovered. Gavin swallowed hard, and Thea almost felt sorry for him. "I'll be at your school musical Monday," he said. "Maybe we can walk Butter after that?"

"I'll take them for a walk," Liv said, putting just enough *fuck you* in her voice to make a point.

Butter danced at the door as Liv reattached his leash and

helped the girls into their fleece coats. She walked out but then ducked her head back in the room. "Don't take too long. We still need to set up your online dating profile."

The screen door slammed.

Gavin made an indecipherable noise.

Thea hid a smile.

"You're not answering your phone," Gavin said as soon as the girls were out of earshot.

"The battery died last night. I didn't feel like charging it."

He stepped closer, his eyes softening with concern. "Are you OK?"

Thea ignored the tiny ping-pong of her heart. "I'm not the one who smells like he spent the night on the whiskey trail."

"I got drunk last night."

Thea turned toward the wall, ready for another blow. "Celebrating your freedom?"

"If you actually think that, I've fucked up worse than I thought."

The crunch of bat against wall wasn't as satisfying this time. "Well, that's kind of a problem, Gavin, because you fucked up pretty bad."

He didn't argue. "Are you really setting up an online dating profile?"

"God, no." Thea snorted, wiping a hand across her forehead. "That's the last thing I need." Another man in her life? More promises that couldn't be trusted? No thanks.

Gavin nodded, relief plain on his features.

"If you're here to pick up some of your stuff, make it quick because the girls won't be gone long."

"I'm not here for my stuff."

"Then what?"

"I w-w-w . . ."

Thea's heart did the ping-pong thing again as she watched him fight against the muscles of his throat.

Gavin finally rushed into his sentence. "I want to talk."

"There's nothing left to say."

"Please, Thea." Goddamn ping-ponging heart. "Fine." Thea shoved his bat at him and stomped toward the kitchen. She turned her back on him to fill a glass of water from the tap and silently seethed as she studied the massive whiteboard calendar that covered a four-foot square of wall space beside the refrigerator. Thea used to relish being impulsive and carefree, but now she lived and breathed by the color-coded control center where she scheduled every minute of their lives—dance lessons, dentist appointments, dinner menus, preschool volunteer days, and, in red letters to denote status-level FORGET THIS AT YOUR PERIL, reminders to find Ava's favorite tights before Monday's school musical.

The calendar also used to be full of charitable and social engagements as an official member of the Nashville Legends' WAGs'—wives and girlfriends—club, but ever since rumors began circulating that she and Gavin were struggling, many of the wives and girlfriends had started to distance themselves from her. They didn't even invite her to their stupid luncheon this month, and that was *before* she'd asked for a divorce.

She'd never felt as though she belonged, anyway, no matter how much she tried. Thea could never shake the feeling when she was around them that she was perpetually *that one*—the girl they all secretly suspected had gotten pregnant on purpose to trap herself a rich, professional athlete.

Little did they know that the very last thing in the world Thea would ever marry for was money. She'd seen firsthand growing up how money corrupted and corroded everything around it.

Nope. She had married Gavin for love.

But seeing how well that turned out, she might have been better off marrying for the cash.

Thea had been completely unprepared for life as a baseball wife. Being a Legends WAG brought its own kind of celebrity and responsibility. Between the charity events and promotional appearances, it was like being yanked into a sorority she never meant to rush. She didn't have anything against sororities. She'd even been in one in college—an artsy collection of theater majors and music majors and feminist studies students who protested cuts to the women's center.

But this sorority was different. This one demanded conformity and total obedience—the opposite of everything Thea once stood for. But Thea had had to figure it all out on her own with infant twins because Gavin was gone more than he was home. And somehow in the process, she got lost until she no longer even recognized herself. How had *Southern Lifestyle* magazine described her last summer in a feature about Tennessee's pro athletes and their families? *Wholesomely pastel*. That was it. And they were right. Her entire Lilly Pulitzer wardrobe had become a walking tribute to cotton candy. She used to wear vintage Depeche Mode T-shirts and black Chucks, for God's sake.

The article was like a bucket of cold water over her head. A wake-up call. She'd sputtered and stumbled and realized she'd become everything she once despised. And Gavin either hadn't noticed or hadn't cared that she had morphed into some kind of sanitized version of herself.

Or, worse, he preferred the sanitized Thea.

At the sound of his clearing throat, Thea finally turned around. The shadows beneath his eyes were more pronounced under the kitchen lights, like twin bruises. He really did look awful. Gavin could never handle the hard stuff. And she didn't just mean alcohol.

She slid her glass across the island toward him. "Do you want an aspirin?"

"Already took some."

"Didn't help?"

"Not really." He cocked a half smile. His hand wrapped around the glass she'd just shared, his thumb rubbing up and down the cool condensation. There was no holding back the zing of surprised longing that made certain parts of her ache and other parts tingle. She had either reached pathetic level *bless her heart* or was just starved for affection if the sight of his thumb distractedly stroking a glass of water could make her pink parts stand at attention. He hadn't touched her since that night—the night of the Big O-No. But despite what he apparently believed, she had always loved being touched by him. She had never faked *that*.

Damn him. "I want to keep the house."

Gavin cocked his head as if he didn't hear her correctly. Like a dog. "W-what?"

"I know it's a lot to ask, but I won't need as much child support if you're willing to pay it off for the girls and me. I'll work, obviously, but—"

Gavin pushed the glass away. "Thea—"

"I think things would have been easier for Liv and me if Dad hadn't sold the house after he left Mom. And since this is the only house the girls have ever known—" Her voice caught. She sucked in a breath to cover it up. "We need to tell them together. I'm not sure when the right time is, though. Before the holidays? After the holidays? I don't know. I don't even know if they'll understand what it means. They still think you're just off playing baseball, but that's not going to hold much longer—"

"Thea, stop!"

The staccato of his voice was as jarring as it was atypical. Thea jumped in her own skin. "Stop what?"

"I don't want this."

"The house?"

"No! Fuck!" He dragged his hands across his hair. "I mean, yes. I want the house. I w-w-want you and the girls in the house."

"I don't understand."

"I want *you*!"

Thea's mouth dropped open. Surprise stole her voice for a moment before cynicism gave it back. "Stop, Gavin. It's too late for this."

Gavin squeezed the edge of the counter until veins protruded from his thick forearms.

"No, it's not."

"It's best to do this now while the girls are still young and won't remember . . ." She couldn't finish the sentence over a sudden thickness in her throat. She didn't have time for this emotional crap.

Gavin's face hardened. "Remember what? That their parents were ever married?"

"I'd rather they never remember *that* than be forced to endure the pain of their family being torn apart."

"Then let's keep our family together."

"You tore it apart the minute you moved out."

"You told me to leave, Thea!"

"And you couldn't go fast enough."

His mouth opened and closed for a moment before he blurted, "I needed time to think."

"And now you'll have all the time you need."

Gavin bent, dropped his elbows on the island, and held his head in his hands. "This isn't going the way I w-wanted."

Thea bolted away from the counter. "Really? How exactly did you imagine this going? Because you seem to think that all you had to do was show up here, and I'd just smile and pretend everything was fine. I've been doing that for three years, Gavin. I'm done."

She headed back to the wall. She needed to hit something again.

"Wh-what the hell does that mean?" he asked, following closely behind.

"It means that orgasms were the least of our problems!" That's what pissed her off the most. He was mad at her for faking it in bed, but didn't he know she'd been faking everything for years?

Thea picked up the bat and swung as hard as she could. Another hole appeared in the wall.

"Thea, wait," Gavin said, wrapping his fingers around the bat to stop her from swinging again. "Please, just listen to me for a second."

She spun around. "We're beyond the listening stage, Gavin. I've asked you to listen to me a thousand times since that night, and you refused!"

"Not everything about that night was awful, Thea."

24

Thea advanced on him, propelled by pent-up rage. "Are you kidding me? You think now is a good time to remind me of your glorious grand slam?"

It would be funny if it weren't so not funny. The perfect pun. The night of his greatest career achievement—a walk-off grand slam in the sixth game of the American League Championship series—was the night of an even bigger home run in bed for Thea.

"I'm talking about what we did after the game," Gavin said, closing the distance between them, lowering his voice to a seductive tone. "*That* wasn't awful."

"Then why did you move into the guest room afterward?"

Gavin held up his hands in a truce-like gesture. "Because I overreacted and fucked up, OK? I know that. And I w-w . . ."

His mouth worked to push out words that his muscles were determined to hold in. He dragged his hand along his jaw and then gripped the back of his neck. He finally looked at the floor with a growl, frustration tugging his lips into a frown.

The front door suddenly flew open for the second time that morning. Gavin bit back a curse as Amelia and Butter ran into the house with Ava and Liv following slowly behind. Amelia stopped in the hallway and held a dog treat as high in the air as her little arm could reach. "Daddy, look!"

Amelia commanded Butter to jump. The dog merely lifted his head and took the treat from Amelia's fingers, but Amelia squealed as if she'd taught Butter to talk.

Gavin smiled softly. "Very cool, baby," he said, his voice strained.

Liv caught Thea's eye as she walked into the kitchen. A few seconds later, "All the Single Ladies" blared from the Bluetooth speakers.

"She's subtle," Gavin said quietly.

"No one is as loyal as a little sister."

"We're going to go jump on the trampoline," Liv said, picking up on the still-unresolved tension in the room.

She turned up the music before going out back with the girls.

Gavin approached Thea cautiously. "Just tell me what it w-w-will take. What do I need to do?"

His face conveyed a beseeching plea that reminded her way too much of the fake *baby, please* tone her father would use whenever he begged her mother for a second chance. Or a third or a fourth. How many times did her mother believe her father's promises and take him back? Too many. Thea wasn't going to make that mistake.

"It's too late for this, Gavin." Thea sighed, repeating her words from earlier.

Gavin's face blanched. "Just give me a chance."

She shook her head.

His eyes pinched at the corners. With a strangled noise, he spun around, his hands stacked on top of his head. His T-shirt tugged over taut back muscles that bunched and bulged as he battled his thoughts. A moment fraught with tension passed before he spun back around. Determination drove his steps as he ate the distance between them. "I'll do anything, Thea. Please."

"Why, Gavin? After all this time, *why*?"

His eyes dropped to her lips, and, oh God, was he going to—

Gavin let out a growl, slid one hand to the back of her head, and slanted his mouth over hers. Thea stumbled back and grabbed the back of the couch to keep from falling, but she didn't need to because Gavin wrapped an arm around her back. A strong, protective, bulging, masculine arm that held her against his hard body. His mouth plundered hers. Over and over. And when his tongue swept between her lips, she couldn't stop herself from responding. She curled her fingers into the front of his shirt and opened wider for him with a sigh. He tasted like toothpaste and whiskey and a shot of long-lost dreams.

But the shot came with a chaser of confusion and betrayal. Was she really this easy? One wild kiss and she was literally weak in his arms? One kiss and she forgot everything that had happened between them?

Thea wrenched her mouth away. "What the hell are you doing?"

"You asked why," Gavin panted, his eyes dark. "That's why."

CHAPTER THREE

"You did *what*?"

Gavin slumped in the passenger seat of Del's truck, the smell of the pizza, chicken wings, and other snacks in the back seat threatening to break the cease-fire in his stomach. It had been several hours since he last threw up, but the spicy odor of buffalo sauce warned that could easily change. "I kissed her."

Del swore. "I specifically told you not to go see her!"

"I know."

"And I definitely did not give you permission to kiss her."

"I didn't know I needed it."

"You do. But more importantly, you need *hers*. Shit." Del banged his hand on the steering wheel. "You might have set yourself back *weeks* with that stunt."

Gavin didn't argue because he had the sinking feeling Del was right. If Thea could've gotten her hands on a frying pan, she might've bashed him over the head with it. After pushing him away, she'd told him he had no right to kiss her like that and ordered him to leave.

But there'd also been a moment when she leaned into him, opened for him, let her tongue tangle with his, and breathed a little sigh. A *real* sigh. It was brief, but in that moment his wife had kissed him back. So maybe he hadn't completely struck out.

Del hung a right and merged onto the freeway. The inside of the car glowed yellow from the lights of oncoming cars heading into downtown Nashville for a night of honky-tonks. They drove for nearly fifteen minutes until Del exited near Brentwood, a subdivision outside the city where many athletes and country stars lived.

Gavin preferred Franklin. A lot of celebrities lived there too, but the historic, tree-lined streets gave it a small-town feel. They lived in a normal neighborhood, not a stuffy mansion-filled subdivision. Their house was within walking distance of a little downtown where the girls could get a library book and an ice-cream cone, and where they had become regulars at the local diner with its cracked vinyl booths. The only tourists they ever got there were Civil War buffs who wanted to tour the local battlefield.

Gavin was skeptical at first when Thea suggested they live there. His salary could afford something more lavish. But when he saw the way her eyes lit up when she pulled up the listing for the 1930s brick Craftsman on her phone, there was no way he was going to push for anything else. And now he wouldn't give up their small-town lifestyle for anything.

Except he almost had.

Five minutes later, Gavin balanced five boxes of pizza and

four cartons of wings up a manicured sidewalk. "Whose house is this?"

By the ostentatious display of sports cars in the garage, Gavin feared they were at Asshole-Ate-His-Apple's house.

He was right. The door swung open, and Mack greeted them with a snort. "Hey, look who's finally sober."

Gavin shoved the pizzas and wings at him. "Hey, look who's still a dick."

"You two need to knock that shit off," Del growled, walking in.

Mack swung the door shut with his foot. "All in good fun, right, man?"

"No. I kind of hate you," Gavin said.

Del turned around. "Everyone here?"

"Yeah," Mack said. "In the basement. Is he ready for his initiation? I have to get that sheep back to the farm by midnight."

Gavin scowled at that, but he trailed behind them through the soaring entryway and past a wide, curved staircase. Beyond that, they entered a kitchen twice the size of his and Thea's. The sound of voices grew louder as they approached a door that led to the basement.

Gavin waited for Mack and Del to go first.

"Food's here," Mack announced, turning a corner at the bottom of the stairs. A round of voices harrumphed manly approval followed by several *about time*s.

"Are we late?" Gavin asked Del's back.

"Nah. They just got here early to finalize the plan."

Gavin grabbed the back of Del's shirt. "Hold up. What plan?"

"The plan to get Thea to take your stupid ass back," Del said, turning the same corner that Mack had disappeared around. "A plan you made a helluva lot harder today."

Gavin sucked in and let out a breath, hovering on the last stair. Finally, mustering his courage with a reminder that this was about saving his marriage, he followed Del.

Ten of Nashville's movers and shakers—professional athletes, business owners, and city officials—stood around an elaborate bar, shoving one another aside as they dove into the pizza and wings. Del dumped the paper bag of other snacks. Several bags of chips fell out. A single green apple rolled onto the floor.

Mack shook his head as he picked it up. "You are one petty bastard."

"Everyone hurry up," Del said. "We gotta get started. Dipshit here kissed his wife today."

The room exploded. Heads swiveled. Chairs toppled. A hockey player in the corner swore in Russian.

"What the fuck, man?" Mack barked. "We told you not to go see her!"

A dude he recognized as Malcolm James, running back for the Nashville NFL team, choked on his beer. "Did you at least ask permission first, or was it a sneak-attack kiss?"

"Sneak attack, I guess?"

Yan smacked the back of his head. "That's grand-gesture shit, man! You can't do that yet."

"Grand gesture what?"

The guys gave him varying degrees of dirty looks as they gathered their plates and headed for a massive game table on the other side of the basement.

The Russian grumbled over the remains of the food, finally

settling on a bag of pretzels. He tucked it under his arm as if someone might steal it. "Too much pizza," he said, glaring as he walked by Gavin. "Cheese. It shoot straight out my ass."

That was a visual he didn't need.

"Gavin, come on. Time to get started."

Swiping his apple off the counter, he dragged his feet toward the one remaining chair.

Del cleared his throat and stood. "Everyone ready?"

The guys nodded, mouths full.

"Good. First rule of book club?"

They finished in unison. "You don't talk about book club."

What. The. Fuck.

Gavin looked around for a hidden camera. This had to be a prank.

"A book club? That's your grand plan for saving my marriage?"

Del nodded at Mack, who rose on one hip and pulled a book from his back pocket. He tossed it at Gavin. It nailed him in the face.

"Nice reflexes. Hope you're better at shortstop."

Gavin bared his teeth. "I play second base, asshole."

Mack shrugged. "Isn't that basically the same thing?"

Gavin ignored him and retrieved the book from the table where it fell. He blinked at the cover. A woman from, like, the 1800s or some shit was leaning on a couch with a dude in one of those old-timey suits standing behind her. His shirt was open.

"*Courting the Countess*," Gavin read slowly. He ground his molars and looked up. "Is this a joke?"

"No," Del said.

"This is a romance novel."

"Yes."

Gavin shot to his feet. "I can't believe you assholes. My life is falling apart, and you're making fun of me."

"I thought the same thing when Malcolm brought me in," Del said. "But it's not a joke. Sit down and listen."

Gavin pressed the heel of his hand to his forehead and shut his eyes. When he opened them again, everyone was still staring at him. Not a weird dream, then. "Wh-wh-what the hell is going on here?"

"If you'd shut up for a second, we'll explain it to you, douche-bag," Mack said.

Gavin returned to his chair. "You guys read *romance novels*?"

"We call them *manuals*," the Russian said.

"And it's a lot more than just reading," Malcolm said.

Gavin went cold. "If you're about to drag me into some kind of kinky swinger shit, I'm out."

Del leaned forward, elbows on the table. "I'm going to tell you something I never told you before."

"Yeah, I'm not sure I want to know."

"Two years ago, Nessa filed for divorce."

The ground shifted beneath Gavin's chair. "What? Why didn't you tell me?"

"One, I barely knew you then. And two, probably for the same reason you're reluctant to tell anyone what happened between you and Thea. It's emotional, personal."

"But you and Nessa are perfect."

"Things are always different behind closed doors, aren't they?"

Yeah, but in Gavin's case, part of the problem was that he was too stupid to know he totally sucked in bed or that his wife had apparently started to hate his guts. The way she'd looked at him today . . . He shuddered. He seriously doubted Del could relate.

"Nearly every man at this table has been on the verge of losing his wife, girlfriend, or fiancée at some point," Del continued, and Gavin recalled the cryptic thing he said last night. *We've all been where he is.* "And every one of us not only got our girls back but repaired our relationships better than ever."

Gavin scanned the faces at the table. They greeted him with nods, smiles, and—from Mack—the finger. Gavin returned the gesture and then shook his head. "I don't understand what any of this means or has to do with me."

"Look, man," Malcolm said, his Hulk-sized hands stroking a beard thick enough to qualify for federal forest protection. "Men are idiots. We complain that women are so mysterious and shit, and we never know what they want. We fuck up our relationships because we convince ourselves that it's too hard to figure them out. But the real problem is with us. We think we're not supposed to feel things and cry and express ourselves. We expect women to do all the emotional labor in a relationship and then act confused when they give up on us."

Gavin puffed out a nervous breath. That hit a little too close to home. *You seem to think that all you had to do was show up here, and I'd just smile and pretend everything was fine. I've been doing that for three years, Gavin. I'm done.* "I-I still don't know what you're talking about," he stammered.

"Romance novels are primarily written by women for women, and they're entirely about how they want to be treated and what they want out of life and in a relationship. We read them to be more comfortable expressing ourselves and to look at things from their perspective."

Gavin blinked. "You guys are serious."

"Dead serious," Del said.

The Russian with the cheese problem nodded. "Reading romance make me know how much my wife and I see world differently, and how I need to be better job of speaking her language."

"Her language?"

"Ever said something to Thea that you thought was totally innocuous only to have her storm off and then claim for hours that she's fine?" Malcolm asked.

"Yeah."

"Or say something you thought was funny only to have her get super offended?"

"Well, yeah, but—"

Yan piped in. "Or tell her that you put the dishes in the dishwasher only to have her get all pissy about how you shouldn't expect a gold star for doing what should be the responsibility of any adult in the goddamn house?"

A chill ran down his spine. "Have you guys been talking to her?"

Yan snorted. "You guys speak different languages to each other." He pointed at the book. "You'll learn hers by reading romance."

"But Thea doesn't even read these kinds of books!"

The guys exchanged glances and then burst out laughing. Del patted him on the back. "Keep telling yourself that."

"I've never seen anything like this in the house."

Derek Wilson, a local businessman he recognized from his TV commercials, spoke up. "She have one of those e-reader things?"

"Yeah. I mean, I don't know. I think so."

"It's full of romance novels. Trust us."

Gavin looked at the book in his hand. "So you're saying I need to d-do w-what the guy in this book does?" Good God, was he actually starting to listen to them?

"Not word-for-word, no," Del answered. "The point is to fit the lessons of it into your own marriage. Plus, that's a Regency, so—"

"What the hell is a Regency?"

"That means it's set in eighteenth- or early nineteenth-century England."

"Oh, great. That sounds relevant."

"It is, actually," Malcolm said. "Modern romance novelists use the patriarchal society of old British aristocracy to explore the gender-based limitations placed on women today in both the professional and personal spheres. That shit is feminist as fuck."

Mack winked. "The sex scenes are also really fucking hot."

Gavin dropped the book.

Mack and Wilson laughed and high-fived. "I loved that one," Wilson said. "At least a BB Four."

"Do I want to know what that means?" Gavin shuddered.

"It's our rating system for how much sex is in it," Wilson said.

"But what does BB stand for?"

The whole table spoke at once. "Book Boner."

Gavin shot to his feet again. "This is ridiculous. My w-w-wife isn't going to take me back because of some stupid books." But what was even more ridiculous was that he was actually starting to consider it. It's not like he could fuck things up any worse than they were.

"The books are just part of it," Del said, picking up *His Naked Countess* or whatever it was called. "We've all been through it and came out on the other end better men, better husbands, and better lovers."

Gavin stopped and looked up at that. "What do you mean?"

"Well, that got his attention." Mack snorted. "Is that the problem, dude? Trouble in the bedroom?"

A heat rash broke out on Gavin's neck. "No," he growled.

"Because you know that problems in the bedroom stem from problems outside the bedroom. You can't fix one without the other."

Orgasms are the least of their problems.

Gavin jerked a thumb in Mack's direction but spoke directly to Del. "Why is this dickweed part of the club? He's not even married."

"I'm here for the dirty parts," Mack said, winking as he chomped into a slice of pizza, devouring half of it in one big bite.

Yan stood and approached him. "Look, I thought these guys were fucking with me too. I didn't even look at the book they gave me for a month. But I'm telling you—we're *all* telling you—we can help you. Book club isn't just about books."

Malcolm nodded solemnly. "It's a brotherhood, man."

"A way of life," one of the city officials said.

Mack slung an arm over Wilson's shoulder. "An emotional fucking journey."

Gavin backed up. "I don't like emotional journeys."

"Just trust us," Del said. "We'll come up with a plan for saving your marriage every step of the way."

"Are you sure you're not just screwing with me?"

"You're one of my best friends," Del said. "Do you really think I'd make a joke out of you and Thea breaking up?"

"No." Gavin sighed. But it seemed too easy. Read some books and, voilà? Thea would take him back with open arms? Was he really that desperate?

He pictured life without Thea.

Yes, he was really that desperate.

Gavin studied the cover again. "Why this one?"

Mack smirked. "Because it's about an idiot who screws up his marriage and has to win back his wife. Sound familiar?"

He swallowed against his rising humiliation. "What do I have to do?"

"Simple," Malcolm said. "Listen to us and read the book."

"Yeah." Del snorted. "And for fuck's sake, do not kiss your wife again until I tell you to."

Courting the Countess

The seventh Earl of Latford had seen many a woman in various stages of undress in his nine and twenty years, but that had not prepared the man for the first breathtaking sight of his wife on their wedding night, looking like an angel in a sheer dressing gown.

Especially since her eyes conveyed the rather clear message that she'd just as soon bathe herself in a pig trough than feel his hands upon her skin.

Bloody inconvenient, that. Because for the first time in his life, Benedict Charles Arthur Seymour was good and truly in love.

"I will do my duty, my lord," his new wife said, her voice flat and hands trembling as she untied the sash at her waist. Her gown floated to the floor in a pool of white silk, leaving her before him in a simple shift that robbed him of speech and thought.

Benedict ordered his feet to remove themselves from their roots in the doorframe separating his bedchamber from hers. As he drew closer to her, his heart shattered with every sign of her discomfort. The clenched fists at her sides. The shaky rise and fall of her chest. The defiant gaze that refused to look away from his.

He had done this. It was his fault.

"You may rest easy," Benedict rasped, bending to retrieve the silky garment from the floor. Her blessedly bare feet were suddenly the most erotic thing he'd ever seen. Standing, he held the robe open for her. "I am not here for that."

Confusion replaced anger for a brief moment in her gaze. She allowed him to hold the gown as she threaded her arms through the silk openings once again. She blushed a pale pink as he tied the sash at her waist, a liberty he should not have taken but could not resist. Dear God, just being close to her was going to destroy every shred of coherent thought in his brain.

"May I ask, then, why you are in my bedchamber?" she asked, stepping back from him.

"I have a gift for you." Benedict pulled the small package from the pocket of his own robe.

Her eyes fell upon the plain brown paper. "I do not require a wedding present, my lord."

"Benedict."

"Begging your pardon?" She arched an eyebrow, a sardonic expression for such a well-bred young woman. Precisely the sort of hidden surprises that made him fall in love with her.

"We are married now. I want you to use my Christian name." He extended the gift farther. "Please."

A heavy sigh escaped the seam of her lush lips. "What is the purpose of this?"

"Does a husband need a reason to give his wife a present?"

"I thought I made it clear that we are not going to have that kind of marriage, my lord."

"Benedict. And I don't recall agreeing to any terms defining what kind of marriage we would have."

"You established the terms of our marriage quite clearly with your accusation."

Regret sliced through him, deepening the wound that had bled inside his chest from the moment he realized how wrong he'd been. But by the time he had learned the truth, it was too late. He'd betrayed her trust when it mattered most. "A mistake for which I will be eternally sorry," he finally rasped.

"And this is an apology?" she asked with a glance at the gift.

"I am not so foolish as to think I can buy your forgiveness, my love. This is just a token of my affection."

Avoiding his gaze, she carefully unwrapped the paper and opened the long, velvet box to reveal the strand of rubies and diamonds that had cost him a small fortune. Her eyes widened. "My lord . . ." she breathed.

"Benedict," he corrected quietly. "Does it please you?"

"It is beautiful. But far too lavish for me."

"Nonsense. You are the Countess of Latford. You should be draped in jewels."

"Thank you, my lord." She turned to set the box on her vanity table. "If there is nothing else . . ."

Her politeness was a cold draft in the room. He wanted the heat back, the one that had scorched between them before he'd let his pride douse it with a single, reckless misunderstanding. Benedict once again closed the distance between them. "Please, my love. I beg you to give me a chance to make this right."

Her lashes fluttered as her pupils dilated. "To what end, Benedict?"

"A long and happy life together."

Her slim, elegant throat worked against a nervous swallow. "I don't believe in such things anymore." She brushed past him and crossed the room to stand beside the bed. "I told you I would do my duty, and I will. I will give you an heir as soon as possible. And then I and the child will away to the country so you can be free of me."

"I don't want to be free of you," he growled.

"My lord, two weeks ago, you accused me in front of the most vicious viper of the *ton* of arranging for us to be caught in a compromising situation to force you into marriage for your title."

"And I have since learned the truth."

"Yet the damage has been done."

"Then let me fix it." He rushed forward in words and steps. "Please, Irena."

Her lips parted. Perhaps it was the use of her name. Or

perhaps it was the strain of his voice, heavy from carrying the weight of an apology he would never stop repeating. Not until she believed it.

"I cannot change what I've done or the horrible things I said. All I can do is try to prove the depth of my regret for what I have done and the sincerity of my feelings for you. If you will let me."

There. A flutter of something other than disdain lit up her eyes. It dissipated immediately, but it had been there, and that mattered.

"Irena—"

"It's too late," she whispered.

"It's never too late. Not for love." He raised her hands to his lips, taking time to kiss each knuckle before meeting her shocked gaze. "And I do, Irena. I love you."

A brittle smile met his words as she tugged her hands away. "Love isn't enough, my lord."

"Benedict," he said, tracing his finger along the delicate line of her jaw. "And you're wrong. Love is all that matters. And I will do whatever it takes to prove that to you."

The arched eyebrow returned. "And how, daresay, do you plan to accomplish such a thing?"

"I am going to court you."

Irena snorted in a particularly unladylike way. "Don't be absurd."

Her laughter made him stand tall, the idea taking root as its brilliance bloomed with certainty. "My love," he said, "we are going to start over."

CHAPTER FOUR

"I am so disappointed in you."

Thea jumped at the sound of Liv's voice behind her. Her hand slipped on the dustpan, and the entire pile of dust and debris from the wall landed back on the floor. She glared over her shoulder. "Why?"

"I leave you alone with a perfectly good bottle of wine, and you ignore it to clean?"

It was Sunday night, and Liv had offered to put the girls to bed so Thea could apparently stare mindlessly, but Thea didn't have time for navel-gazing. She had to clean up the mess from the wall before the girls and the dog decided to play in it. Thea dumped the dirt in a trash can as Liv opened a bottle of Riesling chilling in the fridge. She poured two glasses, handed one to Thea, and plopped down on the couch. "Where's the fun in getting divorced if you can't use it as an excuse to get drunk?"

"I haven't found any part of getting divorced to be fun yet," Thea said, taking the opposite end of the couch.

"Hence, the wine," Liv said, stretching her legs out until her feet rested on Thea's lap. The fact that her legs were long enough to do that didn't help Thea's mood. How had Liv gotten lucky enough to get their father's tall, lean build, and Thea got stuck with the stature of a Smurf? Anytime Thea complained about being short, though, Gavin always said she was perfect because he could prop his chin on her head when he held her.

"You look like you're having second thoughts," Liv said.

"I'm not."

Liv tilted her head and narrowed her eyes, as if she didn't believe Thea's denial. "You're making the right decision."

"I know." Thea took a small sip to cover the twinge of guilt about all the things she hadn't told Liv. And wouldn't. Thea pointed at the pockmarked wall to change the subject. "This might have been a bit impulsive."

"I know. That's what I love about it. The feisty version of Thea clawed its way out with a roar."

Thea raised her eyebrows. "The feisty old Thea?"

"Yeah. Remember her? The one who went through a phase of painting naked and once handcuffed herself to a bulldozer to protect a tree on campus? I've missed her."

Thea stared at the wall and the small progress she'd made. "So have I."

When was the last time she'd done *anything* impulsive? Of course, being impulsive was partly to blame for how she got here. One throw-caution-to-the-wind romp in the back seat of Gavin's car was all it took for sperm to meet egg. And just like that, the mistakes of her own family were repeated. An unplanned pregnancy. A shotgun wedding. A move to the suburbs. A husband who was never home.

Speaking of . . . "You RSVP yet?" Thea asked. Their father was getting married for the fourth time in December.

Liv snorted. "What's the point?"

Thea nodded. "I'm thinking about writing *maybe next time* on the card, but that just seems mean."

"Which makes it perfect."

"What the hell is wrong with these women? How does he convince them to totally ignore his track record?"

"He shows them his bank account."

It really was the only thing that made sense. No woman in her right mind would look at his pattern of chronic infidelity and think, *Oh, yeah, husband material.*

Liv downed the rest of her wine. "She's thirty-two."

"Who?"

"Our new stepmother-to-be."

Thea's mouth dropped open. That was only six years older than her. "Oh, Mom is going to *love* that," Thea said with a snort.

"Speaking of our lovely mother," Liv said, "she called me twice today."

Thea straightened. Neither she nor Liv had talked to their mother in months, each for their own reasons.

"I haven't called her back," Liv added.

"Think she knows about the wedding?"

Liv shrugged and took a drink of water. "No idea, but I am *not* going to be the one to tell her."

Thea winced. Yeah, that wouldn't be pretty. But neither would the alternative explanation. "Maybe she heard about Gavin and me."

"Doubt it. She would've said something about it in her voicemail."

"Or called me directly." Nothing would have made their mother happier than the failure of Thea's marriage.

All your years of judging me, but you'll see. You think you're so in love now and that nothing will ever go wrong. But someday he'll break your heart, and you'll have to apologize to me.

That had been her mother's advice on Thea's wedding day.

Thea let her head fall back against the cushion, eager to change the subject. "How's Alexis coming with the café?" Liv was helping craft the menu for a friend who was opening a cat café and coffeehouse.

Liv gave her a knowing look but played along. "Good. She'll be open sometime in late January, I think."

"Have you decided if you're going to let her use Gran Gran's sugar cookie recipe?"

"Not yet. Part of me still wants to save them for . . ." She shrugged. "You know."

Her own restaurant. It had always been her dream.

Well, *always* was a stretch. There were several years when the only thing Liv dreamed about was finding new and inventive ways to rebel. Bad grades. Bad attitude. Bad boys. Liv reveled in them all during her teenage years. *Restless like a man chasing a worm with a bell on it*, as Gran Gran used to say. Which, honestly, Thea never quite understood but figured it meant Liv was in search of something that didn't exist.

And that was really something to which Thea could relate. Neither one of them had emerged from their messed-up childhood unscathed. They'd just hidden from their scars in different ways.

But no matter how much Liv wanted to open her own business, she had repeatedly turned down Thea's offers for a loan. Liv did things on her own or not at all, even if it meant enduring the hellish abuse of her tyrant boss.

"Thank you for being here," Thea said, rolling her head to look at Liv.

"You don't have to thank me. You were there for me more times than I could ever repay you for."

"That was my job. I was your big sister."

"You were a child."

Thea finished her wine and then stood with a sigh. "I think I'll go to bed."

Liv caught her hand as she walked by. "Everything is going to be fine, Thea."

"You and me against the world, right?"

Liv smiled softly and squeezed her hand.

Upstairs, Thea crept into the girls' rooms to check on them. She bent over Amelia's bed first and smoothed her hair back to drop a soft kiss on her forehead. Then she crossed the room to Ava's bed and repeated the gesture, but she lingered over Ava. Even in sleep, she was more serious than Amelia. She clutched her favorite stuffed animal tightly against her chest, and her tiny pink lips formed a tight line. It was as if the one-minute age difference between them officially made her the big sister with all the big-sister responsibilities.

Thea crept back out of the room and shut the door. With a soft snap, she called Butter to follow. She changed quickly into a nightgown and then went into the bathroom to do the nightly face-teeth-hair thing. On the way back to the bed, she stopped at Gavin's dresser. A tug of regret pulled her heart from its normal rhythm. He'd left almost everything here—most of his clothes and shoes, his collection of baseball caps. On the top of the dresser was a small dish full of the myriad things that he'd emptied from his pockets—loose change and gas receipts and a pack of orange Tic Tacs.

Thea brushed her fingers over the container. She could almost taste them, the hint of them ever-present on his breath when he'd brush his lips perfunctorily over hers before leaving for yet another road trip with the team.

So unlike the kiss he'd dropped on her today.

Thea picked up the Tic Tacs and threw them in the trash. Then she flipped off the light and slid into bed. Butter jumped up, circled several times, and then plopped down on Gavin's side.

Except it wasn't Gavin's side anymore. He'd left. And no amount of begging and apologizing on his part could change that now. Because, really, who the hell did he think he was? He didn't get to march in here and kiss her like that after all this time. As if she'd just melt and forget everything that happened.

Which, okay, she did for a brief moment. It just had been so long since he'd kissed her like that—like he used to kiss her, back before she got pregnant, when they were falling in love like maniacs. Back then, she would never have believed that the man who could barely stand to go a single day without tearing her clothes off would morph into a man who was almost apologetic when he reached for her at night. Who began to reach for her less and less. Who didn't even pay enough attention to her needs to notice that she was left frustrated time and again.

Until that night, that is. The night of the Big O-No.

Thea threw an arm over her eyes and squeezed them shut to block the memories, but like an annoying song that had wormed its way into her brain, the memory wouldn't leave her alone.

They hadn't had sex in two months at that point and were

barely speaking, other than the daily necessities of dealing with the kids and the house and his game schedule. She didn't want to go to the game, but even in her newly woke who-the-hell-have-I-become state, Thea wasn't that petty. She couldn't miss a playoff game. Not with so much on the line. So like a good little WAG, she donned his jersey, posed for photos, sat in the family section, and pasted on her *wholesomely pastel* smile.

And then came the ninth inning. Bases loaded. Two outs. And Gavin was at the plate. He needed to hit just a single to bring in the tying run. A double would mean the win. It was the most important moment of Gavin's career, and for the first time in a long time, it felt important to her too. She didn't have time to explore why, because the minute he swung the bat, she began to sob. Thea knew just from the sound of the bat that he'd done it. He'd nailed a home run. And not just any home run. A walk-off grand slam.

Tears fell down her face as she watched her husband race around the bases, his arms in the air. His teammates waited for him at home plate in a screaming, celebratory melee. The crowd chanted his name. Del drenched him in Gatorade. The announcers called it a Hollywood finish. It was the kind of moment every player dreams of their entire lives but few ever get. And she got caught up in it as much as anyone else. She drank the champagne in the clubhouse. Let him lift her off the ground and kiss her.

By the time they got home, they were just like they used to be. Manic. Crazed for each other. They barely made it to their bedroom before ripping at each other's clothes. And Gavin, oh Gavin . . . he devoured her like he used to.

There was a fierceness in his touch she hadn't felt in so long. An urgency that excited her, thrilled her. And she returned the fervor, the madness. She was drunk on him, on champagne, on desire.

Her orgasm took her by surprise, blinding her, making her shake and cry out. But then Gavin suddenly went still.

"Wh-wh-what was that?"

Thea laughed, joy filling her up and spilling out. "I know it's been a while since we've done it, but did you forget what it's called?"

Gavin planted his hands on either side of her body and raised his torso. "What the hell was that, Thea?"

The coldness in his voice sent a chill through her. "What do you mean?"

He pulled out of her unceremoniously. What remained of her pleasure began to fade, and the desire on his face had been replaced by a mask she couldn't read but didn't need to. Dread soured her stomach. He knew. Oh, shit. He knew.

"D-did you—" He cut himself off. Blinked. Swallowed. "Did you have an orgasm?"

Thea tried to smile but couldn't.

"Oh my God," he breathed, stumbling back. "You've been faking it." A statement. Not a question.

Thea swallowed. "What? No, I haven't."

His face transformed into a mask of such hurt and betrayal that she reached for him. He stumbled away from her. "Don't lie to me, Thea. How long have you been faking it?"

"Gavin . . ."

"How fucking long?" He yelled in a voice so un-Gavin-like that she jumped. Thea grabbed her jersey from the floor and pulled it back on. The shimmery illusion of the past couple of hours was quickly fading, revealing it for the mirage that it was.

At her silence, Gavin planted his hands on his head. "Have you *always* faked it?"

There was no point in lying. And dammit, she was sick of lying, anyway. Sick of wearing a fake smile. Sick of pretending things were fine. Sick of fucking faking it. "Always?" she snapped. "No. Not always. Just since the girls were born."

"That's our entire marriage!"

"Yeah, it is. How the hell did it take you this long to notice?"

He stared at her and, without another word, stormed into the guest room. He never returned to their bed.

What else was it that Gran Gran used to say? *If a man wants to leave you, wave goodbye and lock the doors. You've got better things to do than chase a lost cause.*

Thea did have better things to do. Like finish her degree. Rebuild the career she abandoned for Gavin's. Raise strong, confident daughters. And never, ever again be so stupid as to trust her heart to a man.

CHAPTER FIVE

By Monday morning, Gavin didn't think he could get any more depressed. But then someone knocked on the door of his hotel room at eight in the morning and he realized how wrong he was.

Because standing on the other side of the door was Book-Boner Braden Mack.

"What the fuck are you doing here?"

"Is that any way to talk to a friend who brings you coffee?"

"You're not my friend. You're a pain in my ass." The coffee sounded good, though, so he stepped back and let Mack in. "And you didn't answer my question."

"I'm waiting for Del."

"Why?"

"Because we have work to do." Mack tugged a paper cup from the cardboard drink carrier he was carrying. "I got you a pumpkin spice latte. With cinnamon sprinkles. Seems like your speed."

Gavin turned away with a grimace and an obscene gesture,

but the need for caffeine overruled his pride. He flipped open the tab on the plastic top and took a sip. An explosion of flavor brought his feet to a halt and a moan from his mouth. Sweet holy coffee gods. This shit was delicious. It was a liquid pumpkin pie. Why the hell hadn't he ever tried this before? No wonder women drank this shit.

Mack grinned. "Right? I love these things."

The door vibrated with another insistent knock. It was Del, who barreled inside with an expression that said he wasn't in the mood for bullshit. "You better have coffee for me," he barked.

Mack pointed at the drink carrier. "Pumpkin spice latte, just as you ordered."

Gavin's mouth dropped open. "You drink these too?"

Del dropped unceremoniously into a chair by the window. "I love them, but I'm too embarrassed to order them for myself."

Mack plopped down on the couch and kicked up his feet. "Don't be ashamed for liking them. The backlash against the PSL is a perfect example of how toxic masculinity permeates even the most mundane things in life. If masses of women like something, our society automatically begins to mock them. Just like romance novels. If women like them, they must be a joke, right?"

Gavin blinked. "You sound like Malcolm."

"I'm not just a pretty face, man." Mack set down his coffee and stood. "Point me to your clothes."

Gavin choked into his cup. "Why?"

"We have to pick out what you're going to wear for the school musical tonight."

"You're here to pick out my clothes?"

"Among other things," Del said.

Mack marched to the single closet across from the bathroom

and yanked open the doors. "Dude, this is sad," he said, shoving several hangers aside. "This is all you own?"

"No, shithead. Most of my clothes are still at the house."

"Well, I can't work with this. We might have to go shopping."

"I am *not* going shopping with you."

"Toxic masculinity," Mack tsked.

Del let out a sigh like a beleaguered bus driver who still had three hours to go on a field trip. "I could be home making love with my wife right now."

Mack and Gavin both whipped around with a yell.

Del shrugged. "She was willing. She tried luring me back into bed—"

Mack covered his ears. "Not in front of the children!"

"Then behave!" Del barked. He pointed at Mack. "Stop insulting his clothes and find something. And you." He pointed at Gavin. "Let's hear it."

Gavin glanced around, as if Del had been talking to someone else. "Hear what?"

"What you've learned so far."

"Learned?"

"From the book," Del said, crossing his arms. "You *have* started reading, right?"

Gavin winced.

Del grew several inches. Or so it seemed. "Are you taking this seriously at all?"

"Yes—"

"Because we took a chance inviting you into this club."

"You just gave me the damn thing on Saturday!"

"Oh, I'm sorry," Del said. "Is there a more pressing issue in your life right now that requires your attention? Because I thought saving your marriage was your top priority." He dragged a hand over his head and stared into space for a minute. Then he looked back at Gavin. "How much have you read?"

"The first chapter."

"Christ," Del muttered.

"Look, Del. I gotta be honest. I'm not sure what I'm supposed to be getting out of this book."

"That's because you're not trying. Go get it."

Gavin trudged to the bedside table, feeling like a kid who'd just been sent to the principal's office for not doing his homework. He pulled *His Pissed-off Countess* or whatever it was called from the drawer. Del took it from him and held it aloft like a preacher about to drop some gospel.

"We chose this book for you for a reason."

"Because it's about a man who fucks up his marriage. Got it."

"Not just that." Del opened the book and flipped a couple of pages until he found what he was looking for. He cleared his throat. " 'My love,' " Del read. " 'We are going to start over.' "

"So?" Gavin said.

"That's exactly what you and Thea are going to do."

"I don't get it."

"You're going to court your wife again." Del tossed the book onto the bed. "And we don't have a lot of time, so stand up."

"Why?"

"Because we need to work on your flirting."

Gavin choked on his coffee a second time. "No, we don't."

"You screwed things up by going over there Saturday, so you really gotta work it tonight. Get her to soften up a little so you can press your case. Come here."

Gavin backed up. "No way. Thea hates flirting."

"What?" Mack snorted over his shoulder. "That's bullshit. How'd you get her to go out with you the first time?"

"By not flirting." Which was true. She even told him so once. She noticed him in the coffee shop where she worked precisely because he never trotted out stupid lines on her or tried to be overly familiar. He wondered if she would've found it so endearing if she'd known he was just terrified that she'd laugh at him, but hey, it worked.

Del let out another sigh. "Gavin, all women like to be flirted with. They just like different kinds of flirting. Some like dirty talk. Some like chivalrous overtures. Others like quiet, sweet gestures."

"How the hell am I supposed to know what Thea likes?"

Mack turned away from the closet with an incredulous expression. "How long have you two been married?"

Del interrupted. "This is part of the learning-her-language thing."

"I'm not going to learn it by tonight!" Christ, this was humiliating.

Del nodded some kind of unspoken message to Mack, who whined, "Why me?" before dragging his feet out of the room. He instantly returned, transformed. He leaned in the doorway, crossed his arms over his chest, and cocked a half smile. Then he winked.

Gavin looked over his shoulder and back again. "What the fuck."

"You look amazing. I can't believe I get to be seen next to you."

"Um . . ."

"You should warn a guy before you walk out in a dress like

that." Then he did a long, slow up and down with his eyes. And then it was over. He shrugged and peeled away from the door. "Flirting is about confidence, man. That's all it is."

"I don't have a lot of that right now."

"Not *your* confidence, dipshit. Hers. You want to make her feel like she's the only woman in the room. It's about putting a smile on her face, a spring in her step, a little blush in her cheeks. Say things that she'll replay over and over again when she's in bed."

Gavin nearly groaned at the image that conjured. Thea in bed. Wearing one of those short silk things she wore . . . alone. Or worse, with some other guy. Oh God, he was going to puke.

"Put down your coffee," Del ordered.

Gavin obeyed. Del adopted a weird-ass smile and started walking toward him. His eyes locked with Gavin's, and goddamn, Gavin couldn't fucking look away. He didn't even realize he'd backed up until he collided with the wall. Del flattened his hands on either side of Gavin's shoulders and smiled as he leaned. "Hey."

"Hey," Gavin automatically answered.

"I can't stop thinking about last night."

Gavin gulped. "Wh-what happened last night?"

Del winked. "You want me to remind you?"

Jesus. Gavin flattened himself against the wall. "I feel obligated to tell you that I might be mildly aroused right now."

"You must really be desperate," Del said, still in character. He twitched his eyebrows and glanced at Gavin's mouth. "This isn't even my best effort."

Mack cleared his throat. "Sorry to break up your special moment, but we have a crisis." He held up a gray sweater. "This is the one and only decent thing Captain Douchebag has in his entire pathetic closet."

Gavin knocked Del's arms away.

Del backed out of his personal space. "Just remember to stare into her eyes a lot. Eye contact is key."

"And wink," Mack said, tossing the sweater on the bed. "Women love that shit."

Del added one last thing. "And look at her lips. You want her to think that you're imagining them all over your body."

That part, at least, wouldn't require any work. Gavin spent the better part of his days imagining Thea's lips on his body.

But wait . . . Gavin looked back and forth between them. "That's it? Tell her I like her dress and act like I want her to lick me? That's your entire plan for me?"

"For now."

Gavin sank back down on the bed. "This is hopeless."

"It'd be easier if you'd tell us what really happened between you two."

"Not going to happen."

"OK," Del said with another drawn-out sigh. "Then just tell us *something*. Anything. Tell us one thing she said on Saturday that might help us come up with a plan for tonight."

Gavin fell on his back and stared at the ceiling. Every word she'd spoken on Saturday had taken up permanent residence in his brain, but most of it would reveal too much if he shared it with the guys.

"She wants to keep the house," he said.

Del perked up. "She said that?"

Gavin nodded. "She said it would be easier for the girls if one of us kept the only house they've ever known, and she asked if I would pay it off for her."

Del and Mack looked at each other. "That could work," Mack said.

"It's risky," Del added. "And this isn't like Regency times. Thea is half-owner of all property by law."

"But the symbolism of it could go a long way," Mack said.

"Hey," Gavin said, sitting up and waving his hands. "You guys want to fucking clue me in here?"

"You're going to up the ante."

"Am I supposed to know what that means?"

Del and Mack exchanged a glance that said Gavin wasn't going to like the answer.

He was right.

Del sucked in a breath and let it out fast. "You're going to agree to a divorce."

What. The. Fuck.

"Yeah," Mack said. "But first we're going shopping."

CHAPTER SIX

"Mommy, too hard."

Thea looked down at the face-paint crayon in her hand pressed against Ava's face. She'd volunteered to help with stage props and face paint for the school musical, and though the task provided some much-needed distraction, her mind kept wandering as the clock ticked closer to the moment when Gavin would arrive.

She wished for the hundredth time that Liv could be there for moral support, but her sister had to work a late shift tonight.

"Sorry, honey," Thea said, lifting the crayon from Ava's face.

"Mommy, that's so pretty!" Amelia gushed next to her. "You draw so good."

"So *well*," Thea quietly corrected. "And thank you. That's very sweet."

Thea finished the last of the flowers on Ava's deer face—both girls were playing the part of fawns—and packed up the rest of the paints. Just ten minutes until showtime. The teacher clapped her hands and raised her voice above the excited chatter as she asked the kids to start lining up. Which was Thea's cue to head out to the auditorium. She wished she had lied to Gavin and said she was needed backstage during the show, because she had lost all her energy for the small talk and fake smiles that were prerequisites for appearing anywhere remotely public with Gavin. God grant her the serenity not to sucker-punch the first person who gushed about Gavin's grand slam.

Her stomach clenched as she descended the stairs beside the stage. Her eyes swept across the throng of families looking for seats. A dozen women all wore the same annoyed expression that could only mean their husbands had been late and now they couldn't find more than two red velvet seats together for their families. What she didn't see was Gavin, thank God. Maybe if she hovered long enough they, too, would be unable to sit together.

Relief was short-lived, though.

"Hey."

Jumping at the sound of his voice, she turned. Gavin stood below the staircase, smiling up at her in a thin V-neck sweater she'd never seen before. It wrapped around his muscles as if even cotton couldn't resist him. Good thing Thea could. She'd had a shot in the butt called *broken heart* and was now immune to round biceps and thick forearms and the tantalizing valley between honed pecs—

Ugh. She descended the rest of the stairs. "You found seats?"

He pointed up the aisle. "Tenth row. I put my coat on it to hold the seats."

Gavin waited for her to go first, and then he settled a hand low on her back as if they were together. Just another happy mom and dad. She discreetly moved away from his reach just as a voice rose above the cacophony.

"Hey, you're Gavin Scott, right?"

Aaaand of course. Thea turned around, a string of unintelligible, made-up curse words flitting through her mind. A dad in jeans and a buzz cut held out his hand to Gavin, who stopped politely—as he always did for fans.

Thea pasted on her fake smile and extended her hand, as well. "Thea Scott."

The man limply shook her fingers. How could there still be men in the world who wouldn't shake a woman's hand? He barely spared her a glance as he turned his attention back to Gavin.

"Tough break about that last game," the man said. "I can't believe that last call. The umpire must have been blind."

A vein bulged in Gavin's jaw. He hated it when people blamed the officials for losses. "Our fault for letting one bad call lead to a loss. I didn't play as well as I should have."

"Nah, it was Del Hicks, man. He missed that pop-up. His contract is up, right? Maybe we can get rid of him this year. Shed some dead weight."

"Del Hicks is m-m-m—"

Thea would've known just by the look on the other man's face that Gavin had started stammering. The asshole looked everywhere but at Gavin. As if stuttering was something to be embarrassed about. Thea despised people like him. They claimed to be such huge fans of Gavin's, but the minute he began to stutter, they acted like he had a contagious disease.

Acting on nothing more than instinct, Thea slid her hand into Gavin's and squeezed. His fingers closed around hers, and he exhaled. He started again. "Del Hicks is actually my best friend," he said coldly.

"Oh. Well, I'll, uh, I'll let you guys get to your seats," the man said, his face burning. "Nice to meet you."

Thea turned and tried to tug her hand from Gavin's, but he wouldn't let go. Instead, he pulled her back and brought his lips to her ear, bringing with him the scent of his soap and the teasing whisper of his Tic Tac–scented breath against her skin.

"Thank you," he said quietly.

"That guy was a jerk."

"Thea."

The solemn tone of his voice brought her gaze to his unwittingly. She looked quickly away, though, because the same heaviness of his voice was in his eyes, and that was just too much weight for her to carry right now. "Can you not do that?"

"Do what?"

"Whatever you were about to do. I can't do that with you right now."

"All I did was say your name."

"It was *how* you said my name."

"How did I say it?"

"Like it meant something," she spit out under her breath.

He leaned slowly, purposefully, a shockingly mischievous glean in his eyes. Her heart did *not* start to thud, and her skin absolutely did *not* prickle with goose bumps at the seductive caress of his voice. "And what would it mean if I told you I woke up calling your name this morning?" he murmured.

What the . . . ?

He winked, let go of her hand, and walked to their seats.

Thea stood in the aisle and squeaked out a belated protest.

Then her feet came back to life. "What was that?" she hissed as she sat down.

He hooked an ankle over his knee in a casually male pose. "What do you mean?"

"You know exactly what I mean! Did you just wink at me?"

"I believe so, yes."

"You don't wink."

"That's not true."

"It absolutely is true. A woman remembers every time a man winks at her, because we love winking. It's like catnip. Wink at us, and we roll over and start purring. You haven't winked at me in a long time."

"Then I'm an idiot." Gavin slowly lowered his gaze to lips. "Because I wouldn't mind hearing you purr."

Thea squeaked. "Excuse me?"

"You look beautiful, by the way," Gavin said, nonchalantly pulling his eyes back to the stage. "You should w-warn a guy before w-w-walking out in that dress."

The lights dimmed, and blessed darkness hid the way her cheeks absolutely, positively did *not* flush with heat.

Gavin spared a glance at Thea in the dark theater. Her spine was ramrod straight, her legs crossed tightly. If she clenched her own hands any harder, she'd snap a finger.

He was going to personally disembowel Del and Mack if this didn't work. Not just the flirting, either. He couldn't believe what they wanted him to do tonight. He couldn't believe he'd agreed to give it a try.

The curtain rose over the stage as a recorded orchestra began to play over the speakers. A line of kids danced onto the stage in a mishmash of animal faces and uneven steps. He puffed out a laugh as he recognized their daughters. Even onstage, their personalities were clear. Amelia was flashy, vibrant, dancing to her own beat. Ava was serious, determined to get the prescribed steps correct. Next to him, Thea's hands lost their rigid grip of each other, and her spine relaxed against the back of her theater chair. Whatever anger she held for him was at least temporarily pushed aside at the sight of their girls.

A sensation of falling made his vision swim as he watched her—the way her face reacted to every adorable thing Ava and Amelia did, the gentle curve of her jaw, the dimpled cheek that deepened as she laughed, the tiny crescent-shaped scar below her left ear.

Thea's eyes darted at him in the dark now, and the wariness in her expression brought a chill to his skin.

The show lasted an hour. As soon as the curtain dropped, she whipped her gaze to his. "Stop."

He decided to play dumb, but *oh shit* sweat prickled his armpits. "Stop what?"

"Whatever the hell you're doing," Thea whispered, her eyes darting around them to make sure no one was listening. "You stared at me the whole time. And that whole purring comment? What are you *doing*?"

He tried the half-smile thing Mack used. "Just flirting with my wife."

"Flirting?!" Her hand covered his forehead. "Do you have a fever?"

Heart pounding, Gavin peeled her hand away, turned it over,

and pressed his lips to her palm. "As a matter of fact," he murmured in what he hoped was a seductive tone, "I do."

Thea yanked her hand away and leaned back, staring at him as if he'd just sprouted horns. "You got in a car accident, didn't you? Or fell down the stairs or got hit in the head with a line drive."

Gavin swallowed. "Huh?"

"A head wound. It's the only explanation. You need to see a doctor."

"Maybe we could play doctor?" The uncertain whine of his voice belied any attempt at confident seduction.

Thea's lush, glossy lips parted. But a split-second later, she snapped them shut and ground her molars. Like a soldier called to attention, she shot to her feet. When he failed to follow suit, she glared pointedly at his knees, as if his six-three frame was a deliberate conspiracy against her ability to make a dramatic exit.

He stood, let her brush past him, and then followed her into the slow-moving masses headed for the exit. The staging area outside the auditorium filled up quickly with families waiting for their children. Gavin politely elbowed through, keeping as close to Thea as he could. She walked stiffly, head down, her purse clutched against her side as if it held the nuclear codes.

A few genuine smiles greeted Gavin, and he returned those. But he'd long ago learned how to deftly avoid the other kind of smile—the nervous fan smile that warned someone was one excited *go for it* from asking for an autograph or a selfie. Fans were the lifeblood of professional sports, and he'd challenge any city in America to find a more loyal fan base than Nashville. But professional athletes were also humans who sometimes just wanted a quiet night with their families or to watch their children perform at school.

Or to woo their wives into not divorcing their sorry asses.

When he reached Thea's side, he slid his hands into his pockets. "So I was thinking that after this, maybe we could—"

He didn't get a chance to finish his suggestion that they go out to eat as a family—which was Del's idea—because a woman in a red suit and high heels called Thea's name and click-clicked over with a cheery wave.

"Mrs. Martinez," Thea said in greeting.

"Call me Lydia." The woman smiled. "I'm so glad I caught you."

Thea looked at Gavin and blinked. "Oh, um. Gavin, this is Mrs. Martinez, the principal of the elementary school. Lydia, this is Gavin. My husband."

My husband. Those two words had never sounded more stilted or more promising.

The woman dutifully extended her hand, and Gavin shook it. "Pleasure to meet you."

The principal turned back to Thea. "I just wanted to let you know that I will have your letter of recommendation done by next week. Is that soon enough?"

Letter of recommendation? Thea glanced at him—nervously, it seemed—and then back at Lydia. "That would be perfect, Lydia. Thank you for doing that."

Lydia waved away the sentiment. "It's the least I can do after how much time you have volunteered this year and last."

Lydia raced off again with a *see you next week* tossed over her shoulder.

"Letter of recommendation for what?" Gavin asked.

"Vanderbilt," she said with a forced smile. "I'm going back to school to finish my degree."

"Wh-when did you decide this?"

A firestorm erupted in her eyes. "I've always planned to finish my degree, Gavin."

"Thea, I'm not saying you can't—"

Oh, shit. Wrong thing to say. Very much wrong thing to say. Thea's neck lengthened and flushed red. "Well, thank God for that. Because I definitely wasn't going to do it without your permission."

Gavin raked his fingers through his hair. "Babe, that's not what I meant. Can we just take this down a notch and—"

"Are you seriously telling me to calm down? Because that rarely has the desired effect."

Dear God in heaven, he was going down in a ball of fire. He could actually feel the flames licking his skin. A whistling sound in his ear told him he was one stupid remark away from crashing and dying.

"Mommy, did you see us?"

"Thank God," Gavin breathed as Amelia and Ava ran toward them.

Thea's features transformed. She opened her arms and waited for them to throw themselves against her. "You were amazing!" she said, bending to kiss each one. "The best dancing fawns ever."

"Did you see us, Daddy?" Amelia asked, moving to hug his legs.

"I did, sweetie. You were incredible."

"I'm hungry," Ava said, and Gavin wanted to twirl her around for the segue.

"I'll make you some macaroni and cheese when we get home," Thea said.

The whistling grew louder, but he was going to risk it. "You know what? I'm hungry too. Why don't we go to Stella's?"

Stella's was their favorite restaurant. They'd been taking the girls to the small downtown diner since they could sit up in high chairs.

"Yeah, Mommy! Can we go to Stella's?" Amelia asked.

Gavin held his breath as he met Thea's hard gaze. He swallowed. "You can tell me more about Vanderbilt," he suggested.

Thea shot him a glare that felt like a kick in the balls, but then she pasted on a happy smile for the girls. "That sounds great," she said. "Why don't you take the girls, and I'll meet you there?"

"I want to ride with Mommy," Ava said, gripping her hand.

Gavin flinched as her words hit their mark, but he managed to smile. "Amelia can ride with me, and Ava with you."

They were parked on opposite ends of the lot, so they parted ways on the sidewalk. Amelia held his hand tightly and started to swing her arm back and forth. "Ava th-leeps with Mommy every night," she said, hopping off the curb.

His chest shifted at her lisp. Thea had reassured him several times that it was no reason to worry, but he did. Having a stutter was no reason to be ashamed, of course, but it took Gavin a long time to be at peace with his. He'd endured way too much bullying as a kid and a teenager to not be worried about the idea that his own daughters could face the same thing.

"Every night, huh?" he said, finally catching up to what Amelia had told him.

"She wakes up and gets in with Mommy, but not me. I sleep in my own bed all night. She calls me a baby because I don't like thunder, but she's a baby because she's afraid of the dark."

Gavin paused along a row of parked cars and crouched down

to be eye level with her. "It's not very nice to call each other babies, honey. It's normal to be afraid of things." The words of fatherly wisdom rolled off his tongue, but his brain was distracted. Since when was Ava afraid of the dark? "Even grown-ups are afraid of things. It doesn't make us babies, does it?"

Amelia shook her head. Gavin smiled and stood. They started walking again, but they hadn't taken more than a few steps when Amelia asked. "What are you afraid of, Daddy?"

Losing you and your mom, he thought, his throat thickening. It seemed his daughters were determined to destroy him emotionally today. He swallowed against the lump. "Clowns," he said, exaggerating a shudder. "Big red shoes and squeaky noses."

Then he grabbed her under the arms, hoisted her onto his shoulders, and reveled in her squeal of joy.

CHAPTER SEVEN

"There they are."

Thea pointed as Gavin's SUV turned into Stella's parking lot. She and Ava had been waiting on a bench outside the restaurant for about five minutes. Gavin must have gotten caught in the post-play parking jam. Which was fine, because Thea needed a minute— or five—to calm down. And *not* because Gavin told her to, but because he had. When had a woman ever calmed down because a man told her to do so?

The only thing that was going to make her calm down was for this night to be over. She could've killed him for suggesting Stella's in front of the girls. He should have known they would cling to the idea and beg to do it.

Thea stood as Gavin and Amelia crossed the parking lot. She turned away from his smile, but somehow his hand once again found a place on the small of her back. She stiffened, and he let it fall away.

"Well, look who's here," said Ashley, a waitress who had

worked at Stella's as long as they'd been eating there, when they walked in. "Haven't seen you guys since the summer." She gasped dramatically at the girls' faces. "Oh my gosh, I don't think we serve deer here."

"We're fawns," Amelia corrected happily. "We had a school musical today!"

"A school musical? You aren't old enough for that. I refuse to believe it." Ashley winked at Thea and nodded for them to follow her. "Your favorite booth is open."

This is what Thea loved about living in a small town. They were regulars here with their own booth. Was there anything more comforting than a place where everyone knew your names and the menu never changed? It was the kind of simple tradition Thea and Liv had never known as kids. Would it seem less special for the girls once they stopped coming as a quartet and moved on as a trio?

The girls followed Ashley through the maze of tables decorated with red-checkered tablecloths and vases of fresh flowers that were refilled every morning. Each window was bracketed by white farmhouse shutters on which Stella had draped twine for hanging snapshots of customers and their families. Including theirs. That was going to be awkward in a few months.

The girls slid in on opposite sides of the table, and Thea let out the breath she'd been holding. She didn't want to sit next to Gavin, which was childish, but still.

"Y'all want your usual to drink?" Ashley asked as they all settled in. "Two waters and two chocolate milks?"

"Sounds great," Gavin answered. "Thanks."

"I want the grilled cheese," Amelia said, scampering onto her knees and leaning her elbows on the table. "And applesauce."

"What do you want, honey?" Thea asked Ava. "You want the grilled cheese too?"

Ava shrugged. Thea held in a sigh. She couldn't let this sullen behavior go on much longer, because Ava was venturing into outright disrespect, but Thea wasn't going to say anything now. Tonight was tense enough already. Besides, she wasn't going to punish her daughter for the crime of being a child and expressing her confusion the only way a child knew how. Adults expected too much of children sometimes.

Once, in the weeks after her father filed for divorce, Thea's mother locked herself in her room for days. When Thea knocked one day to complain she was hungry, her mother screamed at her to grow up and to stop being so selfish.

Thea had been ten. She and Liv learned to cook for themselves after that.

Thea planned to make sure the girls received age-appropriate counseling after the divorce—something else she and Liv probably would have benefited from. Hopefully, that would help Ava adjust to the new reality of her world.

The waitress wandered over with their drinks and took their order before leaving them again in strained silence.

"Daisies," Gavin suddenly said, staring at the jar in the center of the table. He smiled at Amelia. "Mommy had a daisy in her hair the first time I saw her."

Amelia giggled. "She did?"

"I did?"

Gavin looked at her. "It was woven into your braid."

"Why did you have a daisy in your braid, Mommy?" Amelia asked.

"I don't know. I don't remember that."

"That's too bad," Gavin said quietly. "Because I've never forgotten it."

"Mommy likes dandelions," Ava grumped.

Thea blinked several times and tore her gaze away from Gavin, who was studying her again like he did during the theater. Like he did on Saturday. As if seeing her for the first time. Maybe he was. It had been years since she felt like he saw her at all.

Thea smoothed Ava's hair. "Dandelions from you will always be my favorite."

Awkwardness hung in the air like a thick layer of humidity. Thea pulled out the crayons and coloring books she always carried in her purse to keep the girls occupied when they were out. This time, though, Thea was using them to occupy herself. She helped Ava color a picture for several minutes until Gavin cleared his throat.

"So," Gavin started, toying with his glass of water. "Wh-when are you going back to school?"

Thea kept her eyes locked on the coloring book. "If I'm accepted, I'll start classes this summer."

"So it's just for one semester?"

She snorted. "I wish. Maybe if I went full time, but that's not really possible with the girls. I hope to be done in eighteen months."

"Eighteen months," he repeated. "That, uh, that seems doable."

"I'm glad you approve."

"And then what? I mean, after you have your degree?"

"I'll pursue an art career. Just like I always planned."

He hesitated a long moment before responding to that one.

"That's, uh, that's great," he said. "I'm glad to see you return to your art."

"So am I."

Their food arrived, and the busy task of helping the girls eat while trying to also get some food into themselves stifled any other conversation, thankfully. Midway through dessert—a brownie skillet that they always shared as a family—Stella herself emerged from the back and wandered over to their table to chat.

"I was just thinking about y'all," she said. "Been ages since you've been in."

"We've been busy," Thea said automatically, the lie so natural that she almost believed it herself. "The girls are in preschool now and taking dance classes, so it's hard to get out."

"Y'all have any plans for the holidays?"

"Nothing concrete," Thea said.

Amelia looked up with a chocolate ring around her mouth. "We're going to see Grammy and Papa in Ohio for 'Sanksgiving."

Ah, shit. Thea hadn't yet told the girls that their plan to visit Gavin's parents was cancelled. She'd hoped they'd forgotten about it since it had been more than two months since she and Gavin had even talked about it. But little girls rarely forgot about trips to see grandparents who spoiled them.

"Well, that was our plan, but, um—" Thea searched the air for an excuse but came up empty. Her ability to lie on command was quickly losing power. "But it turns out we're just going to be sticking around here."

"But I want to go see Grammy!" Amelia whined.

"Me too," Ava said, her voice an octave higher than Amelia's.

Thea rested a hand on Ava's leg. "Sweetie, we'll talk about it later."

"But why can't we go?" Amelia asked.

"Amelia," Gavin said quietly but firmly. "Mommy said w-we'll talk about it at home later."

"But you don't come home anymore!"

The record-screeching silence that followed was so cartoonishly comical, Thea half expected to hear the chirp of crickets next. "Well," Stella said, her cheeks pinking as she failed at pretending she had no idea that Amelia had just announced to the entire restaurant that Thea and Gavin were separated. "It was awfully nice to see y'all again. I'll leave you to your dessert."

She walked away, and then the real chaos started.

"Can we *please* go to Grammy's?" Amelia asked.

"Not this year, honey," Gavin said.

"But why not?"

"I'm too busy with baseball stuff, sweetie."

Ava slumped in her seat, her lips pouty.

"Can Daddy read to us tonight?" Amelia said.

Thea dug her fingertips into her temple. "Honey, Daddy can't do that tonight, OK?"

"Why not?" Amelia asked, her lip beginning to quiver.

"Hey," Gavin said, tugging Amelia against his side. "I will read to you guys soon, OK?"

"But I want tonight!" The dam burst. Tears fell down Amelia's face.

Which made Ava start crying, because that's what twins did.

And when Ava started crying, she got really loud. And suddenly she blurted, "I don't want Daddy to play baseball!"

There was another stunned silence, and then Ava began to sob louder. And then Amelia yelled, "I don't want Daddy to play baseball either!"

And by now the entire restaurant was staring. Gavin let out a quiet *dammit* under his breath and dragged his hands down his face.

Thea's entire body trembled as she wrapped her arm around Ava's shoulders. "Honey, why don't you want Daddy to play baseball?"

Ava wiped a hand across her face, smearing the white dots from her fawn makeup into long streaks down her cheek. "Because it makes him go away, and you guys say mad words at each other."

Thea's eyes shot up and collided with Gavin's. She read her own thoughts in his eyes. "When did we say mad words at each other?" Gavin asked.

"When Daddy hit the big home run." Ava hiccupped. "You made fighting noises and then said mad words."

Heat rushed up Thea's neck and face, followed immediately by gut-clenching comprehension. Ava had apparently woken up that night, and not only had she heard them having sex—that's the only thing *fighting noises* could mean—she then heard their fight afterward.

Thea's head moved as if encased in a Jell-O mold as she once again lifted her gaze to Gavin. They locked eyes—his pained, hers cloudy.

The girls were crying. People were staring. Something cold washed over her skin. Before she could stop herself, she opened her mouth and said, "You know what? How about if Daddy does come home and reads to you tonight? Would that make you feel better?"

. . .

Gavin paid the bill as Thea ushered the girls out to her car. He followed them home in the dark, his hands clenching the wheel and gut churning. How long would it take for him to stop replaying Ava's words? *It makes him go away and you say mad words at each other.* What the hell had he done to his children? To his family?

He pulled into the driveway behind Thea. She refused to meet his eyes as he helped to unbuckle the girls from the back seat. Butter greeted them at the door.

"Baths first and then Daddy can read to you?" Thea asked as she hung up the girls' coats. Her voice had a brittle quality to it, as if she were one tense exchange away from either shattering or going full wrecking ball on the wall again.

"I'll let Butter out," Gavin offered.

Thea responded with a stiff thank-you, and he'd never felt so much like a visitor in his own house. As Thea walked upstairs with the girls, he led Butter to the back door. The smell of dust and drywall clashed with the familiar scents of home—Thea's lotion, the lavender candles she was always burning, the undercurrent of dog, and the ever-present tang of markers and paint from the girls' arts and crafts. By the time Butter was done circling the yard for the perfect spot to piss, Gavin could hear the tub running upstairs. He jogged upstairs and knocked on the closed bathroom door.

"Do you want help?" he asked.

Thea answered *no.*

The sense of being a stranger returned as he hovered outside the door. He looked to his right to the master bedroom. Their bedroom. He walked toward it and stood in the open doorway. Thea hadn't made the bed that morning, and the sight of the rumpled sheets brought a slam of regret to his stomach as powerful as a sucker punch. The last time he'd been in their bed had been that night. One of the most amazing moments of his life, followed almost immediately by the worst.

"What are you doing?" Thea said behind him. He turned around. He hadn't heard the bathroom door open, but his daughters now stood in the hallway with matching towels wrapped around them.

"Nothing," he said. "I just—I'll help get them into their pajamas."

Silence reigned as he and Thea worked together to dry the girls off and thread their arms and legs into matching unicorn pajamas. Thea stood then, collected the wet towels, and told them to pick out a book while she changed her clothes.

The girls settled on a story about a raccoon who gets lost on his way to his grandma's house for Christmas. They had just settled on Amelia's bed when Thea walked back in. She had changed into a pair of sweatpants and his old Huntsville Rockets minor league sweatshirt, the one she'd claimed shortly after they started dating. He'd lost all coherent thought the first time he saw her in it. Something regressively possessive stole over him, as if he'd claimed her. Officially. With a sweatshirt.

Still today, there was something about the sight of his petite wife swimming in his massive clothes that always turned him on. She probably only chose it tonight because it was easy, clean, and familiar. But for him, it held meaning and memory. She'd been wearing that very sweatshirt when she told him she was pregnant. He hadn't been able to reach her for three days. She ignored all his calls and texts, and her coworkers at the coffee shop said she'd been calling in sick. When he finally went to her apartment and convinced her to at least open the door, he was prepared for anything. Or so he thought.

"What are you doing here?" she asked, hugging herself, hands hidden by the cuffs of his sweatshirt.

Gavin braced his hands on either side of the doorframe, his practiced speech replaced by panicked bumbling the instant he saw her face. "Just talk to me. OK? W-wh-whatever it is, just say it."

She stared with empty eyes for a moment and then turned without a word. He watched from the doorway as she disappeared into her bathroom. Moments later, she returned, a white stick in her hands.

Every nerve in Gavin's body erupted as if he'd been struck by lightning. "Wh-what is that?"

She stopped halfway across the small living room. Gavin walked in, shut the door, and crossed to where she stood. She held out the stick. He glanced down and saw a single blue plus sign.

"You're pregnant?" he breathed, dots of light dancing before his eyes.

She snatched the stick back and resumed her cross-armed pose. "I'm pregnant," she said, her voice firm, challenging, determined.

She'd barely finished the sentence before he kissed her.

"Are you ready to read?" Thea asked, interrupting the memory.

"Make room for Mommy," Gavin said. Amelia scooted closer to his side, and Thea squeezed into a tiny bit of space between the girls and the wall. There was more than enough room next to him, but pointing that out probably wouldn't go over well.

Gavin read as the girls snuggled against him, and every few lines he glanced at Thea. She obstinately refused to meet his gaze.

When he finally finished a few minutes later, Thea sat up so fast that the bed shook. She told the girls to give her a kiss and that Daddy would tuck them in.

Ava was the hardest to get to sleep. She only wanted Thea and needed several stuffed animals piled around her to settle down. Amelia was easier. When he tucked her in and told her everything was going to be OK, she believed him. She looked at him with trusting, hopeful eyes, curled her tiny hand into his, and whispered, "I love you, Daddy," before falling asleep. He could barely pry himself up to leave the room.

He closed their door with a quiet click, sucked in a steadying breath, and then walked back downstairs. He found Thea in the kitchen, writing something on her massive whiteboard.

She tensed when he came up behind her. "Are they asleep?"

He had to clear his throat to speak. "Yeah. They were tired."

"So am I."

He watched her re-cap her marker and replace it in the drawer. His eyes drifted to the corkboard and an embossed invitation stuck with a thumbtack. He had to blink twice to make sure he was reading it correctly.

"Your dad is getting married again?"

She slid away from him and walked to the kitchen sink. "Are you surprised?"

"What happened to Christy?"

"Crystal. He cheated on her with the new love of his life." Thea filled a glass with water and used it to wash down the headache medicine she used whenever she felt a migraine coming on.

"When did all this happen?"

Thea shrugged and turned around. "Sometime last winter? I don't remember."

"Why didn't you tell me?"

"I don't know." She sighed. "It didn't seem important."

"How's your mom taking it?"

Thea pressed her fingers to her temple. "I really don't want to talk about my parents right now."

"Sorry. Right. Are you—" He gestured toward her forehead. "Are you OK?"

"Fine." She swallowed and looked at the floor. "Gavin, we need to make some decisions."

Her words were another slingshot that sent him back in time. Whether she realized it or not, she'd said the exact same thing the day she told him she was pregnant.

Thea let him kiss her but not for long. She planted her hands in the center of his chest and pushed him back. "What are you doing?"

Gavin pressed his hand to her abdomen, where his child—their child—grew beneath his fingers. "I'm happy, Thea."

"That's great," she said with more acrimony than he would have expected. "But we need to make some decisions, Gavin."

"What's there to decide?" With his right hand still pressed to her stomach, he used his left to cup her jaw. "Marry me."

An idea took hold. The words had worked back then, so maybe they would work again. It definitely seemed like something Lord What's-His-Name would do, at any rate.

Gavin closed the distance between them. Thea lifted her gaze from the floor just in time for him to slide his left hand along her cheek. "What's there to decide?" he said. "Marry me."

Her head drew back from his touch, her face scrunched in confusion. "*What?*"

His heart thudded nervously. "It's—that's what I said wh-when—"

"I know, Gavin." Her arms wrapped around her torso in a pose that managed to look both tough and vulnerable. "I just wish you wouldn't ruin it by saying it now."

Ruin it? His heart sputtered. "I am not ready to give up on us."

"It's too late."

"It's *not* too late," he said, channeling Lord Always-Says-the-Right-Thing. "It's never too late for love."

Thea snorted. "Are you serious right now?"

Okay, maybe that was a bit much. *Thanks a lot, Lord Asshat.* Still, it was now or never.

And if this didn't work, he was going to kill Mack and Del and throw Lord Claptrap into the fireplace. "What if . . . what if we could start over?"

Thea lifted her hands to ward off his words. "Gavin, stop."

"Let me move home—"

"No." Thea sidestepped him and was halfway across the living room before he could catch up in steps or words.

"Let me move home," he repeated. "And if I can't w-w-win you back, I'll . . . I'll let you go. I'll agree to a divorce."

Thea turned around, an incredulous squint to her eyes. "This is the twenty-first century. I can get a divorce whether you agree to it or not."

Right. Of course. Shit. "I know. Wh-what I mean is, I'll give you whatever you want. I'll pay off the house for you and the girls, give you whatever amount of child support you need. Anything. We don't even need lawyers."

She arched an eyebrow. "Your agent would kill you if you got divorced without a lawyer."

"Why? Are you planning on taking me to the cleaners?"

His attempt at humor was apparently not appreciated, because her lips formed a tight line. "No, but what if you get traded and have to move? Things could get really complicated with custody."

Custody. The word made him want to puke. "Please, Thea. Just give me a chance."

"To do what?" she blurted, throwing her hands wide in an exasperated gesture.

"To prove how much I love you."

Her lips parted again. She stared at him for a moment that lasted forever. "Please stop saying that," she finally whispered, her voice pained.

"Stop saying what? That I love you?"

Her silent nod hit him like an errant pitch. He stumbled back a step. *"Why?"*

"I don't trust those words. Not anymore."

Gavin fought for air. He'd suffered some tough losses in his life. Life-changing ones. And humiliations that burned to this day. But *this* . . . this was as close to total destruction as he'd ever known. If ever there was a time for Lord Benedict to tell him what to say, it was now. But the only voice he heard in his head was a woman's.

Love isn't enough.

When he'd read those words from Irena, Gavin had grumbled under his breath and nearly closed the book. What kind of romance novel declared love meaningless? Wasn't the entire point of all romance novels to prove that love conquers all? He had a sinking sensation that he was about to find out in real life whether that was true. He just hoped Lord Lovelorn would have a better idea on how to prove his wife wrong than Gavin did for his.

"It's late," Thea said quietly, as if softening her tone could possibly soften the blow. "You should go home."

"I am home. You and the girls are my home."

Thea sucked in a tiny breath of air. It was barely perceptible but just enough to let on that his words—his pitiful honesty—had made a mark. It was time to come out swinging.

"You know what? I'm disappointed in you. Because the old you would have jumped all over a crazy proposition like this."

He held his breath as she held his gaze. Her jaw jutted sideways, and her eyebrows pulled together. Not in anger. No. She was considering it. He could tell by the glint of daring in her eyes.

It was that glint, more than anything else, that made him risk everything with his next words. "Come on, Thea," he challenged. "What do you have to lose?"

Thea responded by turning away and walking woodenly to the French doors to the backyard. She stared silently into the darkness outside, her arms once again wrapped tightly around her torso. He'd give anything to see inside her mind, to hear whatever argument she was having with herself. The click of the grandfather clock in the hallway by the stairs ticked off the seconds in excruciating slowness.

The suspense finally got the best of him. "Thea—"

She turned stiffly. "I have some conditions."

Her words hung in the air for a long, stunned instant before they registered in Gavin's brain. Did she mean—? Was she agreeing to—?

He spoke slowly, afraid that if he reacted too strongly, she'd say *never mind*. "Wh-what kind of conditions?"

"This"—she waved her hand in the air, searching for the right word—"*proposition* can't last forever. We'll need a deadline of some kind."

"Spring training," he said. It was perfect. If he failed, he'd at least have something to distract him after he left. He wasn't going to fail, though. Spring training was nearly three months away. More than enough time.

Thea had other ideas, though. She shook her head. "Christmas."

"That's only a month!"

"It will be too hard on the girls if we drag it out longer than that."

He couldn't argue with that. "Fine," he said.

"And you have to sleep in the guest room."

Well, that was a kick in the balls. "How are we supposed to work on our issues if we're not even in the same room?"

"That didn't seem to bother you before."

There was nothing he could say to that that wouldn't sound either self-serving or whiny. "What else?"

"Liv stays."

Ah, Christ. "For how long?"

"For as long as I need her."

He nodded begrudgingly, because what choice did he have? "Fine. Anything else?"

"That's it for now."

"For now?"

The unintentional sharpness in his voice brought a tight line to her lips. "These are my conditions, Gavin. Take it or leave it."

He was taking it. He'd take whatever he could get. Mouth suddenly dry, he swallowed hard. "When do you want me, I mean, when can I come home?"

"Wednesday night."

The night before Thanksgiving. Two days away. "Okay."

"You can be here when I get home with the girls from school."

"Right. Yeah. I, uh, I can do that."

"We'll order pizza for dinner."

Pizza. Sure. What the fuck? This had to be the most ridiculously ill-timed conversation of his life, yet the bizarre normalcy of it had an odd settling effect on his stomach. Somewhere in the middle of all this chaos and emotion, dinner still needed to be eaten.

"So I'll see you Wednesday," she said in what was clearly his dismissal.

His eyes roamed her face, and a chasm opened in his chest. She stood tall but looked small. There was a defeat in her rigid shoulders. He didn't want it like this. Not with her acting like she'd just lost the most important fight of her life. "Thea, is this really w-w-what you want?"

"Do you want to move home or not?" she snapped, staring at a spot over his shoulder.

"I do. I just—"

"Just what? Make up your mind, Gavin."

He let out a tight breath. "Fine. I'll be here Wednesday."

He thought about crossing the room and pulling her into his arms before leaving, more to reassure himself than anything else, but everything about her body language screamed TOUCH ME AND YOU LOSE A TESTICLE. So yeah. Things were off to a great start already.

Gavin settled for a small nod before trudging out to his car. He started the engine but sat in the driveway, watching as light after light went dark inside. Everything he loved most in the world was in that house, and driving away was going to be harder tonight than it had ever been. Because the next time he returned, he had just one month to earn the right to stay. Though her conditions made his task difficult, a batter didn't get to choose his pitches. All he could do was study the field and come up with a game plan.

One month.

That's all it had taken for them to fall in love the first time.

He could do it again.

"Okay, Lord Tight Pants," Gavin said as he backed out of the driveway. "Tell me what to do next."

Courting the Countess

It took two weeks, three days, and sixteen hours for Benedict to realize the fatal flaw in his starting-over plan.

His wife was not a willing participant in it.

He couldn't very well court someone who had no desire to be courted.

Irena had not allowed him more than a few minutes of time alone with her since their wedding night, though she was clever enough to make it seem unintentional. Anytime he attempted to engage with her, she suddenly had a pressing matter to discuss with the cook or a task that needed to be finished elsewhere. Whenever he finished with the business of the estate, she suddenly became consumed with her own. And though the door separating their bedchambers remained unlocked every night, he could not bring himself to enter hers and quench his burning thirst to consummate the marriage. Not as long as she believed that allowing him into her bed was simply her duty. Not until her thirst was as strong as his.

But Benedict was not giving up. He was and would always be a risk-taker at heart—something he and Irena shared. It was, after all, how they met. When he learned that a lowly baron's horse had beaten one of his prestigious thoroughbreds, he was shocked and smitten to discover the horse had been trained by none other than the lowly baron's daughter herself.

Which made them both rebellious gamblers and absolutely perfect for each other in a way that Benedict had never before known was possible.

And now it was time to up the ante.

Benedict poured two fingers of brandy into a glass and positioned himself next to the fireplace in his office to wait for her. When her knock sounded on the heavy wooden door, he downed the amber liquid to calm his nerves and commanded her to enter.

She walked in wearing a day dress of pale blue and an annoyed expression. Her hands were clasped tightly in front of her. "You summoned me, my lord?"

He ignored her sharp sarcasm. Benedict gestured toward the sofa near the window. "Please sit."

She hesitated, probably caught off guard by the formality of his tone, but then she obeyed. She sat in a stiff, ladylike pose—spine straight, hands primly folded in her lap, legs crossed at the ankles and draped elegantly to the side.

"I have another gift for you," he said.

Her sigh could have powered a steam engine. "My lord—"

"Benedict."

"—this has to stop."

"You do not like the other gifts I've given you?" He'd given her seven so far. Earbobs and necklaces and bracelets in every shade of gemstone.

"They are unnecessary."

"You are the only woman I have ever met who would describe earbobs and rings as unnecessary."

"Then you must not know many women."

"Touché." Benedict pulled away from the mantel and crossed to his desk. From the drawer, he pulled out the unwrapped box. It took only a handful of steps to reach the sofa, but it felt longer under the weight of her gaze and the threat of his failure. "Perhaps this gift will be of more use to you."

She accepted the box and wordlessly opened it. Her eyebrows pulled together as she withdrew the slim, silver instrument. "What is it?"

"That," Benedict said, lowering himself to sit beside her, "is a fountain pen."

"I see."

"You dip this part here," he said, pointing to the sharp nib at the end, "into the well, and it draws ink up into a thin capillary, which then holds the ink and deposits it onto the paper when you write. It allows one to write much longer without pausing for more ink."

He watched as she fought a battle between stubbornness and fascination.

Stubbornness won. She replaced the pen in the box. "What use do I have for such a frivolity?"

"You write to your younger sister every day, Irena. I thought this would make the task much easier for you."

The mask of indifference that had held her features in stony neutrality now slipped, revealing a hint of loneliness that tore at his conscience.

"I'm sorry that you miss her so much," he stated.

"I worry about her," she corrected flatly. "The scandal of our marriage has tainted her as well. My parents have become ruthless in seeking her a respectable marriage of her own before it's too late, regardless of what she wants. There is nothing I can do to protect her now."

Guilt threatened to suffocate him—not only for what he'd done but for what he was about to do. He reached over and covered her hands with one of his. "Irena, I have come to a decision."

Her eyes darted to his. "What kind of decision?"

"There will be no heir."

Panic flashed through her eyes, widening the pupils and darkening her emerald irises. "*What?*" she breathed, swaying where she sat.

"You have refused to accept any of my overtures to prove that I love you."

She shot to her feet, the pen clattering to the floor. "And *this* is how you are going to do it? By denying me a child?"

"I will deny you nothing." He rose and grasped her hands in his. "If I cannot win your love again, I will get you with child in whatever cold, passionless manner you require. Then I shall purchase you an estate with an ample stable where you and the child can retire with your beloved horses, and I shall never bother you again. But not until you give me a chance to remind you how much more there can be between us."

Her head shook back and forth in a frantic pattern. "How can you possibly think I would agree to engage in such a cruel bargain?"

"Because you have everything to gain if you win. I, on the other hand, have everything to lose."

Disgust darkened her expression as she yanked her hands away. "Spoken like someone who has viewed the world for too long through the cloudy lens of the male gaze. No matter what happens between us, you maintain your status, your title, your money, your ownership of the entire world. You will remain welcome in every club and every ballroom. You will forever be the victim of a vicious, scheming woman, whereas I will forever be the Delilah who cut off your hair. You stand to lose *nothing*."

Benedict gripped her shoulders. "I stand to lose you!" he exclaimed.

A quiet gasp escaped her lips.

Benedict shifted his hands to cradle the curve of her jaw. "If you think I care about any of it—the money, the title, any of it—you're wrong. None of it matters if I lose you."

She wanted to believe him. He could see it in her eyes. Yet she pulled from his touch, turned away, and walked to the line of decanters on the bar against the opposite wall. He watched with bittersweet bemusement as she poured a stiff serving of brandy and shot it back with practiced precision. His love, always full of surprises.

"I don't understand what you want me to do, my lord."

"Let me court you. Let me take you to the theater, to

balls. Sit with me in the evening and speak with me at dinner. Dance with me. Ride with me in the park. Let us do all the things we did before—"

He cut himself off. She finished in a scathing tone. "Before you accused me of treachery against you and refused to hear my side of the story."

"Yes," he answered calmly.

"And if I refuse to do your bidding?"

He took a deep breath and played his last card. "Then your sister will be ruined."

She rounded on him again. "What does any of this have to do with my sister?"

"You said yourself that our scandal has threatened her reputation. If we can convince the *ton* that ours was—is—a love match, that the rumors were untrue about you, then your sister's prospects will improve as well. But if we remain childless, if the rumors persist about us for long, she'll be forced to marry any cur your parents push upon her. You know I'm right."

Long moments of silence passed between them, each more painful than the last, until finally she spoke. "Benedict, there's something I still don't understand."

Her use of his first name propelled him toward her. "What is it?"

"If you win, what do you get out of this?"

Benedict reached for her hand and drew it to his heart. "The greatest prize of all. I win your love."

CHAPTER EIGHT

Thea woke up the next morning with butterflies in her gut and a foot in her face. Sometime in the middle of the night, Ava had once again awakened, gotten scared in the dark, and climbed in bed with her.

Thea pressed a soft kiss to her daughter's foot and quietly moved out from under her. The mental mom to-do list that never quieted started its slow crawl through Thea's brain. Get groceries. Wash towels. Dump the rest of Gavin's clothes on the guest room bed.

But first, she had to face Liv.

Thea did the bathroom thing and crept down the hallway. The door to the guest room stood open, but Liv wasn't inside. Which meant she'd fallen asleep on the couch again after work. When she worked late shifts, she was usually too keyed up to fall asleep when she got home, so she watched TV for a while until she crashed.

Thea padded down the stairs. The rising sun cast a soft orange glow along the line of family photos that hung in meticulous order down the stairwell. Thea had never missed a year scheduling a family photo, because that's what perfect WAGs did. Were you even a real baseball wife if you didn't have a picture-perfect Christmas card?

Butter whimpered at the door. Thea let him out back and heard Liv yawn and stretch on the couch behind her. Thea looked over her shoulder. "What time did you get home?"

"Around three." Liv stretched an arm high above her head and made a long, tired noise as she sat up. "It was insane last night. We had the most obnoxious group come in late and order everything on the menu." She flopped against the cushions. "I hate bachelor parties."

Butter ran back inside and followed Thea into the kitchen, where he waited for his breakfast with a wagging tail and jumpy paws. After dumping a cup of food into his dish, Thea started brewing the coffee.

"You going to make me drag it out of you, or are you going to tell me how things went last night?" Liv asked.

Thea filled a mug with coffee, cream, and sugar and then sat down on a barstool to face her sister. No easier way to say it than just to say it. "He's moving home tomorrow."

Liv made a face like a possessed doll before squawking, "*What?!*"

Thea held up a hand. "It's only for a month."

"What the hell? Why?"

"It's complicated."

Liv hurtled over the back of the couch with remarkable vigor for someone who'd been dead to the world just three minutes ago. "What's complicated about it? You were so sure about this. What the hell changed?"

"He made me an offer I couldn't refuse." *And hit me where it hurts*, she added silently. The minute he reminded her of how she used to be—impetuous, daring, ready for any challenge—all logic fled, and the next thing she knew, she was agreeing to it.

Liv shook her head. "What could he possibly offer you that would convince you to let him come back?"

Thea summarized Gavin's words from last night. "If he can't win me back by Christmas, he won't contest any aspect of the divorce. He'll give me whatever amount I want in child support, and he'll pay off the house for us."

An eerie calm settled over Liv's face. Her eyelids blinked slowly and her lips went lax.

She turned and walked slowly to the fridge. Thea watched as her sister opened the door, robotically withdrew the orange juice, filled a glass, and then put the carton back. All seemed calm, but Thea knew her sister. Liv was like a sudden summer squall—a heavy quiet followed by a whipping wind and rain.

Thea looked at the clock on the microwave. Superstorm Liv making landfall in T-minus three, two, one—

Liv slammed her glass on the counter. "That manipulative sonuvabitch!"

Thea glanced at the stairs. "Keep your voice down!"

"He knows how much having a family home means to you because of how we grew up. He dangled the one thing that matters most to you in front of your face and knew you'd grab for it."

Thea rubbed her forehead. "Liv, give me some credit, OK?"

"How can I when you're acting just like—"

Thea slammed her mug down, sending coffee over the edge in a hot tsunami. "Don't. Say. It. I am nothing like our mother, and my situation is completely different from hers."

"How?" Liv scoffed.

"Because unlike Mom, I'm doing it for my daughters, not myself." Thea described what happened at the restaurant—how upset the girls were about not going to their grandparents' house for Thanksgiving, about missing Gavin, hating baseball. All of it.

Well, not *all* of it. She left out the things Gavin said that sent her heart into overdrive. *You and the girls are my home.*

Liv was unmoved. "You know the girls are too young to understand any of this."

"They're old enough to understand our traditions and to be sad when they change. At least now they don't have to have a shitty Thanksgiving or Christmas."

"So they have a shitty Thanksgiving and Christmas next year?"

"Hopefully by next year, they will be used to the situation and it won't bother them as much."

Liv started to protest further, so Thea held up her hand. "You weren't there. You didn't hear them cry or see their faces."

"But I can see yours."

Thea ignored the observation, mostly because she didn't want to know what it meant. "I made an impulsive decision. I thought you liked that side of me."

"Sure, when it leads to something fun. This is a disaster."

"Only if you refuse to support me."

Liv took another drink of her juice. "What exactly does he plan to do to win you back?"

"I have no idea."

"You didn't ask?"

"It doesn't matter."

"How could it not matter?"

"Because I've learned my lesson, Liv."

"But what if—"

"I don't know! Okay? I don't know! I have a thousand voices in my head telling me what to do. Yours. His. Gran Gran's. The girls'. I have no idea which voice is mine. All I know is that when he dared me to accept the deal, something snapped in me. So don't judge me."

"I'm not judging you," Liv said, a hint of apology creeping into her voice. "I'm worried about you."

Thea wanted to ignore that observation too, but found herself asking, "Why?"

"You disappeared, Thea," Liv said. "I feel like I just got you back. I can't stand to see you get lost again."

Thea pulled her sister in for a tight hug. "I won't get lost again," she promised. "It's only for a month."

"That's all it took the last time for him to lure you in."

"The last time, I was a willing participant."

"And you're not now?"

"I agreed to let him move home," Thea said, pulling away. "I didn't agree to spend any time with him."

"Something tells me that's going to be harder to avoid than you think."

"Not when he's sleeping in the guest room."

Liv made a whiny noise. "Where am I sleeping?"

"Basement."

"Great. First, he steals my sister. Now he gets to steal my bed?"

Thea walked purposefully to the whiteboard and studied the calendar. Christmas was barely five weeks away.

Five short weeks.

She could do it.

All she had to do was fake it.

The guys—Del, Mack, Yan, and Malcolm—were already eating when Gavin walked into the downtown Nashville diner wearing a morning beard and a scowl. *Not a good day to ask for an autograph,* he conveyed in body language alone as he ignored the too-big smiles from people who recognized him. The place wasn't exactly along the tourist thoroughfare, but it was still busy enough and country enough to be annoying.

He sank into a chair at the table. Del took one look at his haggard appearance and let out a breath. "Fuck. She said no?"

"Worse. She said yes."

"How is that worse?"

"She has *conditions.*"

Mack bit into some egg whites and spoke with his mouth full. "What, like, asthma and diabetes?"

Gavin flipped him off and launched into the recitation of what happened last night. While he talked, Del nodded at a waitress, presumably to let her know their fifth person had finally arrived. Gavin ordered something called the Big Buckle Breakfast because, fuck it, it was the off-season and his wife didn't trust that he loved her.

Mack grimaced when the waitress walked away. "Dude. That shit'll kill you and make you fat."

Gavin lifted up his T-shirt and looked down. Things were flat and tight, just like his trainers and coaches demanded. "I'll risk it."

Mack lifted his own shirt and waved at a washboard that put Gavin's to shame. "Clean livin'." Mack smirked, returning to his heart-happy omelet. "Try it."

"Fuck off, 'Roid Rage. You ate an entire pizza by yourself Saturday night."

Malcolm looked at Del. "Are they always like this?"

Del sighed. "Always."

Yan looked at Gavin. "What are her conditions?"

Gavin let out a long breath and launched into the list. When he finished, even Mack was sympathetic. "Damn, dude. She really won't let you say *I love you*? That's harsh."

"How the hell am I supposed to win her back if I'm sleeping in another room and can't tell her how I feel?"

"Yeah, and if there's no . . ." Mack made the universal sign for sex—he poked his finger in and out of a circle he made with his other hand.

"You're looking at this all wrong," Malcolm said. "This is an opportunity."

"How?"

"She all but dared you to figure her out, to truly learn her language. If she doesn't want you to say *I love you* with those words, you'll have to learn another way to express it, one that she'll accept."

"I don't even know where to start."

"We do," Del said. Then the guys all spoke at once. "Backstory."

"What the fuck is backstory?"

"Everything, man," Mack said. "Backstory is everything."

"It means that whatever happened to your wife before she met you plays a role in who she is today," Malcolm said. "We are all the sum total of our experiences at any given time, and our reactions to things are shaped by them. Just like in romance novels. Whatever a character went through before the start of the book will eventually determine how they react to things that happen in the book."

"But we're talking about my real life here. Not a book."

"Same principles apply," Malcolm said. "That's why fiction resonates with people. It speaks to universal truths."

Gavin's food arrived. He devoured a piece of bacon in two bites. Across the table, Mack puffed out his cheeks and made a round gesture over his stomach, so Gavin ate a second piece with a deliberate glare.

"Tell us about Thea's childhood," Malcolm said.

The bacon turned to a rock in Gavin's stomach. "She doesn't like to talk about it. She always used to change the subject when I would try to get her to talk."

"So it was a bad childhood?" Yan prodded.

"Her dad's an asshole, and her mom is a classic narcissist. They got divorced when Thea was ten. She and her sister had to live with their grandma for a few years because neither parent wanted them."

"Didn't want them? What does that mean?" Del asked.

"Her father remarried pretty quickly after the divorce, and his new wife didn't want the girls to live with them, and her mom was just too selfish to want the responsibility." Gavin ate a quick bite. "I found out last night that her dad is getting remarried again for, like, the fourth time in a couple of weeks."

The guys all met one another's gazes with a stunned expression. Del spoke. "You didn't know this?"

"No."

"When did Thea find out?"

"Not sure. She found out that he was getting a divorce from his third wife last spring, but I think the wedding invitation only arrived in the past couple of weeks while I've been gone."

Del leaned forward. "How does Thea feel about it?"

"She's not going to the wedding, if that's what you mean."

"Did she say why?"

Gavin tried to recall that part of the conversation from last night. "She said there's no point because he's just going to cheat on this one and leave her too."

The guys stared at him.

He blinked. "What?"

Mack snorted. "You are some kind of stupid."

"You think her dad's wedding has something to do with Thea letting me move home?"

Del smacked the back of his head. "No, dumbass. It has something to do with her kicking you out in the first place."

Gavin opened his mouth to protest but then shut it. He couldn't argue without revealing the embarrassing truth about what actually led to him leaving.

"And not wanting you to say *I love you*?" Yan continued. "Of course she doesn't trust those words, Gavin. When has she ever been shown that love is reliable, that it can last, that it can be trusted?"

"Words don't matter, Gavin," Mack said, uncharacteristically sober. "Actions do. And if she's skittish from her childhood, then it doesn't matter how many times you say the words to her. You made her doubt your love when you left."

"Just like her father," Del said pointedly.

"She kicked me out," Gavin growled.

"Maybe it was a test," Yan said.

Gavin swiveled his head to stare at his teammate. "A test," he repeated.

"Maybe she wanted to see what you would do if she told you to leave. Would you fight for her, or would you just walk away? You walked away, so . . ."

Gavin's breakfast began to rot in his stomach.

Mack snorted. "There it is. There's the lightbulb."

He was too sick to his stomach to take the bait. *Love isn't enough.* Was Irena right?

"Look," Malcolm said calmly, "we never said this was going to be easy. In fact, you need to be prepared for Thea to make this as hard as possible. She's going to resist you at every step at first."

"She already is."

"Which is why you'd better have done some more reading," Del said.

He sighed. "I read some last night."

"And?" Del prodded. "Anything stand out to you?"

Gavin glanced around the restaurant. He gave a one-shouldered shrug. "I don't know. Maybe."

"Read it to us."

"*Here?*"

"Unless you want to wait until Easter to save your marriage," Yan said.

Gavin looked around again. A few people were still staring,

but most of the other diners were absorbed in their own meals and conversations. Gavin dug into his coat pocket and pulled out the book. He splayed his hand wide on the cover so no one could see what it was.

Flipping to his current page, he read the paragraph he'd underlined last night. " 'More than anything, she feared that she would awaken some morning and realize her entire life had passed her by,' " he read. " 'That at some point, she had become less than. Less than w-w-what she used to imagine. Less than w-wh-what she used to hope for. Nothing more than a silent accessory to a man. Nothing more than her own mother, a passive face at a glittering table.' "

Gavin set the book down and waited for something smart-assy from Mack. Instead, he heard silence. Glancing up, he found all of them staring. "What?"

"You tell us, bro," Del said. "Why did that stand out to you?"

Gavin felt hot. He shouldn't have read it out loud. He should have chosen some stupid-ass, meaningless paragraph just to satisfy them. He knew exactly why it stood out to him. Because at some point during their three-year marriage, Thea had changed into her own version of *less than*. Gone was the carefree, impulsive woman he'd fallen in love with—the woman who would wake up at all hours of the night to paint, the woman who once kissed him so passionately in his car that they'd ended up in his back seat down a dark road, the woman who once handcuffed herself to a bulldozer to protest the removal of a century-old tree, the woman who picked fights with him just for the makeup sex.

And the worst part was, he'd been so preoccupied with his career that he hadn't noticed the changes in her until it was too late. Until the night *it* happened, when it had been so long since they'd picked a meaningless fight with each other that the real one was too big to come back from. "Y'all need anything else?" The waitress appeared out of nowhere. Gavin jumped in his chair. The book fumbled in his hands and fell, cover up, in his eggs.

"Oh, I love that author," the waitress gushed.

Gavin grabbed the book, wiped it with a napkin, and started to stammer. "Present for my w-w-wife," he said.

The waitress raised a single eyebrow and smacked down the check. "Whatever floats your boat, honey. I won't tell."

She sauntered off, and Gavin dropped his elbows on the table. He dragged his fingers through his hair and stared at the cover of the book. Lord Smugness was too busy ogling Irena's cleavage to offer advice.

But maybe he already had.

"And if I refuse to do your bidding?"

He took a deep breath and played his last card . . .

Gavin surged to his feet. Lord Boob Man wasn't the only one with another card to play. He dropped thirty bucks on the table and shrugged on his coat.

"Dude, where are you going?" Mack said.

"To up the ante."

"Excuse me?" Del said.

"I have some conditions of my own."

"Hey!" Mack yelled as he stormed off. "Can I have the rest of your bacon?"

CHAPTER NINE

The street outside the girls' school was at a dead stop in a pre-holiday traffic jam. Even with the extra twenty minutes Thea had built in for just that reason, she was still barely on time when she finally found a parking spot and jogged inside to pick up the girls. Preschoolers had to be picked up inside, rather than by the bus loop like older kids. And on days like this, it seemed nearly every kid in school was being picked up instead of taking the bus home.

Thea's heart smiled, as it always did, at the sight of the girls sitting side by side on the bench next to the main office. Their little mouths moved at a rapid pace, chattering to each other about something Thea couldn't hear over the shouts of other children, the conversations of other parents, and the general after-school chaos that vibrated through the hallways. Their connection was so strong—best friends already. They would always have each other, even if the rest of the world let them down.

After waiting to be buzzed in to the locked inner door by the school secretary, Thea strode in with a thank-you wave to the office staff. The girls jumped up at the sight of her, both extending colored-paper crafts.

"We made turkeys," Amelia said.

"Nice job!" Thea adjusted Ava's backpack, which had slipped down to her elbows. "Ready to go home?"

They ran ahead without answering. Thea reminded them to walk but couldn't fault them their excitement. Kids were always squirrely the day before a holiday break. The thrill and antici- pation of a holiday, of a day off, of a fun family tradition, made it hard to sit still.

Of course, it didn't take long for Thea and Liv to realize their holidays looked a lot different than other kids' in their classes. They'd spent one Thanksgiving hunched over TV dinners because their mother had taken the passive-aggressive tactic of refusing to cook a holiday meal to punish their father for some thing or an- other. Her parents never actually fought. They preferred the tense prison of silence.

Thea caught up with the girls on the sidewalk and took each of their hands. Their fingers were cold in hers, and Thea wished she'd thought to send gloves with the girls that morning. It was unseasonably chilly for this part of Tennessee.

"So guess what?" she said, unlocking her Subaru in the park- ing lot.

"What?" Ava asked, waiting to climb into her booster seat.

Thea bent through the back door to help her with the harness before rounding to the other side to repeat the process with Amelia. Then she looked at both girls with as big a smile as she could muster.

"There's a surprise waiting for you at home," she said.

"What is it?" Amelia asked breathlessly.

"Is it a kitten?" Ava asked.

"Nope, not a kitten." Thea shut Amelia's door and went around to the driver's side. As soon as she got in, the girls picked up the guessing game again.

"Is it a hedgehog?" Amelia asked.

"Nope." Thea started the car and eased out of her parking spot into the slow-moving traffic.

"Is it a giraffe?" Ava asked. Amelia giggled.

"Nope, not a giraffe."

"A lion?"

"Nope." Thea turned left at the stop sign. "It's not any kind of animal."

It was, in fact, something potentially far more dangerous. Nervous tension had been Thea's constant companion since Monday night, and now that the day was finally here—the day of Gavin's big return—she was a twitchy mess. She had no idea what to expect when she and the girls got home. She didn't even know what she would *say*. She only knew what she had to do.

Which was to stay as far away from him as possible.

The girls picked up their earlier conversation in the back seat as Thea drove the rest of the way home. Crisp leaves fell from the trees and danced through the air as Thea turned onto their street. Even from several houses away, her eyes zeroed in on the dark SUV in the driveway.

Tension coiled around her lungs as she pulled into the driveway. She'd just shut off the car when the front door opened. Gavin strolled out onto the front porch with a casual wave, as if he'd never left.

Amelia spotted him first from her window and shouted, "Daddy!"

"Yep. Daddy's home," Thea said, swallowing hard.

"Is that the surprise?" Ava asked, and Thea couldn't tell from her tone if she was disappointed or excited.

"That's the surprise!" Thea forced cheeriness into her own voice. "Daddy's home just in time for Thanksgiving."

Amelia squealed, drowning out whatever response Ava might have had. But both were eclipsed by the roaring in her own ears as Gavin jogged down the porch steps and headed their way.

Two observations hit her at once. First, it looked like he hadn't shaved since Monday. Second, she liked it. Which he probably knew, because she used to tell him he was sexy when he hadn't shaved.

He also wore the kind of outfit he knew she liked—loose-fitting jeans that hung low on his trim hips and a flannel shirt worn open over a snug T-shirt. He had pulled out the big guns. Good thing her heart was made of Kevlar.

"Hi, Daddy!" Amelia yelled.

Gavin's smile grew as he waved at the girls in the back seat. Nervousness bled into resolve. The girls were happy. That's what mattered right now. Thea would take this one day at a time for their sake.

Thea followed Gavin with her eyes as he rounded the hood. He stopped by her door, a quizzical pull on his brows.

Oh. Right. She was just sitting there.

Thea took her keys from the ignition and grabbed her purse from the passenger seat. Gavin backed up a step as she opened her door. With a swallow, he shoved his hands in his back pockets. "Hey," he said, low and sexy.

"Are you growing a beard?" she blurted.

He smiled and dragged one hand down his jaw. "That depends."

"On what?"

"On whether you like it."

She shrugged and turned to open Ava's door. "It's your face," she grumbled.

"True, but I would definitely have an opinion if you decided to grow a beard."

The girls giggled. Bending, she unbuckled Ava's harness. Gavin walked around to Amelia's side and did the same with her car seat. Thea avoided his eyes as she pulled Ava from the car and set her on the ground. "Go see Daddy," she said.

Gavin got Amelia out and hoisted her in his arms, then waited for Ava to slowly round the back of the car. "Hey, squirt," he said, squatting to hold his other arm open for her. Thea held her breath as Ava hesitated for a moment. But then she exhaled as Ava willingly went to Gavin. He stood, both girls easily in his arms, and met Thea's eyes over the hood of the car.

"Anything need to be brought in?" he asked.

"The turkey."

His eyebrows did the quizzical thing again. "You're taking a turkey to Del's?"

"Del's? What do you mean?"

"I just figured that since we canceled on my parents . . ." He shrugged.

"You just figured you'd make plans for us without talking to me?" she finished.

"It's what we did last year, so yeah, I assumed we'd go again this year."

"Yeah, Mommy, we want to go to Del's," Amelia piped in.

"I want to go to Del's and play with Jo-Jo," Ava said.

Resentment prickled her along her spine.

"Is that OK?" Gavin asked.

"No, it's not OK. I bought a fresh turkey for us to have at home."

"I guess you should've asked me first, huh?" Gavin said.

"Asked you first?" Her voice came out an incredulous squeak as Gavin left her standing in the driveway to carry the girls inside.

Thea whipped around and stormed to the hatchback. Did he really think it was a good idea to spend Thanksgiving with other people this year? And not just other people, but other Legends players and their wives? Right. That's exactly what she needed.

Thea grabbed two grocery bags and carried them inside. She hoisted the heavy bags onto the kitchen island, wincing as the glass jars inside clunked against the granite countertop. Her eyes focused on a bouquet of fresh daisies that hadn't been there when she left the house earlier, and she bit back a growl.

She started unloading the bags, pulling out more Thanksgiving ingredients that wouldn't get used tomorrow, when she heard the door open. Gavin returned a few moments later and set the two other bags on the island.

"Hey," he said.

Her hands froze inside the bag, fingers wrapped around a bag of fresh cranberries.

"Hey," she said, resuming her unpacking, nonchalantly sliding sideways to get away from his heat.

"I put up a tarp."

She looked at him. He pointed at the wall, now covered by a blue plastic sheet.

"Oh."

"We'll have to talk at some point about what we're going to do about that."

"*I* am going to finish tearing it down."

Gavin cleared his throat. "About tomorrow."

"What about it?"

"I'm confused. You're the one who said you wanted the girls to have a good holiday. They like going to Del's, and that's what we did last year, so I didn't think it would be a big deal."

"It's a big deal."

"Why?"

"With everything that's going on with us, do you really think I want to spend tomorrow with a bunch of people who are going to be watching our every move?"

"They're our friends, Thea."

"They're *your* friends, Gavin."

"What does that mean?"

"Except for Nessa, I can't stand most of those women. Or, more to the point, they can't stand me."

Gavin shook his head as if her words made no sense. "What are you talking about, Thea? Since when?"

"Since forever." Thea filled her arms with canned goods and walked to the butler's pantry.

"Is there more to that answer?" Gavin asked behind her. He stood in the doorway, arms braced against the frame and blocking them both in.

"It doesn't matter," she snapped. "We'll go to Del's tomorrow, and then I never have to hang out with those women again."

She plowed past him and searched out the girls in the living room. They were sitting on the floor and watching a cartoon on PBS. Thea crouched down and kissed them both. She was doing this for them. She had to remember that.

Which she was able to do through much of the evening—during pizza, the girls' bath, and bedtime. After getting both girls to sleep, she went to her own bedroom without a word to Gavin and shut the door. If she could make this her nightly routine, she just might survive this.

She had just stripped down to her bra and panties when the door opened.

Thea whipped around as Gavin strode in. "What are you doing?"

He closed the door and leaned against it, swallowing against his dry throat at the sight of her bare skin. "You established your conditions, Thea. Now it's my turn."

Thea's eyes did a *you have to be joking* bug out before she shook her head with an angry exhale. "No. You don't get to set any conditions."

"First," he said, peeling away from the door. "We attend the team Christmas party."

Every year, the Legends hosted a black tie post-season bash at the ballpark for players, families, and other staff.

"No." Thea shook her head. "Absolutely not."

He sauntered closer. "Second, we go on a date every single week. Just the two of us."

She laughed openly. "No."

Gavin took another step. "A real date, Thea. Not grocery shopping or some other mundane activity you can think of to avoid being alone with me."

"Sorry. Next?"

He closed what remained of the distance between them. "We kiss good-night. Every night. Starting tonight."

"You can't be serious," Thea said, her jaw clenching. "No. No way."

Gavin stepped back. Time to play his card. "OK, fine," he said, raising his hands in a wide shrug. "Then let's call this off right now. Let's go get the girls, tell them we're getting a divorce, and we'll let the lawyers figure out who gets them on Christmas and which one of us keeps the house."

The first chink in her armor was a rapid blink of her eyes. She wouldn't do that to the girls, and Gavin knew it. Still, he found no joy in watching her eyes flicker with a pain that told him how right the guys were yesterday morning. There were things he needed to find out about his wife.

Thea clenched her jaw. "I can't believe you would use the girls against me like this," she seethed, shaking.

He winced inwardly but plowed forward. "You've left me with few options, Thea. Your conditions would have made it impossible for me to win."

"*Win?* Is this a game to you?"

He lowered his gaze to her lips. "A game? No. A competition? Yes."

Thea braced her hands on the edge of her dresser behind her as Gavin inched ever closer. Her eyes darted to his lips and lingered there. Blood roared through his ears as logic and reason failed him. Because instead of backing away like he should have, he leaned closer. Dipped his head. Nudged the tip of her nose with his.

"What're you doing?" Thea whispered. She might have been aiming for angry, but the breathless anticipation in her voice gave her away. She was as turned on as he was.

"Sealing the deal," he rasped.

Then he palmed the back of her head and he kissed her. He kissed her like he had last weekend, open-mouthed and probing. And just like last weekend, she greeted his passion with a split-second of resistance before all but melting into him with another one of those sighs that sent a surge of lust to his groin. Gavin changed the angle of his mouth and went deeper, pouring everything he couldn't say and she didn't want to hear into the push and pull of his lips against hers.

Thea's hands fisted the front of his shirt. And when she pulled back enough to suck in a shaky breath, he took advantage. He lowered his lips to the hot, sensitive skin of her throat.

"I'm going to fix everything," he whispered, heated and fervent. "I swear to God, I am going to make you trust me again, Thea. I'm going to make things perfect again."

And just like that, she went stiff in his arms. She pushed him away and turned her face.

"What's wrong?" Gavin panted, holding her hips to keep her from slipping away.

"There's no such thing as perfect," she said flatly.

Gavin begged for Lord Seduction's guidance on what to say but came up empty. His delay gave her time to grab his wrists and pull his hands from her body. "I need you to leave now."

"Thea—"

"Go, Gavin."

Gavin stepped back and wished he was wearing a longer shirt to hide the hard bulge in the front of his jeans. Thea slid to the right and turned around, hands pressed to the top of her dresser as if she needed help standing up. He'd probably pay for it later, but he couldn't stop himself from stepping closer once again. He lowered his mouth to her ear. Her shoulders tensed.

"I know what you're doing," he whispered. "And I know why. But I'm not going to let you push me away again. Not without a fight."

Her breath caught. "Why are you doing this?" she rasped. "What do you possibly get out of this?"

A smile spread his lips wide. *Thank you, Lord Benedict.* "I get the best prize of all," Gavin murmured, dragging a finger down the nape of her neck. "I win you."

A strange sound woke Thea the next morning.

It sounded like rain, but the sky outside her window was lavender and clear.

It wasn't until her skin felt the warm brush of humidity that she realized what it was. Thea shot up and kicked free of the sheets. The bathroom door stood ajar, letting out a soft billow of steamy air.

No. Oh, hell no. Gavin was using her shower? It was bad enough that he was essentially blackmailing her into kissing him every night. But the shower? That was *so* not going to happen every day.

The water suddenly turned off, and Thea sprang out of bed. She stumbled on her morning legs like a newborn colt learning to stand for the first time, and caught herself on the bedside table. She was not going to be in there when he got out, because there was no way she would give him that satisfaction. She heard the glass shower door open. Time to run. But just as she stepped forward to bolt, her pinkie toe collided with the same table that had saved her moments earlier.

"Motherfu—" She bit off the curse and hopped on one foot. But she was still in newborn-colt mode, and she toppled backward onto the bed. Dammit! She had to get out of there before—

The bathroom door swung open wide. And out walked her

husband wearing nothing but a towel tied loosely around his hips. Another hung around his neck.

Sweet Jesus. His torso glistened with droplets of water that he'd missed in his hasty swipe with the towel. Gavin never dried off completely after a shower, and at this moment, she hated him for it. A line of water dripped between his massive, toned pec muscles, before getting lost in the tangle of dark hair that spanned his rock-hard abs.

His hair was wet. His chest was wet. She was suddenly wet.

Dammit! Why, dear God, WHY did she have to be married to a man whose job literally depended on him being in peak physical shape?

"Hey." He smiled, dazzling white teeth sparkling, or actually not, but that's how it seemed because he looked like a fucking TV commercial. "Happy Thanksgiving."

Thea shot back to her feet, pinkie toe still throbbing. She welcomed it, though. It fueled her rage. "You're cheating!"

"Um, what?"

"You're using my shower. That's cheating."

"What are you talking about?" He laughed.

Where did he get off laughing about anything? "You using my shower was *not* part of our deal."

"We never specified which shower I'd use, Thea. But I can use the girls' shower, if that's another one of your conditions."

"Oh, stop with the innocent act. You did this on purpose."

"Yes, I purposely took a shower. I don't normally accidentally take one."

"You know what I mean! You're doing *this*"—she waved in the general direction of his chest and abs and, dear God, the towel was starting to loosen—"on purpose."

He raised his eyebrows and glanced down at himself. "I'm afraid I don't know what you're talking about."

"You're walking around half naked just to tempt me!"

"I swear that wasn't my intention, but if that's the outcome, I'll take it." He waggled his eyebrows and turned away from her. He used his strong, thick forearm to clear a circle in the cloudy mirror. She watched as he picked up his electric razor and began to trim the edges of his beard. He tilted his head to the side and tackled the soft whiskers below his jawline.

Oh, that was—that was just plain *dirty*. He wasn't even trying to play fair.

Gavin had called this little proposition a competition.

No. This wasn't competition.

This was war.

And she could play dirty too. Without thinking it through, because impulsivity seemed to be her worst enemy, Thea grabbed the hem of her sleep tank and whipped it over her head.

Gavin stilled. The razor hovered just above the skin of his throat. His eyes darted from his mirror image to hers. His Adam's apple bobbed in his throat as he stared at her outraged half-nakedness. Meeting his eyes in the mirror, she smiled and yanked down her sleep shorts and panties.

Gavin's eyes darkened, and he did that slow-swallow thing again. His eyes did a long walk down her naked body and then meandered back up a different path, stopping on parts of her that reacted to his perusal with hot and heavy immediacy.

She planted her hands on her hips. "There. How do you like it?"

"Remind me," he said, his gaze settling on her breasts. "Which part of seeing you naked is supposed to be punishment?"

Then he winked, and boom, her nipples hardened. What

the . . . ? Thea looked down at her round, pink areolas, now tight and pebbled. Jesus. Her tits were like Pavlov's dog around him.

And he knew it too. His lips curled up at the corners. "If you think I mind this game, you're wrong. Because I definitely just won this round."

Thea jerked the shower on, yelped when scalding water beat down on her skin, and skidded backward. "Why do you take such hot showers?" she grumbled, yanking the faucet handle in the other direction.

He returned to his beard trimming. "I had no idea my shower habits would be the cause of our first argument."

Thea grabbed the bottle of body wash. She was going to make him pay for this. She was going to soap herself up head to toe and make him watch. "It's not our first argument," she said casually, squeezing a large dollop of pink scented goo into her hand. "We argued last night."

"That wasn't an argument."

"What do you call it?"

"A negotiation."

"And what do you call this?" Thea spread the body wash on her stomach in a slow circle. She was rewarded with a strangled noise from the other side of the shower door.

Thea looked up and met his gaze in the mirror once again. She tilted her head innocently as she slid her hands higher to lather her breasts. "You were saying?"

His eyes no longer held hers. His gaze was firmly on her hands as she twirled suds around her nipples. "I missed that last thing you said," she mused, pinching her nipples.

Gavin's jaw popped and clenched with a deep swallow. He lowered the razor again and turned around. Through the steam on the glass, she could see him just enough to watch his eyes once again travel the length of her. Her hands moved with him, sliding down to the underswell of her breasts, to the indentation of her belly button, and lower.

The door suddenly swung open, and Gavin walked into the shower, towel and all. He backed her against the shower wall and planted his hands on opposite sides of her. His chest rose and fell as if he'd just finished a round of push-ups. "How far you going to take this, Thea?" he rasped.

"Take what? I'm afraid I don't know what you're talking about."

He clenched his jaw again. "Give me one w-w-word, and I will replace your hands with mine."

Thea didn't bother to hide her smugness as she pushed his arms aside and leaned into the water to rinse the suds away. "Sorry, that's not on the table." She leveled a glance at Gavin over her shoulder. There was a muscle jumping in his tight jaw, and it made her smirk. "But don't worry. I'm a big girl. I know how to take care of myself."

Gavin's eyebrow twitched, and the desire in his eyes dissipated into something else. Something that looked a lot like the same flash of hurt she'd seen the night when she admitted that she'd been faking it in bed.

He turned and stormed out, not even bothering to shut the shower door.

Thea sank back against the slick, wet wall. This didn't feel like a victory.

Thea stood under the water until her skin chilled. Then she dressed quickly and opened her bedroom door to listen for the girls. Their giggles combined with Liv's voice assured her that at least one Thanksgiving tradition would not be destroyed today. Liv was sneaking them an early piece of pumpkin pie. She heard nothing that indicated Gavin had gone downstairs to join them, and the guest room door was closed.

Thea went back into her room and entered her closet to stare at her clothes. Last year, when they went to Del's, Thea had dressed up because that's what WAGs did. They wore their best clothes and showed off to one another. And dammit, she did not have the energy for that this year.

She finally settled on a pair of leggings and a long tunic sweater. Her hair was going up in a messy bun, and she was not going to spend more than a couple of minutes on makeup. For the first time in a long time, she didn't care what they thought of her. She had only a few weeks left as a WAG, anyway.

When she came out of her closet, she found Gavin sitting on the bed. He was dressed in jeans and a black T-shirt that tugged impatiently over his biceps as she leaned on his knees.

"What are you doing in here?"

He looked up. "What did you mean by that? What you said in the shower."

Thea moved to her dresser, her bare feet silent on the plush carpet. "Nothing. I just was trying to be coy."

"OK, but just because I feel like torturing myself, and, trust me, this question has tortured me every night since you-know-what, do you?"

She had a hard time following his sentence. "Do I what?"

"Take care of yourself wh-when we're done? Sneak off into the bathroom and finish yourself off when I finally roll off you?"

"Are you seriously asking me if I masturbate?"

"No. I'm asking if you ever masturbate after sex with me."

Thea opened a drawer and thought again about lying. But once again, she couldn't bring herself to do it. Lying. Faking it. Pretending everything was perfect. None of those things had done either of them any good. She withdrew a pair of socks and turned around. "Yes, sometimes I do."

Gavin's face fell and flushed red.

"If you didn't want to know the answer, why did you ask?"

"Just because I wanted to know doesn't mean the answer doesn't hurt."

"Why should it hurt? Everyone masturbates. You going to tell me you've never masturbated?"

He shot to his feet and surged forward. "Hell yes, I masturbate. Every time I'm on the road, I lie in that hotel bed and think of you, fantasizing about coming home and getting the real thing." His face twisted into a pained sneer. "Except even that wasn't the real thing, was it, Thea?"

Thea drew herself tall, even as the slap of his words stung. "Yet you're so eager to go back to when things were *perfect*."

The hard edges of his face softened with an apology she didn't want to hear. "Thea—"

"Get out of my room, Gavin."

CHAPTER TEN

Thea wouldn't look at him when Gavin walked into the kitchen a few minutes later. He couldn't blame her. He'd damn near strangled himself after he said what he did, but he was humiliated, and humiliation was his own personal Kryptonite. Always had been. Beastly things came out of his mouth when his pride was on the line. And holy shit, knowing his wife had to take matters into her own hands because he routinely left her unsatisfied in bed was almost more than his fragile ego could handle. So he lashed out and threatened to destroy whatever tiny amount of progress they'd made last night.

Thea stood at the island, covering pies they would take to Del's with tinfoil. His ugly words hung in the air between them.

He settled on something safe to break the taut silence. "Where are Ava and Amelia?"

"Doing yoga in the basement with Liv."

The smell of coffee lured him to the counter by the stove. He filled a mug, dumped some shit in it—he'd never understand people who could drink it black—and turned around to lean against the counter. Minutes passed in silence. Gavin finally set his cup down. "I'm sorry."

She didn't even look up. "For what?"

Gavin crossed the kitchen to stand next to her. Her hair had fallen across one cheek as she looked down. He brushed it back over her shoulder. "I w-w-was an asshole. I'm sorry."

"You should never be sorry for speakin' your truth." She said it in a strange, Southern drawl, the one she used when quoting her Gran Gran. For as long as Gavin had known Thea, she'd had an endless well of her grandmother's sage wisdom to draw upon.

Thea moved away from him and pointed in the general direction of all six pies. "These pies need to go out to the car."

Gavin reached for her hand.

She yanked it from him. "There's no point, Gavin. This will all be over after Christmas, anyway."

She stormed away before he could answer. He heard her padded footsteps carrying her back upstairs. Gavin plunked his elbows on the counter and lowered his head into his hands.

"Rough night in the guest room?"

Gavin jumped and looked up. Liv had materialized out of nowhere. She'd worked so late last night that this was his first run-in with her since coming home. "What are the girls doing?"

"Running with scissors."

His expression must have been thunderous because she backed down. "God, chill. They're watching TV with the dog. I just ran up to get them some orange juice."

She filled two small sippy cups, gave him a quizzical look,

and returned the juice to the fridge. She started to leave but he stopped her.

"Liv."

She turned around.

"Thank you for being here for Thea and the girls. I know you've been a big help."

She snorted. "I didn't do it for you, asshole."

"I know. All the same . . ."

She rolled her eyes and headed toward the basement, but she stopped at the last minute and turned back around.

"Hey, Gavin?"

He looked up once more. She smiled in a dangerous way. "If you do anything to hurt my sister again, I will poison your protein powder. Happy Thanksgiving!"

Then she disappeared into the basement.

He busied himself for the next several minutes carrying all six pies out to the car and then wandered to the living room to call his parents just to get it over with. They still had a landline, and an unexpected voice answered the phone.

"You owe me for this," his younger brother, Sebastian, hissed by way of saying hello.

"What're you doing there?"

"Filling in for you. Mom was crying about how she wasn't going to have any family with her this year for Thanksgiving, and the next thing I knew, I was packing my duffel bag. I've been up since five, since Mom has to get the turkey in early enough for us to eat by two."

Gavin pinched the bridge of his nose. "You'll survive. Let me talk to Dad."

"He's in the shower. Talk to Mom."

He tried to protest because there had to be a rule of some kind about the amount of time one had to wait between a conversation about jerking off and a phone call with one's mother. But Sebastian had pulled the phone away from his ear.

A moment later, his mother got on the line. "Hey, honey! Happy Thanksgiving!"

"Hey, Mom. How big is the turkey this year?"

It was a running family joke that his mom always bought a turkey three times the size of what they actually needed. His mother lived in fear of people starving to death in her presence.

"Almost eighteen pounds," she said. "He's a big 'un."

Gavin could picture her instantly. She was probably wearing her ruffled apron, the one she only wore on holidays. And she'd have her hair twisted on top of her head so it didn't get in the way while she cooked. Pretty soon, she'd pour herself a mug of hot spiced cider from the slow cooker and she'd turn on Christmas music, because in the Scott household, Thanksgiving Day was officially the start of the Christmas season.

"I sure wish you guys were here," she said. "I miss you and the girls. And Thea. Gosh, I've tried to call her several times for the past couple of weeks but keep getting her voicemail. Oh—did she get my email?"

"I have no idea."

"Oh, well, she probably just didn't tell you. I asked what the girls want for Christmas this year."

"You could just ask me."

She made a psh noise with her lips.

"You think I don't know what my daughters want for Christmas? Geez, thanks."

"I think Thea probably already has a color-coded spread-sheet with links of where to buy everything and what's already on sale."

Despite his mood, Gavin smiled. Yes, that sounded exactly like Thea.

"Hey, maybe you guys can come here for Christmas!" his mom said. "You could spend Christmas Eve here, and the girls could open their stockings here. Oh, Gavin, it would be so fun."

An ache bloomed in his chest at the picture she painted. It would be fun, but there was no way Thea, who had just appeared at the bottom of the stairs, would agree to it.

"Hey, Thea's standing right here. Do you want to talk to her and see if she got the email?" Gavin held out the phone. "It's my mom."

Thea gave him a look that could extinguish a fire. But she sucked in a breath and put on her best voice. "Hey, Susan. Happy Thanksgiving."

Gavin listened to Thea's half of the conversation, and the ache spread. His parents adored Thea. They said she was the daughter they always wanted and joked that Sebastian was going to have to work extra hard to even come close to finding a wife as perfect as Gavin's.

That was the main reason he hadn't yet told them that he and Thea were having trouble. It would devastate them. But that wasn't the only reason. His parents had the perfect marriage, and they'd be so disappointed to know that Gavin couldn't live up to their model.

Thea said goodbye, ended the call, and handed Gavin his phone. "You need to tell them, Gavin."

"Tell them what?" he countered, bitter at her constant reminder that this was a temporary thing for her. "You gave me until Christmas to win you back. Until then, there's nothing to tell."

Del and Nessa lived outside Nashville in a mansion-filled sub-division that was home to several of Music City's rich and famous. The twenty-mile drive took only a half hour in the sparse holiday traffic, and if it weren't for the girls in the back seat, it would have been a silent trip.

"Mommy, can we swim?" Ava suddenly asked.

Del had an indoor pool, and it had become part of the tradition that after everyone's dinner had settled, the guys took the kids swimming. Thea turned in her seat to look at the back seat. "I brought your bathing suits."

The girls let out a cheer. At least they would have fun today.

Gavin pulled along the curb in front of Del's house. A ribbon of nervous tension tightened around Thea's chest. This would normally be the time when she would adopt her perfect WAG smile and pretend to love every minute of this.

Screw that this year. She and Gavin unbuckled the girls and sent them running up the sidewalk. Just as they reached the front portico, the door swung open. Del's wife, Nessa, walked out looking stunning, as usual. She wore wide-legged black slacks and a slim camel turtleneck. It was the kind of effortlessly classy outfit that only tall people like her and Liv could actually look stylish in. Nessa gathered the girls against her legs for a quick hug and then looked up with a smile and a wave.

Thea waved and leaned into the back to grab one of the pies.

Gavin did the same, and he followed her up the sidewalk. Nessa shooed the girls inside and took the pie from Gavin.

"I'll help Thea carry stuff. You go out back and stop Del from killing himself."

"What's he doing?" Gavin asked.

"That fool bought a turkey fryer."

"Oh, shit." Gavin took off at a jog.

Nessa turned back to Thea. "I'm so glad you're here," she said, nodding for Thea to come in. "Del said there was a chance you guys might go to Gavin's parents' this year. It wouldn't be the same without you."

Thea didn't know what to say to that, so she said nothing as she followed Nessa into their massive, gleaming white kitchen. The heavenly aroma of the turkey in the oven mixed with the scent of spiced cider in a slow cooker. Sage and garlic from the stuffing made her mouth pool with spit. It smelled just like Gran Gran's house used to. Those three Thanksgivings when she and Liv had lived there were the best of her life.

The girls ran through on their way to the stairs, chasing after Del and Nessa's daughter, Jo-Jo. "She's been bouncing off the walls, waiting for you guys to get here," Nessa laughed, lifting the pie high in the air to avoid a collision. Then she set it down on the counter with a dramatic sigh. "I swear, she woke me up before dawn asking if you were here yet."

Thea laughed. "The girls have been excited too."

And, honestly, if it were just going to be their two families, today wouldn't be so bad. Nessa was genuine and kind and funny, the only one of the other wives and girlfriends that Thea would remotely call a friend. Mostly because Del and Gavin were such good friends. And the twins adored playing with Jo-Jo. Today could have been OK. But it wouldn't be. Because pretty soon, she'd be swimming with the sharks.

Nessa took the other pie from Thea and set it on the counter. Thea could tell just from the way her eyes pinched at the corners what was coming next.

"So . . ." Nessa said, leaning closer. "I hope you don't mind, but Del told me that Gavin has moved home. Are things going OK?"

"Great," Thea said automatically. Wait. No. She wasn't going to do that anymore. Thea straightened her spine. "Actually, it's not going great. He came home last night, and we haven't stopped fighting since."

"Del saw Gavin last week. He said he's never seen Gavin so broken up."

Thea bristled. *Gavin* was broken up? "It hasn't been a picnic for me, either."

"Of course not," Nessa said quickly. "I just . . . I know a little about what you're going through. These men of ours, they're not great at expressing themselves. Give it time."

Thea wanted to press her—because how could Nessa know anything about marital trouble? She and Del had the perfect marriage. But she was cut off by a knock at the front door, which was followed immediately by an impatient dinging of the doorbell. Nessa swore and rolled her eyes again. "Lord give me strength. I have no idea why Del invited him."

"Invited who?"

"Well, well, you must be Mrs. Thea Scott."

Thea turned around and came face-to-chest with an impressive set of pecs beneath a tight white T-shirt. She looked up and was nearly blinded by a sparkling smile that may or may not have brought a little whimper from her mouth. Her eyes cata-logued the gloriousness of thick dark hair, mischievous brown eyes, and a jawline that could cut glass. He winked, and angels began to sing.

"Braden Mack," he said, lifting Thea's mouth toward his lips. "Pleasure to finally meet you."

His lips brushed her knuckles, and Thea's mouth went dry.

"I— How do you know who I am?"

"I know your husband, but obviously not well enough be-cause he failed to mention how beautiful you are."

Thea tried to respond but could only squeak.

Nessa cleared her throat. "Mack, it's too early for your brand of charm. Why don't you go out back and help the men?"

Braden stroked Thea's wrist with his thumb. "They need advice about women?"

"No, they're trying to fry a turkey."

Braden dropped the act and Thea's hand. "Oh, shit." He took off through the back door.

Thea swallowed and shivered. "Whoa. I feel like I just met the god of seduction."

"Lord, don't tell him that. His ego doesn't need any help."

Thea and Nessa wandered to the glass doors to watch him walk. She licked her lips and then looked up. Her eyes collided with Gavin's unmistakably jealous glare. "Oh, crap."

"I'm going to kill him."

The minute Gavin looked through the glass door and saw Mack kiss Thea's hand, something hot and red took hold of his senses, which were already scrambled from the past twenty-four hours. And now the asshole was headed their way, waving and swaggering like nothing had happened.

"He's just doing it to get you riled up," Del said. "He hits on all our wives."

"And you let him get away with it?"

"He doesn't mean anything by it."

Gavin curled his hands into fists as jealousy surged. It was childish and immature and completely irrational, but Braden-Fucking-Mack was exactly the kind of interference he and Thea didn't need right now. Gavin had been competing with smooth-talking, cock-swinging fuckboys like Mack his entire life. He sure as shit wasn't going to compete with him for his own wife.

And fuck if he didn't feel like a loser for even thinking about that. This wasn't high school. Thea was his wife, not the girl he wanted to take to prom. But logic and reason were scarce quantities in his life these days. Case in point: the argument about masturbation this morning.

"You dipshits are gonna burn the house down," Mack joked as he sauntered toward them. He pointed directly at Gavin. "Yo, Scott. Why didn't you tell me your wife was so hot? No wonder you're wound so tight."

Gavin swung his fist before he could talk himself out of it, before he even realized he'd decided to do it. The punch landed squarely below Mack's eye and caught him enough by surprise that Mack stumbled back, a hand over his cheek and a wounded look in his eyes.

"What the hell?" Mack pulled his hand away to look at his fingers, presumably for any signs of blood. "What was that for?"

"I don't know. I guess my toxic masculinity doesn't like you hitting on my wife."

"Are you kidding me?" Mack said. "I hit on everyone's wives! It's my specialty. You don't have to punch me for it."

Gavin took a step forward. Del wrapped an arm around Gavin's chest and held him back. "Easy there, Creed."

The glass door slid open. Nessa and Thea ran out wearing matching expressions of shock. Thea's held a hint of something a lot more sinister, though, and Gavin knew he'd just fucked up. Again.

"What is going on?" Thea demanded.

"Nothing," Gavin grumbled, shaking out his hand. Dammit, that hurt. Contrary to stereotypes, professional athletes didn't go around throwing punches very often. Gavin had been in exactly one bench-clearing brawl in his entire career, and he'd only managed to knock someone's hat off before the umpires broke it up.

Thea looked at Mack. "Are you OK?"

"You're worried about *him*?"

"He's the one who got hit!"

Mack cocked a half smile and milked the situation for all it was worth. "Don't you worry about me now, darling. I get this response from a lot of husbands."

Gavin made a strangled noise.

Thea glared at him. "Inside. Now."

Gavin followed on wooden legs as Thea stormed back inside, stalked a path through the kitchen, and ducked into Del's first-floor study. She slammed the door and whirled around.

He was in so much trouble. "Babe—"

"I swear to God, if you try to *babe* me right now, our entire deal is off."

He shut his mouth. The word *deal* left a sour taste. That's what his entire marriage had been reduced to.

"What is wrong with you, Gavin? You're acting like a lunatic! This is how you plan to win me over again?"

"I'm sorry—"

"What if the girls saw you hit him? Do you know how much that would scare them?"

No. He hadn't thought about that. She was right. He was acting like a lunatic. *A slimy-bellied worm wanker,* came the whispered reply. Great. Lord One-liner had now surged past helpful tips into Shakespearean insults.

"What right do you have to march back into my life after a month of the silent treatment and decide to go caveman on a guy just for kissing my hand?" Thea seethed. "Do you seriously trust me so little?"

"I trust you, Thea. It's him I don't trust."

"Oh, that is so insulting." Thea pressed a hand to her forehead dramatically and adopted a breezy Southern Belle accent. "I'm just a fragile little damsel in distress who can't take care of herself around such strong, virulent men. Save my virtue, dear husband." She leveled him with a gaze. "This little jealousy act might impress me a little more if you hadn't left me."

"You kicked me out, Thea." Why the hell did everyone forget that part?

Perhaps because you left her long before that, you lily-livered bastard.

Thea shook her head and stormed toward the door.

"Thea, wait," Gavin said, reaching for her. "I'm sorry. You're right. I'm being an asshole."

With a steadying breath, she walked out, leaving him alone with the voice of Lord Shitty Timing. Worm wanker? Seriously? What the hell even was that?

When Gavin finally emerged from the study, he ran headlong into a line of stern faces and crossed arms at the end of the hallway. Apparently, several more people had arrived while he was in the study. And apparently, none of them were too happy to see him.

Del, Yan, and Malcolm glared like he'd just been caught watching soccer. Del gave an angry jerk of his head toward the stairs to his basement. "Downstairs. Now."

"I need to find Thea."

"She's with the girls. Go."

With a resigned sigh, Gavin followed the men down the stairs to Del's finished basement. He rounded the corner and stopped. Mack sat on the couch, an ice pack pressed to his cheek.

Gavin turned around. "No. No fucking way. I'm not talking to him."

Del grabbed his arm. "Mack has something he wants to say."

"Your wife is hot."

Gavin growled. Del smacked Mack upside the head.

"Just kidding," Mack said. "I mean, not about her being hot. Your wife really is hot."

"I'm going to fucking kill you."

Mack stood. "I'm sorry that I caused a problem between you and your wife that did not need to happen. I just can't help it that I have natural charisma."

"For fuck's sake, Mack," Del complained.

Mack looked at the floor. "Sorry."

"There," Del said, looking back and forth between them. "Better? Everyone friends again?"

"We were never friends," Gavin said.

"Chill, man. I won't touch your apple again."

"Sit down, Gavin," Malcolm said, motioning toward the couch. Gavin obeyed and braced for an ass-chewing that he knew he deserved.

"What just happened up there?" Del demanded.

"Well, Del. You might have heard that my wife and I are trying to work through some problems right now."

"Judging by the look on her face when she left the study, you're doing a pretty shitty job of it," Yan said.

Gavin sank against the cushions and stared at the ceiling, sullen and obstinate.

"It's been one day," Del barked. "How can you fuck up already?"

Mack snorted. "Have you met him?"

"Give us an update," Malcolm said calmly.

"I think I'm going crazy. I keep hearing a British accent in my head telling me to say and do things."

"It happens to all of us eventually," Mack said.

Gavin lifted his head to see if he was joking. Mack's expression suggested he wasn't. "You hear the voice too?"

"It's your subconscious," Malcolm said. "At some point in this process, every one of us has had to fight a British aristocrat in our brain that identifies things we would otherwise prefer to ignore."

Perhaps because you left her long before that, you lily-livered bastard. "So I should listen to him?"

"Unless he starts telling you to kill people, yeah," Del said.

Gavin thought about blaming Lord Tight Pants for punching Mack. But that one was totally his own fault. As was his worm-wankery this morning when he asked her if she ever masturbated.

Gavin leaned forward to prop his elbows on his knees. He

dropped his head into his hands. "She keeps pointing out that this is only until Christmas. I don't think she's going to really give me a chance."

"Look, man." Del sat down across from Gavin in much the same pose as the night when they found him drunk and despondent in his hotel room. "We could help you a lot more if you would just tell us what really happened to break you guys up."

Gavin stood. "Not going to happen."

"Fine," Malcolm said. "But just remember this. The point of all this is to court her, Gavin. Not seduce her."

"What's the difference?"

Mack snorted again. "It's a fucking miracle you got married at all."

Gavin flipped him off.

"The difference," Malcolm said, "is to make her want *you*, not prove how much you want her."

CHAPTER ELEVEN

Hell. That was what the next two hours were for Thea. Unmitigated hell. After fleeing the study, she helped Nessa finish the cooking and pretended she couldn't hear the other wives and girlfriends whispering behind their glasses of wine.

I heard they broke up.

He punched Braden Mack!

Did he really move out?

But just when Thea thought things couldn't get worse, a high-pitched female voice rose above the rest.

"Hello? Where is everyone?"

Thea crossed herself and uttered a prayer. *God grant me the serenity to not slap the shit out of her.*

"We're in the kitchen," Nessa called.

Rachel Tamborn, former model, professional WAG, and archnemesis to all nonconformers, swept into the room on click-clacky stilettos and in a cloud of expensive perfume that left a frustratingly pleasant ambiance in her wake. Her hair was glossy. Her makeup perfect. Her dress a skin-toned, form-fitting bandage that had the added insult of looking amazing on her. Her husband, Gavin's teammate Jake Tamborn, strolled in behind her.

Rachel greeted Nessa with an air kiss on each cheek. "Thank you so much for having us," she crooned. "I just couldn't deal with either of our families this year, and I gave our cook the day off, so poor Jake was going to starve without you guys."

"Of course," Nessa replied smoothly. "The more, the merrier."

Rachel pulled back and glanced around the kitchen as if she'd never seen one before. Only then did she notice Thea. Her eyes widened. Her glossy lips parted. Thea half expected fangs to appear. But then she suddenly seemed to remember other people could see her.

She held open her arms. "Oh my gosh! Hi, Thea!"

She click-clacked over and hugged Thea with the accuracy of a boa constrictor. "I'm soooo glad you are here," Rachel said, pulling back. "I've missed you!"

"You've missed me?"

"Well, I mean, you weren't at the last game—"

Oh, slinging arrows already.

"—and you missed our last luncheon—"

"I wasn't invited—"

"And with everything else, I just assumed you wouldn't be here."

Wow. There was sooo much to unpack in there. Thea couldn't help herself. Impulsive Thea was in control of her mouth all of a sudden. "Why wouldn't we be here today?"

Rachel's smile turned sugary. "Oh, I mean, you know . . ."

Thea stood firm. "No, I don't know what you mean." Thea stared, her eyebrows raised, daring her to finish.

Rachel finally clasped her hands in front of her. "So, you and Gavin are back together?"

Ah, there it was. What Thea had been waiting for. "That's not really any of your business, Rachel," she said quietly.

Rachel's eyes widened just enough to show she was shocked that anyone would dare stand up to her. Jake cleared his throat and sidestepped his wife. "Good to see you, Thea," he said, loosely hugging her in the way people do when they feel sorry for someone. "You look adorable, as always."

Rachel nearly broke a tooth. "You do always look so adorable," she said, her eyes doing a slow, disdainful walk up and down Thea's outfit. "But this is a new look for you, isn't it? I guess comfort really does trump style some days, doesn't it?"

"Absolutely. Just like class trumps beauty."

Jake winced. "Where are Gavin and Del?"

Thea gestured toward the back door. "Out back frying a turkey."

"That's not good." Jake took off.

Rachel clasped her hands in front of her body and pasted a smile on her face. Thea nearly laughed because it was a purposefully fake smile. The kind where you want someone to know it's fake, not because you want them to feel better but because you want them to feel worse. For God's sake, Rachel was pretending to pretend.

It had always been like this with Rachel. Always. Beneath her friendly facade was an ugly underbelly of competitive wifedom that revealed itself the very first time Thea met the other wives and girlfriends. She'd innocently asked a group of WAGs what they all did for a living, and it was like someone had scratched a needle across a record.

"*This*," Rachel had said.

As if that explained it all.

Over time, it did.

For many of the wives and girlfriends, being a baseball wife *was* their profession. For some, that was simply because balancing the demands of their husbands' careers with the demands of raising children was more than a full-time job.

But for others, this was their identity. As if they'd been groomed for it like the debutantes of old. They flaunted their relationships with their rich, handsome men as if it were the natural order of things that all the beautiful people were destined for each other.

And then there was Thea. The outsider who barely understood the rules of the game, who had married a baseball player because she got pregnant, who'd joined their exclusive club without having to put in any of the work that the rest of them did. She didn't have to slug it out for years when he was a prospect or during the long, impoverished minor league years.

And Rachel hated her for it.

Thea used to pretend she didn't care, but in reality, she did. Being an outsider was a lonely place to be.

But soon she'd be free of their animosity, and it was that thought that allowed her to focus on helping Nessa without straining to hear what was being said behind her back.

Finally, the food was ready. Nessa yelled out back for the boys to bring in the fried turkey, and Thea offered to help set everything out.

After Thea and Gavin fixed the girls' plates and got them settled at the kids' table, they joined the rest of the grown-ups in the dining room. Thea sat next to Nessa, because she desperately needed an ally. Unfortunately, she was right across from Rachel.

Twenty minutes into dinner, Del stood at the end of the long table. "Everyone shut up."

Conversations quieted as everyone focused on Del, who held a beer in one hand and his wife's fingers in the other.

"Nessa and I want to thank you all for being here today to celebrate Thanksgiving with us. Some of you we love to have. Some of you we just put up with."

Everyone laughed, but Thea suspected there was a lot of truth in his words. Thea smiled at Rachel, who smiled back. Thea could've sworn blood dripped from one corner of Rachel's mouth.

"So I could stand here and do a long speech about being thankful and all that shit, but I don't feel like it," Del said. "Because Nessa and I have something to announce. Something we've been keeping quiet for a couple of months now."

Nessa jumped up, her arms spread wide. "I'm pregnant!"

There was a happy pause and then a chaotic eruption of applause and congratulations and all the other things that normally greet a pregnancy announcement. Gavin stood and reached over to shake Del's hand. "That's awesome, Del. Congratulations."

A few minutes later, Nessa sat back down, and Thea pulled her in for a hug. "I'm so happy for you guys."

Nessa laughed weakly. "I've been dying to tell you, but we've had two miscarriages, and we just wanted to be sure."

Thea grabbed Nessa's hand and squeezed it. "I'm so sorry. I had no idea."

"I guess I also didn't want to upset you, because I didn't know what was going on with you and Gavin. It felt wrong to throw our good news in your face when you guys were having trouble."

Somehow, that felt worse—knowing that someone withheld good news out of fear that Thea couldn't handle it. It was even worse, though, when she looked up and realized Rachel had heard every word.

Rachel pounced immediately. "Thea, what about you and Gavin? Are we going to hear any good news anytime soon now that you two have patched things up?"

"Not unless you're talking about me finishing my bachelor's degree." She smiled.

"Oh, you never finished college?"

"Not yet."

"And why's that?"

Jake slung an arm over the back of Rachel's chair. His fingers appeared to dig a little too tightly into her shoulder.

"Well, Rachel, as I'm sure you know, I had to quit college because I got pregnant."

"Oh, that's right. I knew that. You guys hadn't been dating very long, right? And didn't Gavin get called up to the Majors right after that? What amazing timing for you."

Thea felt the pressure of Gavin's hand on her knee under the table.

"Thank you for that accurate recitation of the timeline of our relationship, Rachel. Can we hire you to write our Wikipedia page?"

Gavin's fingers dug into her knee as Rachel's mouth dropped open again.

"Remind me where you went to college, Rachel," Thea said.

Tension soaked the air as half the table hung on their every word while the other half ate as if it were their last meal.

"I was a pre law major at Ole Miss."

"You didn't go to law school?"

Rachel turned a luminous smile at her husband. "I did not. I happily gave it up for Jake's career."

Jake pretended to be fascinated by the stuffing on his plate.

"But surely you still wish to be a lawyer, don't you?" Thea prodded, because the impulsive side of her was operating her voice like a puppet.

Gavin's hand tightened on Thea's knee. She shoved it away.

Rachel preened prettily before answering. "No, I don't," she said. "We all make sacrifices to support our husbands. Most of us don't mind."

Rage colored her vision red. Rachel had no fucking idea how much Thea had sacrificed for Gavin's career. She was just about to tell her when Soledad Feliciano, Yan's wife, broke the tension.

"So, Thea," she said in the kind of nervous tone one might use with a rabid dog, "with your art background, you might be able to help us with some design ideas for the new logo for our charity softball game."

The softball game was another WAGs tradition. Every summer, some of the Legends' wives and girlfriends competed in a game against the wives and girlfriends of the Nashville hockey team to raise money for school supplies for needy children. For years, the game had been called WAGs vs. HAGs, because, you know, there's an "h" in hockey. Ha-ha, so funny. It was astonishing how few people failed to see the problem with it, but maybe someone had finally convinced them that they needed a new name.

"I didn't know we were getting a new logo," Thea said.

"It was decided at our last meeting." Rachel smiled.

The one Thea hadn't been invited to.

"I'd be happy to," Thea finally said, "*if* we can also get rid of the term WAGs."

Rachel sputtered into her wineglass. A fork fell against a plate, and someone at the table uttered a blasphemy.

"Why on earth would we do that?" Rachel asked, wiping a splatter of wine from her cleavage.

"Come on," Thea said. "Wives and girlfriends? It's so limiting. What if a woman makes it to the Majors someday? What would her boyfriend be called?"

"Since I highly doubt there are any female players who are anywhere near good enough for that, I don't think that's something we need to worry about," Rachel said.

"Fine, then what about a gay player? The term *WAGs* is completely heteronormative. Don't we want something more inclusive?"

"What exactly do you suggest?" Rachel asked.

"How about spouses and partners?"

Rachel paused for a moment and then said, "That would make us SAPs."

"You're right. It sure would." Thea stood and picked up her plate. "I think I'll check on the kids. Anyone need anything?"

Thea walked out of the silent dining room and around the corner. It wasn't long before Gavin appeared. "What the hell was that?" he asked.

"That," Thea said, setting down her plate, "was the kind of bullshit I've had to put up with from Rachel and her friends the entire time we've been married. I just decided to stand up to her for a change."

"She *always* treats you like that?"

Thea snorted. "Um, yeah. From day one."

His eyes pinched at the corners. "Why didn't you tell me?"

"Why didn't you know?"

Gavin shook his head, opened his mouth to say something, and then apparently thought better of it. He swallowed instead.

"Don't worry about it," Thea snapped. "It won't be a problem much longer, anyway."

She spun on her heels and left him standing there. And she spent the rest of the day with the kids, carefully avoiding his every attempt to get her alone.

Ava started complaining about a stomachache around six o'clock, so Gavin made their excuses. Nessa dished up some leftovers into a tower of plastic containers and carried them out to the car while Gavin got the girls ready to leave.

"It will get better," Nessa said quietly, loading containers in the back of the car.

Thea sighed. "Thanks, but I don't think Rachel is ever going to like me."

"I'm talking about you and Gavin."

Thea looked up.

"Give it a chance to get better, Thea," Nessa said.

The front door opened, and Gavin walked out carrying Ava. Amelia scampered ahead of them. Nessa squeezed Thea's arm and lowered her voice. "Call me anytime."

Thea shut the door to the trunk as Nessa walked up the sidewalk. She paused to kiss the girls goodbye and give a one-armed hug to Gavin. Thea opened the door to Ava's side and took her from Gavin without meeting his eyes.

"I'll buckle Amelia in," he said.

The drive home was as silent as the trip there. Gavin clenched the steering wheel. Thea stared out her window, watching other families in other cars. Smiling, laughing families. Did those husbands and wives start their holiday arguing about masturbation? The thought brought an absurd burst of hysterical laughter from her mouth, which quickly became a frustrated sigh. She felt more than saw Gavin's head turn in her direction, but she kept her eyes locked on the passing scenery. The lifeless, gray sky matched her mood.

By the time they got home, Thea practically threw herself from the car. She unbuckled Ava and carried her to the porch, fumbling at the door with the key. Butter greeted them in the foyer with excited barks.

"Mommy, I don't feel good," Ava whined.

"I know, honey. Let's get your coat off—"

Vomit covered the floor before she could finish her sentence. Ava began to cry. Butter began to sniff.

"Butter, no!" Thea grabbed the dog's collar just as Ava heaved again. Another round of what-the-hell-did-she-eat splashed onto the floor. Behind her at the door, Gavin let out a quiet curse, and Amelia yelled, "Gross!"

Gavin rushed in and took Butter's collar.

"I'll clean this up," Thea said. "Can you take her up and start a bath?"

"No!" Ava cried. "I want Mommy."

"I'll clean it up," Gavin said. "Amelia, honey, just stay back for a second."

Too late. Ava turned and heaved all over her sister. Amelia shrieked. Gavin cussed out loud this time. Butter barked like he'd found his own particular heaven and tried to start licking Amelia clean.

"Butter! Stop it! Girls, come on. Let's get upstairs," Thea soothed. "Ava, hold it if you can until we get to the bathroom."

Both girls crying, Thea followed them upstairs and into their bathroom. Kneeling, she told them to put their arms up and then peeled their shirts from their bodies. She'd be lucky if she could salvage either garment. She told them to finish getting undressed as she started the bath. Downstairs, Gavin said something particularly unkind to Butter before presumably putting the dog out back.

"Mommy, I don't feel good," Amelia hiccupped, her face pale.

Oh, no. Thea took Amelia by the shoulders and steered her toward the toilet—a split second too late. And now there were two floors to be cleaned.

"It's OK, sweetie," Thea said, rubbing a circle on Amelia's back. She turned around to check on Ava, who now stood naked and shivering. Balancing on one foot, Thea leaned over and checked the temperature of the water. "Go ahead and get in the bath, Ava."

Turning back to Amelia, she gently moved her to the side of the toilet and told her to lean over in case there was more. And yep, there was. Amelia shivered with a pitiful whimper. Thea smoothed her hair back. "It's OK, honey. It'll be over soon."

She finally got Amelia into the tub a few minutes later. Gavin appeared in the doorway as she lathered Ava's hair. He looked at the floor, grimaced, and used a leg to block Butter from coming in.

"Amelia's sick too," Thea said. "Can you grab some clean towels from the closet?"

"Which closet?"

Resentment pounded at her temples. "The same closet they've always been in," she said in a clipped voice as she dumped water over Ava's head.

"Which one is that?" he snapped.

"Seriously? How long have we lived here?"

"I don't spend a lot of time paying attention to towels, Thea."

No shit. "The linen closet in the hallway."

Gavin disappeared and returned a moment later with one hand towel. "This is all I could find."

The pounding became a jackhammer. "I just put an entire stack of clean towels in there yesterday."

"Well I didn't find them. What do you want me to do?"

"There are clean ones in a basket in my room."

A vein popped along his jaw. "*Your* room?"

Thea shot to her feet. "Forget it. I'll get them."

She stormed to the linen closet, retrieved the stack of towels that Gavin had to purposely not see in order to miss them, and stormed back.

"Where were those?"

"In the closet." She dropped the stack on the floor and finished rinsing Ava's hair. "OK, sweetie, go to Daddy."

"I want Mommy," Ava whined.

"You're going to have to settle for me, squirt." Gavin picked her up from the water. He knelt to dry her off, his body brushing against Thea's as he did. She scooted over, which earned her an annoyed scowl.

"I'll get Ava into her pajamas," Gavin said. He stood, Ava in his arms. Tucking Ava's head into his shoulder, he walked out of the bathroom.

Thea finished Amelia's hair and then paused to gaze at her daughter, who still looked pale. "You feeling any better, honey?"

Amelia nodded and yawned. It was going to be an early bedtime tonight.

"Come on, sweetie." Thea hefted Amelia from the tub and dried her off. Then she carried her into the girls' bedroom. Gavin sat on the floor, threading a shirt over Ava's head. He looked up.

She looked away.

Gavin's neck burned with frustration at Thea's dismissal. He tugged Ava's sleep pants up. "Let's get you into bed."

"I want Mommy."

Wow. Would that ever not hurt? He wished someone had told him that having children could devastate a man in ways unimaginable before. Gavin stood and picked Ava up. "Mommy's getting Amelia dressed."

He glanced backward. Thea had set Amelia on her bed and was helping her into a nightgown. Amelia pressed her face into Thea's neck as Thea caressed the back of her head with a soft, soothing whisper that Gavin couldn't hear. But he felt her voice all the same. Tender and loving. Gavin was officially jealous of his own kid.

Ava yawned, so Gavin set her on the bed and lifted the covers for her to scoot beneath. Thea had skipped the toddler bed thing with them and moved the girls straight into twin mattresses. They were way too small for Gavin's long frame, but he made do. He laid down next to Ava and smoothed her wet hair from her face.

"You feel any better?" he whispered.

She nodded, yawning again. "My tummy doesn't hurt anymore."

"That's good. You probably just ate too much at Uncle Del's."

"I had three pieces of pie."

Yikes. "How'd you get three pieces?"

"Mack said we could have as much as we want."

Gavin was going to kill him. "You need to ask Mommy or Daddy for stuff like that, honey. You know that."

"But Mommy would say no."

Gavin chuckled. "Probably. But that's because she knows that if you eat too much, you'll get sick."

Ava's eyelids grew heavy, and she snuggled her favorite stuffed animal to her face. The duck had once been bright yellow, but it was now faded into a dull hue from too much love. Gavin rubbed his hand up and down her tiny back, the warmth of her skin seeping through her pajama top.

"Daddy," she whispered, eyes flying back open.

Oh, shit. Please don't puke in my face. "What, honey?"

"I have to have a kiss good-night before I fall asleep." Then she lifted her head from the pillow and puckered her lips.

Something warm and devastating spread through Gavin's chest. He kissed her, rolled onto his side, and tucked her under his arm. She was asleep in seconds. Gavin turned his face into her wet hair and breathed in the scent that was uniquely Ava. He'd always heard people say they'd do anything for their kids. That they'd walk to the ends of the Earth to protect them, do whatever it took to make them happy. It's not anything a man can understand until he feels it himself, though. He wondered if his parents ever felt like this—completely slayed with love for him and his brother. Maybe that's what his dad meant one day after the girls were born and he found Gavin staring at the girls in their NICU cribs. His father clapped him on the back and said, "Oh, son. You have no idea what you're in for."

Gavin had laughed along, but his father was right. Gavin had had no idea how his life would change because of them. No clue how they would literally expand the size of his heart inside his chest, sometimes to the point of pain. No clue that the fear of something happening to them could render him useless, speechless. No clue that loving them would make him love his wife even more, something he didn't even think was possible.

And he'd almost thrown it all away. He was still throwing it away. If his father could have seen the way Gavin had been behaving, he'd shake his head in disappointment.

Behind him, Thea's quiet voice broke the silence as she told Amelia to close her eyes and dream good dreams. A thick wall of emotion clogged his throat. A few minutes later, Amelia's bed creaked as Thea stood. Then her petite silhouette cast a shadow over Ava's bed. Gavin rolled his head to peer up at her. She stubbornly refused to meet his gaze as she leaned over to peer at Ava.

"She fell asleep fast," he whispered.

Thea pressed the back of her hand to Ava's forehead for a moment and then did the same thing to her cheeks. "Neither of them has a fever."

Gavin had long ago stopped asking how Thea knew for sure. *The best thermometer is a mother's hand.* He knew that Gran Gran–ism by heart now. And it was always proven right. Thea probably knew the girls' normal temperatures better than her own.

With a weary sigh, she straightened. "I'm going to take a shower."

Gavin eased onto his back, careful not to wake Ava as he removed his arm from her waist. "I'll clean up the bathroom."

Thea grimaced. "I forgot about that. I'll do it since you handled the other one."

"I got it, honey. Go take a shower."

She blinked and stiffened at *honey*. "I said I'd do it," she said, obstinately refusing to accept even the smallest olive branch.

"Christ, Thea. Can't I even offer to help without it becoming a fight?"

Ava stirred at his sharp voice. Thea shot him a dirty look. "Fine. Clean the bathroom."

She stomped out of the room. Gavin swallowed another blasphemy. By the time he was done with the bathroom, the shower had stopped running, but he needed a time-out before he attempted to talk to her again. He stalked to the guest room to change into running clothes. The only thing that was going to ease the tension in his muscles was the pound of the pavement and a dripping sweat.

Gavin carried the trash downstairs and threw it into the bin in the garage. Butter followed forlornly and flopped onto the kitchen floor.

"She shut you out too, huh?" Gavin crouched and scratched the dog's ears. Butter thumped his tail and sighed. Yep. Just a couple of dudes licking their wounds after the alpha in the house let loose a vicious bark.

Gavin whistled for Butter to follow him to the front door. At the sight of Gavin reaching for his leash, Butter started bouncing on his front paws and yipping. Gavin tugged a wool skull cap over his hair, grabbed a pair of gloves, and headed out. He thought briefly about going back in to tell Thea where he was headed, but he was still just pissed enough to know they both needed some space.

Outside, the crisp air was a slap to his lungs and forced him to take his first deep breath in hours. He followed his normal route, hating life for the first ten minutes as he always did when running. Just because he was a professional athlete didn't mean he actually enjoyed running. It was a necessary evil. But his body finally adapted to the punishing pace and fell into the zone. Tension eased from his shoulders with every stride. Butter kept pace, tail wagging, tongue flopping, and apparently forgiving him for shoving him outside earlier. At least someone forgave him.

Gavin ran for two miles until he came to one of the city recreational parks. He slowed to a walk and stopped at the baseball field nearest the parking lot. A chain-link fence encircled the diamond, and two dugouts flanked home plate. The lights over the field were dark now, but streetlamps from the parking lot illuminated the dusty infield and the worn, eroded hill of the pitcher's mound. Gavin sat down on the cold bleachers, which, come summer, would be filled with parents and grandparents who all thought their kids were the cutest and most talented to ever play the game.

He'd spent most of his youth at fields like this, and it was at those dusty fields where people first started to notice and whisper about him for something other than his stutter. Where coaches began to gather and say, "Is that him?" Where scouts eventually began to show up in college sweatshirts to introduce themselves to his parents and watch for proof that the kid from an Ohio suburb was as good as everyone said he was.

One-in-a-million chance. That's what they always said. It was a one-in-a-million chance that he'd get to the Majors someday. But once the dream was planted in his head, Gavin wanted nothing else. Nothing was going to stop him. He would work harder than anyone else because out there, on those grubby fields, he was more than the kid who couldn't read aloud in class. More than the boy who was too nervous to talk to girls.

Butter flopped to the ground at Gavin's feet with a pant. His phone vibrated in his pocket. He pulled it out and saw a text from Thea.

Did you leave?

Fuck. He should have told her. He thumbed a quick answer. *I went for a run.*

Seconds passed before the dancing dots indicated she was responding. *Don't lock the door when you get back. Liv won't be home until late, and Butter will bark if she has to use her key. I'm going to bed.*

The cold unspoken message was clear: Don't even think about a good-night kiss.

He was fucking this up.

Before he could change his mind, Gavin called up his recent calls list and scrolled to find his parents' number. His father answered on the third ring, voice heavy with sleep.

"Hey, old man," Gavin teased. "Sleeping off the turkey?"

"Just dozing," his dad said. "Waiting for your mom to get home."

"Where is she?"

"Your brother talked her into going to a movie."

"Ah." Gavin bit his lip.

"Everything OK?"

"Yeah."

"You sure?"

Gavin cleared his throat. His dad knew instantly something wasn't right.

"Christ, Gav. What's wrong?"

"There's, uh, there's something I haven't told you and Mom."

"Oh, shit. Is it one of the girls? Are the girls OK?"

"The girls are fine. Just . . ."

"Are things OK with Thea?"

Fuck. He sucked in a breath and let it out. "No."

Gavin heard the creak and snap of his father's old recliner. Gavin could picture him standing. "Tell me what's going on, son."

Gavin let out another shaky breath and gave his father the basics—they'd been having trouble, had a big fight, he moved out for a couple of weeks; he was home now but things weren't going well. He left out the most humiliating aspect, obviously.

His father let out a heavy breath. "Why didn't you tell me sooner?"

"I don't know. I didn't want to worry you, I guess. It's not like you and Mom ever went through anything like this, so—"

His father's boom of laughter caught him by surprise. "Is that what you think?"

"Well, yeah."

"Wow. We were better at hiding it than I thought."

Gavin sat up straighter. "Wh-wh-what are you talking about?"

"Son, you can't be married to someone for almost thirty years without going through hell a couple of times. If you asked your mother, she'd tell you there were times when the only reason she didn't leave me was because she couldn't afford to raise you boys alone. And I know because she told me that to my face."

A noise pounded in Gavin's ears, something that sounded a lot like the crumbling of the illusion that was his childhood. "But you guys never fought."

"Not in front of you, but we fought plenty. Still do."

"About what?" Gavin felt like he'd just been told Santa Claus wasn't real again.

"Hell, you name it. She gets pissed at me for walking past dirty dishes without putting them in the dishwasher, and I get pissed at her for not writing down her debit card expenses in the check register."

Gavin snorted. "Dad, nobody uses a check register anymore."

"Ah, Christ. Don't you start in on me too."

Gavin stared blankly at the dark field in front of him. He wasn't sure if he was devastated or relieved to learn his parents weren't perfect. "Look, Dad, I get what you're saying but you and Mom apparently fight over stupid shit. Thea and I have bigger problems than that."

"You really think your mother would threaten to leave me over dishes? We struggle with the big stuff too."

Gavin scuffed his shoe in the dirt.

"Son, there's something I never told you, but I'm going to tell you now. But you gotta let me finish before you react."

Gavin tensed. "OK."

"When you first told us about Thea, that you'd met a woman, we were so happy because *you* were happy. Finally. But when you told us just a couple of months later that she was pregnant and you were getting married? Well, we weren't real happy."

"Wh-what? Why?"

"I told you to let me finish."

Gavin grumbled an apology.

"You were a sure thing for the Majors, Gav. We knew that by the time you were a senior in high school. But you were also, well, naïve about girls, let's just say that."

Oh, great. Even his parents thought he was a fucking loser.

"We worried that it would make you easy pickings for some girl to take advantage of you somehow because of the money you were going to make someday."

Swift anger stiffened his spine. "Thea isn't like that."

"I know, son. As soon as we met her, we knew. And you know how we knew?"

"How?"

"She didn't ignore your stutter. She didn't pretend it didn't exist. All your life, you thought you needed to find a woman who would love you despite the stutter, but you should have been looking for a woman who loved you because of it, because it was part of who you are. Thea is that woman."

Yes, she was. And Gavin was on the verge of losing her.

His father suddenly broke off, and in the background, Gavin heard the telltale squeak of his parents' back door.

"Your mom's home," his father said in a hushed tone.

Shit. "Don't tell her about Thea."

"I won't." Then louder, he said, "Hey, I'm talking to Gav."

His brother shouted something in the background that sounded a lot like *you owe me*. Or it could have been *blow me*. Either was possible.

His father came back on the line, but a moment passed before he spoke in a low voice. "Listen to me, son. Whatever you did wrong, you fight like hell to fix this with Thea, you hear me?"

"I'm trying."

"Try harder."

Then his own goddamn father hung up on him. He was officially batting zero lately.

With a short whistle, he urged Butter to his feet and started a slow jog back down the park path toward home. The house was dark and quiet when he walked in the front door. Butter made a beeline for his water dish and managed to slobber half of it on the floor. After wiping up the mess, Gavin walked upstairs. He needed a shower, but he found himself drifting to the door of her bedroom.

Their bedroom.

He raised his hand to knock, fighting against the resentment that he had to request entry to his own bedroom. She didn't answer right away, and the second-long delay was just enough to make him sweat.

"Come in," she finally said.

The door creaked softly. The bedside lamp was the only light source, painting everything in a soft yellow glow. The room smelled like her lotion. Thea sat on the bed, back against the headboard and her computer on her lap. Her hair was wrapped in a twisty towel thing that she always wore after showers, and she'd donned one of his T-shirts as a nightgown. His heart thudded a heavy beat. What would she say if he admitted that all those times he'd sought release on the road with his own hand, he'd been picturing her just like this—warm and soft and unintentionally sexy?

Butter bounded into the room and leapt onto the bed. Little bastard actually smirked as he lay down and settled his head on Thea's bare legs.

"I'm home," Gavin said dumbly, his mouth suddenly dry.

She met his gaze over her laptop. "OK."

"What are you doing?" He nodded at the computer.

"Emailing your mom about what the girls want for Christmas."

"Right." Seeing how he mauled her last night, it was ridiculous how nervous he was to ask if he could kiss her now. But this was different. He wasn't sure why. It just was.

Thea finally let out a long breath and turned her attention back to her computer. Fuck it. Gavin surged forward. The sound of his feet on the carpet brought her eyes back up in what he would pretend was anticipation but was probably more likely surprise.

He waited for Thea to say something, do something. Waited for her to make the first move, to lift her face or reach for him. He begged her silently, with his eyes and his quickened breath, to do it. Because even though it was one of his conditions, it had to be her choice. He wasn't going to force it on her.

Her nostrils flared slightly, and he could swear that her body swayed just a touch toward his. Her tongue darted out from between her plump lips and licked the bottom one. His gut clenched in response.

"Good night," he said gruffly. And before he could talk himself out of it, he bent and brushed his lips lightly across hers.

There. Give him a gold fucking star. He'd kissed his wife.

Thea looked up at him with wide eyes. "Good night," she murmured.

"Want me to tuck you in, or is that something you can handle yourself too?"

Thea's eyes narrowed for a split second until she realized he was attempting to tease her. She rolled her eyes, but her lips twitched at the corners. He wanted nothing more than to kiss her again and see if he could coax another moan out of her like last night.

But he'd made this bed.

It was his own fault he didn't get to lie in it.

He settled into the guest room, cracked open his book, and hoped Lord Know-It-All had some wisdom for fixing the mess he'd made.

CHAPTER TWELVE

The puke-opalypse was over.

The girls woke up squirrely, hungry, and begging for pancakes. Thea woke up tense, hot, and hungry for something else. Her dreams had been vivid.

Thea tugged on a pair of leggings and followed the girls downstairs. Gavin's door was shut, so he was either still asleep or—

Or he was already awake, showered, and making coffee when she entered the kitchen. Wow. OK.

"Daddy!" Amelia raced toward him and threw her arms around his legs.

"Morning, baby girl," he said, resting a hand on her head. "You all better this morning?"

"I want pancakes," she said.

"I'm sure we can make that happen." He looked at Ava. "You want pancakes, squirt?" She nodded and hugged her duck.

Gavin looked over his shoulder and met Thea's gaze. He lifted the corner of his mouth in a half smile, an apology emanating from his eyes. "Morning," he said. "Coffee?"

"Um, sure." She shuffled forward and sat at one of the barstools. A moment later he set a steaming mug in front of her.

"Want me to make the pancakes?" he asked.

"I can do it." She raised the mug to her lips. He'd doctored it perfectly with vanilla creamer and sugar.

"I know you can," he said calmly. "But I'm asking if you'd like a day off from it for a change."

It was a truce. A pancake peace offering. It would be petty to keep arguing, and even though petty was her favorite mood these days, she relented. "OK. Thank you."

Gavin smiled as if she'd just agreed to let him move back into the bedroom.

"Where's Liv?" Thea asked as she stood.

"Basement, I guess. Haven't seen her."

Thea changed direction and walked to the basement door. She opened it and listened but heard nothing. She crept down the stairs, rounded the corner, and nearly burst out laughing. Liv lay prostrate across the bed, still fully clothed. Her hair spread around her head in a violent swirl.

She started to tiptoe away.

"I'm awake," Liv muttered.

Thea turned around. "Sorry."

Liv groaned and rolled onto her back.

"Bad night?"

"People who go to restaurants on Thanksgiving are the worst people in the world. I never want to make another pumpkin pie in my life."

Thea leaned against the wall and sipped her coffee. "What time did you get home?"

"What time is it now?" Liv yawned.

"Eight."

"Then four hours ago."

Thea choked. "You worked until four?"

"I hate my life."

"No, you don't. You hate your job."

"I worked until four in the morning on Thanksgiving. My job is my life."

Thea walked back upstairs. The sight that greeted her in the kitchen stole her breath. The girls sat on barstools on their knees so they could reach the mixing bowls. Each awkwardly stirred batter with child-sized whisks that had been a gift from Liv. Gavin stood between them, an arm around each, hovering in case one of them tipped over or started to spill something. With murmurs of encouragement, he waited patiently as they worked the whisks through the thick batter. Every few moments, one of them would look up for approval, and Gavin gave it with gentle smiles and kisses on their heads.

Her heart shifted sideways. Even when her parents were married, her father never did things like this with her and Liv. He didn't travel like Gavin, but he was far more absent in their lives than Gavin ever was in Ava's and Amelia's. By the time her father finally left for good, Thea couldn't bring herself to care. He'd been gone all their lives in the way that mattered most.

Gavin looked up and caught her gaze. She tried to rein in her expression, but she wasn't quick enough. Gavin's eyebrows pulled together. She forced a smile and a breezy tone. For the girls' sake. Not his. "Looks good, girls."

Amelia did a little shimmy in her chair and lifted her whisk. "I'm done, Daddy." Batter dribbled onto her hands and the counter. Gavin wiped both and asked Ava if she was ready too.

Ava shook her head. Her batter needed to be perfect. "I'll help her finish if you want to start cooking," Thea offered.

They worked in quiet tandem for the next ten minutes. Gavin flipped pancakes as Thea got out the syrup, whipped cream, and chocolate chips. She cleaned off the counter and set plates in front of the girls' chairs. After getting the girls settled with their food, Gavin fixed a plate for Thea and himself. They ate standing up on opposite sides of the island, each hovering in case they needed to save either of the girls from getting syrup in their hair. Neither spoke as they ate, except to the kids.

Gavin swallowed a last huge bite of pancakes and leaned back against the other counter. "So, I was thinking."

Thea looked up. Gavin bit his lip, as if afraid to finish his thought.

"Since the girls are feeling better, I was thinking of taking them downtown to do a little Christmas shopping this afternoon. You could kick back here, maybe dig out your paints or just relax?"

The girls both perked up at the word *Christmas*. Or maybe *shopping*. Both were powerful words to them.

"What do you think?"

"Can we, Mommy?" Amelia asked, smearing syrup across her cheek.

Thea could hardly say no. Her entire game plan revolved around keeping her distance from him, and what better way than for him to leave the house? But the Christmas festival was the kind of thing they did together as a family before. It was hypocritical of her to be hurt that she wasn't included in his plans. This is what it would be like from now on. She needed to get used to it as much as the girls.

"Sure, sounds great," she finally answered. "I'll get some more work done on the wall while you're gone."

She poured another cup of coffee and carried it upstairs to change. A few minutes later, Gavin walked in. He had her cell phone. "Dan just tried to call you."

Her father. Thea set the phone on the dresser. It was way too early to even think about him.

Gavin hovered in the doorway. "Wh-what do you think he wants?"

"I haven't RSVP'd for the wedding yet."

"Are you . . . are you OK about him getting married? I mean, are you upset?" he asked.

Thea knitted her brow. Where was this coming from? "I don't really think about it," she admitted.

"Do you want me to deal with him?"

"Deal with him?"

"If you don't want to talk to him, I can answer the next time he calls. Or I can just call him myself and tell him to back off. Do you want me to?"

Her heart shifted in her chest with an unidentifiable emotion. She tried to picture Gavin dealing with her father in any way whatsoever. He'd met Dan in person exactly once—a few months after the twins were born and Dan stopped on his way through to a business retreat of some kind. And as far as Thea knew, Gavin had only spoken to her father on the phone a handful of times since then. Yet the thought of not having to deal with her father, of not having to call and let him know she wouldn't be at the wedding, was hot fudge sundae–level tempting.

"No, thanks," she said. "I'll talk to him eventually."

Gavin nodded. "If you change your mind, let me know."

"OK," she said slowly. "Thanks."

After Gavin and the girls left, Thea decided to take out her confusing emotions on the wall. The banging and crashing brought Liv up from the basement like a zombie in search of brains.

"Coffee," she grunted.

Thea pointed at the pot. "You might need to heat it up."

"Where is everyone?"

"Gavin took the girls downtown for some shopping."

"How long are they going to be gone?"

"Not sure. Why?"

"You and I should go get pedicures or a massage or something," Liv said, stifling a yawn.

"I don't think I—" Thea stopped herself mid-sentence. She was about to run through the litany of reasons why she couldn't. She had to get groceries, fold some laundry, plan the family menu for the next week. But why shouldn't she do something relaxing and totally for herself today? Gavin had the girls, and even if they weren't gone very long, he could be home with them all day. And since Liv had the day off, why the hell not?

Thea nodded. "You know what? You're right. Let's go crazy and get sushi too."

"This reminds me of watching you get ready for your wedding."

Thea met her sister's gaze in the mirror of the dressing room.

It had taken some major coaxing on Liv's part, but Thea had finally agreed to hit the mall for some shopping. A mall on Black Friday was pretty much the last place Thea wanted to be, but Liv reminded her she needed to replace her Southern Belle wardrobe.

"I remember you trying to zip me into that dress," Thea responded, turning to see how the black dress she was trying on looked from behind.

"It fit."

"Barely."

"You were pregnant with twins."

"My ass had its own zip code."

"You were happy."

"Was I?"

Liv sat up straight, and one eyebrow went stratospheric. "Weren't you?"

"I was nervous," Thea clarified. "I wasn't sure if I *looked* happy."

Liz snorted. "Nice save."

It wasn't a save. Thea *had* been happy. Terrified, but happy and hopeful and one hundred percent naïve. If only she'd known then what she knew now.

"Well, Gavin definitely looked happy that day. Never would've guessed that he'd end up being just another asshole."

Thea slipped out of the black dress and started to put her own clothes back on. "I don't want you to hate him, Liv."

"I don't hate him. I'm disappointed in him."

Thea once again met her sister's eyes in the mirror. "What do you mean?"

"You guys were my OTP." One true pairing. "It sort of gave

me hope that maybe there actually were some decent men left in the world."

"He is a decent man."

Liv gathered a stack of clothes into her arms and shoved them at Thea. "Why are you defending him?"

"I'm not. I just—" Thea hefted the load of clothes she'd decided to buy higher in her arms.

"Just what?"

"I just think it's dangerous to expect anyone to be perfect."

Liv snorted. "Well *there's* a cryptic statement."

One that Thea had no intention of expanding on, but Liv wasn't easily swayed. By the time their food arrived at a nearby sushi restaurant, her sister was primed and ready for attack.

"So, what gives?" Liv asked, dipping a spicy tuna roll into soy sauce.

"What do you mean?"

"Why are you going easy on him, all of a sudden?"

"I'm not. All I did was point out that he's not some kind of evil mastermind."

"Something has changed. What is it?"

He offered to deal with Dad for me. He kissed me and made me want to forget everything bad. He made pancakes with the girls. Thea shook her head. "Nothing."

"Don't shut me out, Thea." Liv looped her pinkie finger with Thea's. "You and me against the world, remember?"

Thea sucked in a breath. Liv wasn't going to let this go. "Okay, there is something I haven't told you."

"I knew it," Liv hissed. "What did he do?"

Thea explained about his conditions, leaving out the part about kissing. That one was too personal.

Liv's jaw practically broke because she clenched it so hard. "And you say he's not an evil mastermind. He's blackmailing you!"

"It doesn't matter. Just because I go out with him doesn't mean I'm going to cave."

It was dark by the time Thea and Liv returned shortly after dinnertime. Gavin and the girls were hanging out in the living room when they walked in. He looked up with a smile that made Thea's heart swipe right.

At the sound of Liv's knowing snort, Thea wiped her expression clean.

"Have fun?" Gavin asked, draping an arm over the back of the couch.

"Yeah," she breathed, bending to kiss the girls.

"We were just going to watch *Elf,*" Gavin said.

"Can we all watch it?" Ava asked.

"Sure," Thea answered, glancing up at her sister. "Maybe Liv will make us some caramel corn."

"Sure," Liv drawled in a sickly, sweet tone. "And then we'll just be one big happy family!"

Thea smothered her groan with a sigh.

When the movie ended, Gavin offered to put the girls to bed so Thea could continue her day of pampering with a long bubble bath. It sounded too heavenly to refuse, but when she emerged from the bathroom forty-five minutes later, she realized his suggestion hadn't been entirely altruistic.

Gavin was sitting on their bed, reclined against the headboard with his legs crossed casually at the ankles. A present rested next to his hip, wrapped way too beautifully for Gavin to have done it himself. His present-wrapping skills usually involved an entire role of tape and a wad of paper five times bigger than was necessary.

"Did you need something?" she asked, crossing her arms over the plush robe that covered her nakedness.

Oh. Right. The good-night kiss. Her heart skidded sideways.

Gavin held out the present. "I got you something today." When she made no move to accept it, he rose from the bed and brought it to her. "It's nothing big, but I thought of you when I saw it."

Reluctantly, Thea took the present from his fingers and slid a fingernail under a strip of tape along the back. The red-and-gold paper fell away in a single sheet and fell to the floor.

And then so did her stomach.

It was a book.

But not just any book. *Their* book. The one she'd been reading the day when he finally approached her in the coffee shop after weeks of shyly smiling. *W-w-what are you reading?* he asked.

And it was that book that he offered to read aloud to her when she came down with what she thought was a stomach flu three months into their relationship.

"Where did you get this?" she asked, because it was the only thing she could think to say. It's not like it was hard to find a copy of a Faulkner novel.

"The bookstore downtown." He cleared his throat. "I was thinking maybe w-w-we could read it again since we never finished it."

No, they hadn't. Because that stomach flu ended up being morning sickness, and the book was quickly forgotten. Thea wasn't even sure what happened to her old copy. Probably packed away in a box in the attic along with her other neglected college textbooks.

The high from the day began to dissipate like a mist in the air. "I know what you're doing, Gavin, and I-I appreciate the sentiment. But—"

"Yesterday sucked," he blurted, cutting her off. "I know that." He stumbled over his next words. "I w-w-want to try this again. Can we pretend the past twenty-four hours never happened?"

"Pretending everything is fine doesn't solve anything, Gavin." Her tone was combative and defensive, but that's how she felt. Why bother hiding it?

"I just w-want us to read together like we used to," he said.

"And then what? After you read, then what?"

"And then I'll kiss you good-night and go back to my room. And tomorrow night, we'll do it again, and the night after that."

Thea sank to the mattress. Gavin must have mistaken it as a sign of her softening, because he approached the bed. "I'm trying to put us back together, Thea. Can't you meet me halfway?"

At her silence, Gavin sidestepped her and sat down on the bed. He reclined into the same pose as when she walked out of the bathroom, only this time he cracked open the book. He looked up and cocked an eyebrow, daring her to join him.

Thea rolled her eyes. "Fine. We'll read." She stomped around to her side of the bed and climbed in next to him, holding her robe closed as she did. She fluffed the pillow behind her head and fell back against it. Her head clunked the headboard. She tried again.

His quiet chuckle vibrated the bed. "Comfortable?"

"Fine."

His smile actually made noise. "Just checking."

Thea let out another annoyed breath. "Are you going to pick up where we left off?"

Gavin made an mmm noise. "I think maybe we should start over."

CHAPTER THIRTEEN

Gavin started over by lying to his wife bright and early Monday morning.

"I have a training session," he told her, pouring cereal into the girls' bowls. They sat sleepily in matching red T-shirts in their booster seats at the island countertop. "I'll be back around noon."

"OK," Thea said, handing him the milk over the girls' heads. Their fingers touched in the exchange, and she didn't react, which was progress. A pleasant truce had settled between them since Friday night. He read to her and kissed her chastely before bed every night. She hadn't exactly warmed up to him yet, but she'd let him put his arm around her while watching a movie with the girls on the couch last night. It was like working with a skittish stray dog.

"I like a lot of milk, Daddy," Amelia said.

"I know, baby." He filled her bowl to the brim and then

splashed half as much into Ava's, who he secretly believed wanted less just to be different from her sister.

"Can you write everything on the whiteboard so I'll know what your schedule is?" Thea said, putting the milk back in the fridge. She looked at the girls, who were still in the yawning-and-staring phase of waking up. "Eat. We're gonna be late." She looked back at him. "I gotta run into the school to pick up my letter of recommendation, and then I'm meeting with the guidance counselor."

"I know. I saw it on the whiteboard."

Butter barked at his empty dish and smacked the bowl with his paw. He somehow managed to spill his water instead. Thea did a little hop and pirouetted over the puddle, grabbed a handful of paper towels, and dropped them over the mess. All while answering a question from Amelia about where her pink headband was. "It's in the drawer in your bathroom, honey. Do you want to wear it today?"

Amelia nodded, milk dribbling from the side of her mouth. Thea did the same little dance back over to the counter, another paper towel in hand, and wiped it up. "OK, I gotta get dressed or we're going to be late."

She whirled out of the kitchen, and Gavin could've sworn he felt an actual breeze as she went by. Thea in the morning was like a well-choreographed dance routine. He fed the dog and cleaned up the wet paper towels.

Then he called up his calendar app, uncapped the pen with his teeth, and started jotting down his various training sessions and other appointments, meetings, and required events through the end of December. When he was done, he saw that Tuesday night was open on the schedule. It also happened to be a night off for Liv. He and Thea hadn't set a date yet for their first night out, but he wasn't going to waste an opportunity. He got a different colored pen and wrote DATE NIGHT.

At the sound of her feet on the stairs, he quickly put the pen away as if he'd been caught sniffing pine tar. She walked back into the kitchen in a skirt, cardigan, and tall brown boots he'd never seen before. They must've been part of her haul from Friday. She held Amelia's pink headband in one hand.

"I put stuff on the whiteboard," he said.

"Thanks." She looked at it and then did a double-take when she saw what he wrote for tomorrow night.

"Is that OK?" he asked, feeling like he'd just asked her out for the first time all over again.

She avoided his gaze. "I'll have to make sure Liv will watch the girls."

"We could get a babysitter, if she can't."

She nodded noncommittally, which wasn't a *no*. "Here's your headband, honey. Are you done eating?" she asked the girls. Both nodded. Thea picked up their bowls, carried them to the sink, and rinsed them out. She spoke as she put them in the dishwasher. "Will you get propane for the grill today? We're out, and I was thinking of steaks for dinner."

"Sure. Do you need anything else while I'm out?"

"I don't think so, but I'll text you if I think of anything. OK," she said with an exhale, turning to the girls. "Let's get your coats on."

Gavin helped them both off their seats. They worked side by side to thread arms into sleeves and tug on backpacks. Butter, sensing their departure, flopped dramatically on the kitchen floor.

"Butter's sad," Thea told the girls. "Go give him kisses."

They wobbled over, crouched down, and gave him gentle kisses before promising they would be back soon.

"Now come kiss Daddy," she said.

"Geez, I'm second to the dog?" he teased.

"You're less pathetic-looking than the dog."

"Wow. High praise."

Thea laughed quietly. The sound made him want to pump his fist in the air.

Gavin picked up the girls, kissed their cheeks, and carried them to the car. After helping to buckle them into their car seats, Gavin walked around to the driver's side. Thea's eyes did a shy dodge to the right as she tossed her purse over to the passenger seat.

"We'll be home after school," she said.

Gavin propped an arm on top of her door. This was still a line they hadn't yet crossed—the casual goodbye kiss.

"So . . ." he said.

"See you later?"

He nodded, glancing at her lips. Her breath caught, and she looked at his.

"Bye," he murmured, his feet inching forward.

She turned and slid into the car.

A half hour later, Gavin walked into the diner, once again the last to arrive. The guys had managed to grab a table in the corner this time, farther away from the prying eyes of tourists. Still, Gavin tugged his hat lower on his forehead.

Del shoved a cup of coffee in his direction. "Update."

"We're going out tomorrow."

"Just the two of you?"

"Yep."

"Where are you taking her?" Malcolm asked.

"I'm not telling you that."

"Why not?"

"Because knowing him"—he nodded at Mack—"he'll show up to spy on me."

"I'll wear a disguise. You'll never know I'm there."

The waitress came back with the coffee and took their orders. Gavin ordered the Big Buckle again and pointed at Mack. "Don't touch my bacon."

"The way I hear it, no one is touching your bacon."

The waitress squeaked out a laugh.

"OK, focus," Del said. "Where are you taking Thea?"

"Art Supplies Plus."

Mack choked on his coffee. "What?"

"It's that huge arts and crafts warehouse place near downtown."

"I know what it is. You can't take your wife there for a date!"

Gavin snorted. "You don't know my wife. It's like a toy store for her. Our pen drawer at home is organized by color, and she has an entire basket full of washi tape."

"What's washi tape?"

"It's, like, pretty tape for decorating. I don't know. She loves that shit, though."

Del nodded. "Nessa has two full drawers of it. Sometimes I catch her staring at them with this weird smile on her face."

Mack pulled out his phone and started typing.

"What are you doing?" Gavin asked.

"Looking up washi tape."

"Why?"

"Obviously, I need to know this shit for the future Mrs. Mack."

"This is good," Malcolm said. "I like it. It shows you support her decision to go back to school and that you understand some of her passions."

"Then what?" Del asked.

"I was thinking dinner."

"Where?" Yan asked.

"I don't know."

"Huh," Mack said distractedly. "This shit is a legit phenomenon." He turned his phone around. "There are entire Pinterest boards devoted just to washi tape."

"What kind of boards?" Del asked.

"Pinterest."

"What the hell is Pinterest?" Gavin said.

"I feel like I'm with a table of baby boomers." Mack sighed. He leaned and turned around the screen of his phone. "Romance novels might be the manuals, but Pinterest is where they post the pictures."

"It's a website?" Del dug out his phone. "How do you spell it?"

"You'll need to create an account. Just look at mine for now." Mack gave Del his phone.

"Can we maybe get back to talking about my date?" Gavin asked.

They ignored him.

"What do you use it for?" Del asked, scrolling with his thumb.

"I get all my best outfit ideas from it." Mack pointed at Gavin. "You should really be using it."

"Fuck off."

Mack typed a few things. "There are probably pictures of all of us on here too."

"Why?"

"Because we're famous and good-looking." He looked at Gavin. "Well, some of us."

Del made a strangled noise. "Christ, I'm all over this goddamn website. Why the fuck didn't I know about this?"

"Half of these were probably posted by your team's social media staff, dude. Chill."

"Wait, this woman here has an entire board of pictures of me."

Mack peered at the screen. "Yep. Oh, look. She calls herself a super fan."

"She's a fucking stalker! What if my wife sees this?"

"Maybe it is your wife." Mack took his phone back. "Let's search for Gavin."

"Let's not."

Mack typed again and hit the search button. Then, "Damn, Gav." He turned the screen around, and Gavin found himself staring at a collage of images of himself, some shirtless and sweaty from various workouts at spring training last year.

"Someone loves you," Mack said.

"If it's not my wife, I don't care."

Mack aww'd. "That's adorable. He's blushing."

"Are you guys seriously looking yourselves up on Pinterest?" The waitress busted them with a tray of food.

"We were looking for outfit ideas for our friend here. He's fashionably challenged."

She smiled at Gavin. Like, *smiled* smiled. "He seems fine to me," she said, setting his food in front of him. Gavin scratched his beard to show off his wedding ring.

Mack snorted. "Subtle."

"OK, back to Gavin's date," Del said. "We left off on where to take her to dinner."

"Let me do some searching." Mack said. He typed and talked at the same time. "Best . . . Nashville . . . restaurants . . . to get . . . you . . . laid."

"Man, fuck off."

Mack barked out a laugh. "Holy shit. There's actually a list like that."

Gavin grabbed the phone. "Really?"

"Things might be looking up, Gav Man. No more five-knuckle shuffle for you."

Gavin shoved the phone back at Mack. It didn't matter. He wasn't out to get laid tomorrow. He'd settle for making her laugh again and maybe a slightly longer good-night kiss.

"Gavin, listen," Del said. "Ultimately, whatever happens tomorrow night will depend on how you handle things, so don't spend so much time planning out the perfect date that you forget the most important thing."

"What's that?"

"Talking. Getting her to open up to you. You're moving into the next phase of our plan."

Mack laughed. "Aw, yeah. This is where it gets good."

"Oh, Christ." Gavin scrubbed a hand down his face. "What?"

"Son," Malcolm asked, as if he weren't only a year older than Gavin, "what do you know about the G-spot?"

Gavin sputtered and coughed.

"Listen," Malcolm said. "Your wife doesn't want you to say *I love you*, but that doesn't mean you can't express it."

Yan nodded. "You just can't use those exact words. They're not part of her language anymore. Hell, maybe they never were."

"You have to tell her you love her in a way she wants," Del said. "A way that makes her feel good and safe. A way that will break through her walls and her fears."

"Wh-what does this have to do with the G-spot?"

Malcolm smiled broadly. "You're going to find and stroke her *emotional* one."

"Every woman has one," Del said. "A place somewhere deep inside her that only the right man can reach."

Del's voice trembled. He paused to press his hand to his mouth. Mack patted him on the shoulder. "It's cool, man. Let it out."

"We all have a void," Del said a moment later. "Something that's missing in us. Something we need but don't want to admit or don't even know we're missing until we find it in that other person. If you want to fix this thing with Thea, figure out what she's missing inside. Stroke that broken part of her until it doesn't hurt anymore. That's how to say *I love you* to Thea."

"That's really all it is, Gavin," Malcolm said. "Your wife has a void. A hole. Find it and fill it."

Malcolm's words were greeted with an uncomfortable silence, like the kind when a middle school teacher accidentally says the word *erect* in front of twenty twelve-year-old boys. Everyone wants to laugh, but no one is brave enough to do it first.

Mack finally came through. "Gavin hasn't filled Thea's hole in a while."

"Someday I'm going to hurt you when no one is looking."

Del grunted in frustration. "Look, it's great that she agreed to a date. That's progress. But don't go into it thinking it's going to be easy. She's going to be skittish. She might even try to pick a fight with you tomorrow night."

Yan nodded. "Don't forget that she's in full resistance mode. You just have to keep calm, keep cool, and be patient."

Calm. Cool. Patient. He could do that.

Mack shoved the phone in his pocket. "And I swear, you'll never notice me tomorrow night."

"Now," Del said. "Let's talk about the book. How far are you?"

"About halfway."

"Perfect," Malcolm said.

"Why is that perfect?"

"Because," Mack said, "shit's about to get real."

Courting the Countess

The one redeemable quality to the entire farcical evening, if there could be one at all, was that Irena would finally get to look upon her husband's face and utter the words every woman longed to say to a man who had for too long been convinced by society, his family, and the church itself that he was always right.

Folding her hands primly in her lap, she stared at Benedict on the seat opposite her in their carriage and tried her best not to smile. "I told you so."

Benedict managed to look chagrined as he tugged at his cravat. But he suddenly pounded a fist against his thigh. "The audacity of that woman."

"To which woman do you refer? There were so many."

"The duchess."

"Ah. Of course." The Duchess of Marbury had been suc-cinctly malicious in her rejection of Irena at the ball. Whereas other, less powerful women in the room had taken to loud gossip and serene looks of disdain from across the room, the duchess had mastered the most effective insult of all. She simply refused to speak or look at Irena upon their introduction.

"I don't care what title the woman possesses. No one gives my wife the cut direct. No one."

"Don't think too harshly of her, my lord. We women must steal our power where we can, and in the world of the *ton*, that power is sadly limited to the reduction of other women."

"If she were a man, I would call her out."

A bubble of laughter burst forth from her chest, as up-lifting as it was unexpected. Benedict met her eyes with a surprised gaze. "Are you laughing at me?"

"I'm sorry," Irena said, holding her fingers to her lips. "I just . . . that is an image I will never forget."

"Be careful, my dear. Your laughter is such a welcome sound, I may be driven to homicide yet."

"How very romantic."

"I did say I would do anything to prove my love."

"Perhaps it's a good thing, then, that you will be gone the next few days," she mused. Benedict had to travel to his estate to deal with some matters there. Irena would never admit it to him, but she was not looking forward to his leaving tomorrow.

The carriage bumped uncomfortably across a rut in the muddy road. Irena winced as the bones of her stays dug into her rib cage.

"Are you unwell?" Benedict asked.

"I will be fine as soon as I can remove this bloody monstrosity of a gown."

He cocked a half smile. "I don't suppose now would be an appropriate time to tell you that I find it exceedingly arousing when you speak like that."

"No, it would not."

"Still, if you should find yourself in need of assistance in removing said gown, I am at your service."

Heat stole across her skin, pooling in places that cared little that her dignity demanded self-righteous indignation. Her dignity, however, had fallen under his spell as much as every other part of her body. Especially when they'd danced tonight. He'd held her unfashionably close, even for a husband and wife in a waltz. His hand upon her back had burned straight through the silk of her gown and left an imprint upon her skin. The spinning sensation had continued long after the music had ended.

"I'm sorry this evening didn't turn out the way you'd hoped," Irena said, irrationally nervous all of a sudden.

"I got to hold you in my arms. It turned out exactly as I'd hoped."

His words sent a shiver down her spine and raised goose bumps along her arms. It was a miracle she could hear anything over the thud of her own heart. She was a fool for letting him get this close again, but she was also a fool for thinking she could continue holding him at bay. Not when her body demanded the same thing his did, and not when her heart seemed determined to follow.

The carriage slowed in front of their home. A footman opened the carriage door, and Benedict alighted himself to the cobblestone street. Turning, he extended his hand to help her down, and when he tucked her hand in his arm, the warmth of his body once again set hers ablaze. If things progressed as they had the previous two times they went out together, he would escort her to her room and bid her good night with a chaste kiss on her hand. And then, an hour later, he would join her in the library to read by the fire.

Something told her he would want more tonight.

Or maybe that was just her own desire talking.

He escorted her into the house and directly to the stairs. Neither spoke until they stood outside the closed door of her room.

"Thank you for seeing me to my room," she said.

This should have been the point when he would raise her hand to his lips. Instead, he stepped closer. "Irena," he said, his voice hoarse.

"Yes?" she breathed.

Benedict dipped his mouth close to her ear. "May I kiss you good night?" he murmured.

No. Her mind demanded she say the word. But when he nuzzled the tip of his nose against her jaw, her body acted on its own, turning her face to meet his.

The first brush of his lips was so feather-light, a mere mingling of breath, that she wondered if she'd imagined it. But then the pressure intensified as he molded his lips to hers, as his fingers wove into her hair, and as the fingers of his other hand laced with hers and curled it close to their hearts. And suddenly everything she'd been fighting—memories and longing and desire—waved the white flag of surrender. *She* surrendered.

Benedict leaned into her until her back pressed against the door of her bedroom. His mouth explored hers with a passion and tenderness that set her heart soaring to dangerous heights.

His brow came to rest on hers. "And now the evening is perfect." He stepped back with a wink. "Meet you in our secret place?"

It was a silly routine for a married couple. But their secret rendezvous had quickly become her favorite part of the day. She nodded. "I will be there."

By the time she walked into the library an hour later, he was already there. He had tossed several pillows from the couches onto the floor and spread a large blanket before the fireplace. Irena set her candle onto a nearby table and let him hold her hand as she lowered herself to the blanket. Then she watched as he crouched before the hearth and struck up a fire. An orange glow chased away the darkness.

Benedict sat down behind her and settled onto his back. With one arm propped behind his head, he displayed the sort of easy maleness that the other wallflowers giggled about at balls. He looked up at her and stretched his other arm across the blanket until his fingers brushed the fabric of her dressing gown. "I missed you," he said quietly.

"It has been an hour."

"That's a long time."

"What are we reading tonight?"

Benedict handed her a book she had never seen before. Her fingers traced the embossed title as a lump filled her throat. "How did you know?" she whispered.

"You mentioned once that you and Sophia used to dream of visiting America to see the wild horses. I ordered this book immediately. It only arrived today."

Her heart shifted sideways in her chest at the gesture.

"Why did you wish to see the wild horses, love?"

Her throat thickened with unshed emotion. Did one ever truly get over the death of a beloved sister? "Because they were free," Irena whispered. "We used to hatch secret plans late at night on how we could escape. We could dress as boys and stow away on a ship. Or we could book passage and pretend to be orphans seeking family across the sea. I would have gone. I would have done it for her."

"Tell me about her," Benedict said quietly.

"She loved horses as much as I do."

"Was she as talented a rider as you?"

"No. She could have been, but she never had the freedom to explore that interest as I did."

"Why not?"

"She was the oldest of three daughters. The expectation to marry well fell squarely on her shoulders. She was, after all, considered the beautiful one in the family."

Benedict unleashed an inventive string of curse words that secretly delighted her. "You're the most beautiful woman I've ever seen, Irena. The moment I set eyes upon you, I lost all ability to speak."

"I do not require compliments, my lord. I'm well aware

of my own attractiveness, which, of course, no lady is supposed to admit, but such is the world. English society seems to rest upon the requirement that women are pitted against each other until we all emerge envious of the other."

He was silent at that. Only for a moment, though. "Were you envious of your older sister?"

Irena shook her head. "Never. But she envied me."

"Why?"

"I didn't carry the same burden she did. Her entire life was about securing a husband she didn't want just to please my parents."

"And when she died, that burden fell to you."

Irena avoided his eyes but nodded. His hand found hers. "Talk to me, my love. Trust me."

She met his eyes. "She felt guilty for falling ill. Before she died, she made me promise that I would never marry for anything less than true love."

Benedict sat up slowly until their faces were inches from each other. "And did you?"

Time moved in hour-long seconds as he stared at her mouth, waiting for her answer.

A discreet throat-clearing sent them jumping apart, as if they'd been once again caught in a compromising position. Of course, they were married now, so there was no need to be embarrassed, but Irena's cheeks blazed all the same.

Benedict turned toward the intrusion. Benedict's longtime butler lingered several feet away. "What is it, Isaiah?"

"My lord, I apologize. A rider from Ebberfield has arrived with urgent news."

Ebberfield was the name of the Latford estate in Dorset.

"What kind of news?" Benedict asked, tense.

"It is Rosendale. He's been in a terrible accident."

Her husband's body went rigid. "I'll go at once."

Irena placed a hand on his arm. "I'll go with you."

"No. You'll slow me down."

"I am a better rider than you are, my lord."

"Irena, please," he said, suddenly every bit the lordly earl. "I command you as your husband to stay here."

His words were a cold slap. She stepped back, hands trembling.

Benedict cursed and closed the distance between them. "I'm sorry," he rasped. His hand dove into the loose curls at the back of her neck and drew her forward. His mouth was on hers before she had time to react. It was a hard, desperate kiss, and when he pulled back, it was only far enough to move his lips to her forehead. "Forgive me, but there are things I cannot talk to you about right now."

Then he turned and left her.

CHAPTER FOURTEEN

"I can't believe you're actually going to do this."

On Tuesday night, the sound of Liv's voice in the door of her bathroom made Thea jump as she put on mascara. A half-moon of brown polka dots appeared under her right eye. Great. Not that she cared how she looked. It wasn't like this was a real first date. It was a technicality. A part of their deal.

Thea cleaned up the mascara mistake with a cotton swab and decided good enough was as good as it was going to get. She stepped back and surveyed the final results in the mirror. OK, so slightly more than good enough.

"When all else fails, show a little leg, huh?" Liv snarked.

"I know you didn't just quote our mother to me."

Liv plopped down on the bed. "I'm just saying that you're putting in a lot of effort for a man who you're not trying to impress."

Thea stepped into her black patent heels. "It's just a stupid dress."

"That says, *Press me up a wall and do me, big boy.*"

"It says, *Aren't you the one who talked me into buying this last week?*"

"Yeah, but that was before I knew he'd blackmailed you into going on a date."

A quiet throat clearing in the doorway brought their heads around in guilty, no-we-absolutely-weren't-talking-about-you swivels.

"Ready?" Gavin asked with a yes-I-know-you-were-talking-about-me quirk of his lips.

Thea tried to answer, but all that came out was a little squeak, because *damn*. Her husband cleaned up good. He wore a pair of dark gray twills she'd never seen before but seemed to have literally been tailor-made for him. She'd also never seen that shirt before—a plain, slate-blue button-down that fit just tightly enough to tug over his shoulders and biceps. He had the sleeves rolled up to reveal muscular forearms. She mentally fanned herself. Men should spend more time developing their forearms. They had no idea the impact a flex of that hair-dusted whatever muscle that was right there could have on a woman.

"You look nice," he said.

"So do you."

"New dress?"

"Yes. New shirt?"

"Yep."

"I like it."

"This is your cue to get out, Liv," he said without taking his eyes off Thea.

"And this is your cue to—"

"Liv," Thea admonished. Her sister pursed her lips and scooted off the bed.

Gavin moved into the room with a smile that seemed almost bashful. "W-where's your purse?"

"On the dresser. Why?"

He pulled a folded bandana from his pocket. "Because you need to put this in it."

"Um, should I be afraid?"

He answered with a slightly less bashful smile. "You'll see."

Downstairs, they kissed the girls, dodged dog slobber, and told Liv not to show the twins any stupid YouTube videos. She said she couldn't make any promises and then shooed them out the door.

Gavin helped her into the car and then went around to his own side.

"So . . ." He did a throat-clearing thing after merging onto the freeway. "D-did you hear anything from Vanderbilt today?"

"Not yet. But it should be sometime this week."

"W-what if . . ." He didn't finish the question, but he didn't need to. She knew what he was asking.

"If I don't get in? I don't know. I haven't let myself think about that."

"You'll get in," Gavin said with a confidence he couldn't possibly have. "And we'll celebrate when you do."

Thea made a noncommittal noise.

A few minutes later, Gavin signaled for an upcoming exit. "Blindfold," he said playfully.

"Here?" She looked around. They were in a nondescript, big-box store parking lot.

"Yep. Here."

Heart hammering, Thea tied the bandana around her eyes.

This was both ridiculous and endearing. Which made it dangerous. She was supposed to be going through the motions of this date, not actually enjoying herself.

"Can you see?"

"Not a thing."

"Good. No peeking."

The car turned two more times until Thea sensed Gavin pulling the car to a stop again. Bright lights turned her vision from dark to reddish through the fabric of the bandana.

Then she sensed him leaning toward her. "OK. Ready?"

She laughed. "Ready."

Gavin's fingers fumbled with the bandana. Careful to not pull her hair, he untied it and let it fall. Thea reared back for a moment in the suddenly bright light. Then . . . "You brought me to Art Supplies Plus?"

"I thought w-we could pick up some stuff for your classes."

Thea stared at him, her heart thudding a warning. He wasn't going through the motions. This was the kind of date meant to break her down. Her husband was seducing her with markers and blank canvasses.

A flash of uncertainty flickered in his eyes. "Is-is this OK?"

"Yes," she said. "I . . . thank you."

Inside, she grabbed a shopping cart and gave him an *are you sure* look. "You really want to do this?" she asked, trying to keep her tone light.

"Don't you?"

"Yeah, but be forewarned, Gavin. I'm like a kid in a candy store in places like this."

He smiled. "I know. I've seen our pen drawer at home, Thea. I'm prepared."

. . .

He wasn't prepared.

Thea in an art supplies store was like watching a crazed animal released at the Running of the Bulls in Pamplona. Gavin offered to push the cart while she shopped. It was partially self-serving, because it gave him a better view of her in that dress.

Jesus, that fucking dress. The minute he'd walked into the bedroom, he turned into one of those cartoon characters whose eyes bug out and tongues hang from their mouths.

He followed her up and down several aisles before she let out a loving exhale. "Washi tape," she whispered, her hand over her heart. There was an entire aisle of it. Rows and rows of the stuff in every pattern and color imaginable. Thea studied individual rolls of tape with a critical eye, throwing some in the cart and returning others to the display. As if they couldn't afford to buy the entire inventory twice. But that wasn't Thea's style. Frankly, he'd been amazed that she'd spent as much money as she did on herself on Friday.

"Look at these." Thea thrust a collection of school-related tapes in his face. "The girls would love these."

Gavin returned them to the shelf. She watched him with a confused expression "Why'd you do that?"

"We're here for stuff for you, not the girls." He reached over her and grabbed some others that looked like re-creations of Van Gogh paintings. "What about these?"

She plucked them from his fingers and threw them in the cart.

"Have you ever heard of Pinterest?" he asked a few minutes later.

Thea looked at him as if he asked if she'd ever heard of Elvis. "Seriously? I live on Pinterest."

"You have an account on there?"

"Um, yeah. Why?"

"What do you use it for?"

Thea let out a shrugged breath. "God, what don't I use it for? Recipes. Craft projects I want to try. Parenting tips. Cute dog pictures. Why?"

His cheeks got hot. "There are . . . pictures of me on that site."

Thea snorted out a laugh. "I know."

"You've seen them?"

"Did you just discover Pinterest or something?"

"Sort of." He tilted his head. "So you've seen pictures of me on there?"

She shrugged. "Yeah. I have a board dedicated to the Legends, so the site's algorithm automatically sends me related pins to consider, and that often includes you. Especially since . . ."

She let the sentence drop. Since the grand slam, she meant. She did not want to go there.

"So, you'll just be sitting at your computer searching for pot roast recipes or whatever, and suddenly there's a picture of your husband that some woman has posted?"

"Gavin, women have been posting pictures of you on every social media site since the day we met. Sometimes they even post pictures of us and photoshop me out of them. I'm used to it."

"If there was a website where strange men posted thousands of pictures of you, yeah, I w-wouldn't get used to it."

"That's different. I'm not famous like you are."

"You're the most important person in the w-w-world to me, so I beg to differ."

Her lips parted, and a kaleidoscope of contrary emotions danced through her eyes. As if she didn't believe him but desperately wanted to. Then, before he knew what was happening, she rose on tiptoe and placed the softest of kisses on his lips.

It was over so quickly that he almost didn't believe it happened. She backed up with a small head shake. "Sorry, I don't know why I did that."

Gavin tried to ease the tension with a joke. "I should take you shopping for w-w-washi tape more often," Gavin mused.

The joke worked. Thea relaxed. "Wait until you get me in the paintbrush aisle."

"How fast can we get there?"

Thea playfully pushed at his chest.

Sadly, nothing happened in the paintbrush aisles. Nothing good, anyway. But after studying about twenty different brushes in various sizes between two different rows, Thea suddenly grabbed his arm and tugged him down so she could whisper.

"OK, you're going to think I'm paranoid after that Pinterest conversation, but I think you might actually have a couple of crazy fans following you right now."

The hair on the back of Gavin's neck stood on end. "What are you talking about?"

"There are these two strange guys who keep showing up wherever we are in the store. They're too obvious. I don't know. Like they're watching you but trying really hard to look like they're not watching you."

Gavin tried to keep his face neutral. "What do they look like?"

"I'll point them out if we see them again. I'm probably just being paranoid."

"Just stay close to me," he said, tensing. This was the one thing he hated about being a ballplayer. His family was exposed. All joking about Pinterest aside, it sucked to know he couldn't even go out with his wife without worrying that someone was going to stare enough to make her uncomfortable.

They checked out, and on the way out, he gave one last look back to see if the weird men she'd mentioned were still there. Seeing no one, he relaxed but kept his hand on her back as they walked. Gavin loaded the bags into the back of the car and then helped Thea into her seat again.

"So where to now?" she asked as he pulled onto the street.

He almost suggested a dark road and the back seat, but that was probably pushing his luck. "Dinner," he said, turning left.

"Good. I'm starving."

"Me too," he said, looking pointedly at her. Her shy smile expanded his chest.

A quick drive on the freeway took them into the city. Even on a Tuesday, traffic sucked and crowds surged. Gavin inched through a stoplight and turned into a parking ramp near the restaurant. He pulled up to the valet stand as Thea reapplied lipstick and fluffed her hair in the mirror. His chest expanded again. She was so beautiful that it sometimes literally hurt to look at her. Like now.

After exchanging keys for a ticket with the valet attendant, Gavin once again put his hand on her back as they walked out to the street. They were a few blocks away from Broadway, the main tourist thoroughfare through downtown Nashville. But it was still crowded with both locals and out-of-towners who wanted something off the beaten path.

They walked mostly in silence for a block, stopping and going with the flow of tourists in search of bourbon and music. He kept her tucked protectively against his side, especially when the inevitable began.

"Dude, I think that was Gavin Scott," a guy in cowboy boots said as they passed.

Thea looked up with a grin. "Dude," she said with a snort.

"Just keep walking, and hopefully they'll leave us alone."

A few feet later, another man recognized him. "Hey, aren't you—"

Gavin held up his free hand in a polite wave that said *not now, please.*

Since the grand slam, he got recognized more than he ever used to out in public. Which almost made him choose a different spot to bring her tonight, but the restaurant was a famous steak place that he knew Thea would love. It also featured live music and a dance floor, because there was no other kind of restaurant in Nashville. When Gavin made the reservation, he'd requested as private a table as possible. He didn't use his own celebrity much, but he'd laid it on thick to ensure he got what he wanted. It paid off, because the hostess treated them like royalty when they arrived and led them to a private loft overlooking the dance floor.

The table was set for two with a candle in the center next to a vase full of daisies. The hostess said a waitress would be by soon to take their drink orders, and then she left them blissfully alone.

"Did you ask them to do that?" Thea asked, pointing to the daisies.

"I did."

The gesture obviously made her uncomfortable. "I'm sorry I don't remember that day, about the daisy."

"I noticed you a long time before you noticed me, so I w-wouldn't expect you to remember it."

"Not a *long* time," she argued.

"It was a pretty long time."

"How long?"

"Two months."

She rolled her eyes. "That's a lie."

He laughed and held up his hands. "I swear."

"You were coming to that coffeehouse for two months before I noticed you?"

"Yep. Broke my heart every day until you finally looked up one day and smiled at me."

"But I *noticed* you before we smiled at each other."

"Fine. How long?"

She shrugged. "I don't know. A few times."

"Yeah, well, I hated coffee and only started going there hoping to see you again, so . . ."

Thea's lips parted. "You did?"

"Yep."

"How come you never told me that before?"

"Once I finally got up the nerve to talk to you, there was too much else I wanted to talk about, I guess."

And because there were things they never talked about, like her parents. He'd tried several times, but Thea always shut down those conversations. He was dumb enough, apparently, to think that meant there was nothing worth talking about. But when he asked her if she wanted him to deal with her father, the wall went up like it always did. At least he now recognized the wall for what it was. At least he now knew that the wall needed to be knocked down.

The waitress interrupted quietly and asked if they wanted a bottle of wine. Gavin motioned for Thea to do the honors, because she was way better at that shit than he was. She quickly scanned the wine list and ordered a French-sounding chardonnay.

The waitress delivered the wine, poured two glasses, and then took their orders. Gavin moved his chair around to be closer to her and clinked his glass against hers.

Thea lifted an eyebrow. "Are we toasting?"

"Yes."

"To what?

He considered saying something glib, like to washi tape. But he opted for something more mature and meaningful. "To our first date."

Thea smiled into her wine, but then she glanced over his shoulder at the bar below and narrowed her eyes.

"What's wrong?"

"You remember those two guys I told you about at the store?"

His spine went rigid. "What about them?"

"They're here."

"Where?" He followed Thea's point down to the bar. Two men quickly turned away. One wore a cowboy hat and sunglasses, the other a Detroit Red Wings jersey. He couldn't see faces from this far up, but he'd know that cocky stance anywhere.

Braden-Fucking-Mack in a shit-assed disguise.

CHAPTER FIFTEEN

He was going to kill him. Trying to keep his voice neutral, Gavin asked, "You're sure it's the same guys?"

"Yeah. But it's probably just coincidence, right?"

Gavin threw his napkin on the table. "Stay here."

"What?" He stood, and Thea grabbed his arm. "What are you doing? Gavin, you can't confront them!"

"Trust me."

The two "guys" knew they'd been busted the instant his feet hit the stairs. Gavin followed them with his eyes as they pushed through the crowded bar toward a dark hallway in the back with a neon RESTROOMS sign illuminating the floor in a pink glow.

Gavin dodged dancing couples and drunk assholes in pursuit and finally threw open the bathroom door with both hands. "I know you're in here, Mack," he barked.

"No one by that name in here," came a voice from the second stall.

Gavin banged on the stainless steel door. "Out. Now."

The door opened. Gavin backed up, fists forming against his thighs. Mack walked out, hat in hand. "Why aren't you answering our texts?"

Gavin felt something like a growl rip through his chest. "Are you fucking kidding me? That's all you have to say to me? What the fuck are you doing here?"

"Trying to help you."

Gavin walked down the aisle, banging on other doors. "Who else is with you?"

A second door opened, and out walked the Russian hockey player with the bad digestive system. "Ask wife if she want to dance."

"Seriously?" he squawked in Mack's direction. "You dragged him along?"

"He's right," Mack said. "She keeps looking at the dance floor. Ask her to dance."

"I am doing just fine on this date without your help, thank you very much. And by the way, that hat and those glasses are the worst fucking disguise I've ever seen. Do you really think no one recognizes you?"

"No one has yet."

"They're probably just too embarrassed for you. They think you've gone crazy. And you know what? You are crazy. Certifiable. Don't you have a goddamn life?"

"What about my disguise?" the Russian asked, looking down at his rival Red Wings' shirt.

"It sucks."

"No one recognizes you, anyway," Mack said. "You were right about that washi tape, by the way. She kissed you!"

Gavin grabbed a handful of Mack's shirt. "I swear to God—"

A toilet flushed. Gavin felt a blood vessel burst in his brain. A short, round man walked out of the stall at the end and stopped to stare at them. Mack began to whistle and look around. Gavin clenched his jaw so tightly he heard a bone crunch.

The man looked at Gavin. "I know you."

Gavin let go of Mack's shirt. "No, you don't."

"You're Gavin Scott."

"No, he is not," the Russian supplied. "Gavin Scott much bigger man. And not so ugly as this one."

The man snorted and washed his hands. In the mirror, he looked at Gavin. "You should ask her to dance. If she's looking at the dance floor, she wants to."

Great. Now he was getting advice from strangers in the goddamn bathroom?

The man dried his hands. "I heard nothing," he said. Then he left.

Gavin pointed at Mack. "You are going to leave. Now."

"Just listen to us," Mack said. "You're doing really well, but dance with her, and use it as a chance to get her to talk. It happens all the time in the manuals. Remember when Irena and Benedict danced the waltz? It brought them closer. People reveal secrets when they dance. It's easier to talk to a shoulder than to a face."

That made an absurd amount of sense, which pissed Gavin off.

The door opened again, and in strode a security guard in a gray uniform. He surveyed the scene. "Everything all right in here?"

"Yep," Mack said. "Nothing to see here."

"A woman said she was worried that her husband might be in trouble."

Gavin extended his hand. "My name is Gavin Scott, and I'm a player for the Nashville Legends. These two men are harassing my wife and me, and I'd like you to throw them out, please."

"Let's go." The security guard took Mack's arm. He hesitated when he realized Mack was solid muscle. "Um . . ."

Mack ignored the guard. "When you get home, ask if you can kiss her in the driveway. In your car. She'll love it. I read it in this one book, and I tried it on a girl once, and I swear, she melted on my lap like butter."

"This man is clearly unhinged," Gavin told the security guard.

"Have you been drinking, sir?" the security guard asked.

Mack nodded. "Yes. Good. I'll pretend I'm drunk. Make sure Thea sees this when he throws us out. You can follow us out and be all, *get the fuck out of here*, and be all alpha male and shit."

"You're insane."

Mack put his hat back on. "I'm telling you, she'll open up with you after all this. You'll be thanking us later."

The security guard pulled on Mack's arm. "Look, I don't know what the hell is going on in here, and I'm not sure I want to know, but you two, out."

He shoved Mack toward the door. The Russian followed. "My disguise does not suck."

A small, curious crowd had formed outside the bathroom, because who isn't curious when a security guard goes into the john at a bar? Mack turned to look over his shoulder and made as big a scene as possible. "I love you, man," he cried, stumbling for effect. "I'm a huge fan. Huge."

Gavin pinched the bridge of his nose.

"Yes. Huge fan," the Russian said, inexplicably throwing his arms high in the air.

"Out you go," the security guard said, pushing them to the door.

Gavin ignored the looks and questions from people as he walked back around the dance floor. He looked up to see Thea leaning over the railing, biting her lip. He took the stairs two at a time.

She rushed over to him. "What happened?"

"Nothing. It's fine."

"What did you say to them?"

"I told them that I was enjoying a nice evening with my wife and that I would appreciate it if they would leave us alone."

"Don't do that again. Do you hear me? They could have been crazy! I don't want you to do that again."

"I won't."

"I'm serious."

Gavin put his hands on her hips and pulled her against him. "Do you w-want to dance?"

"*Dance?*" Thea scanned Gavin's face for signs of another head wound. Had one of them hit him in the bathroom?

Uncertainty flashed across his face. "I thought maybe you w-w-wanted to."

"I—"

"We don't have to."

He started to step back, but Thea covered his hands with her own. "I didn't say that. We just, we've never danced before."

"I know. It's long overdue, don't you think?"

Yes, but not much about their marriage was normal. They were doing a lot of things for the first time that most married couples did long before they got married and had children.

"I like dancing," she finally said. Wait. No. What was she thinking? This wasn't supposed to be a real date. She was supposed to be going through the motions. The washi tape and wine were scrambling her brain. She backed up.

"So do I," Gavin said. He caught her hand with one of his and pulled her back. He curled their fingers together. "So should we?"

Thea looked around the dark loft. They were safe from prying eyes, and the band was playing a slow song.

Nervous butterflies took flight in her stomach as Gavin wrapped an arm around her waist and pulled her against him. His other hand curled around hers, and he tucked them both against his heart. It was manly and gallant and sexy as hell, and that was *before* he began to move.

Which. Wow. He swayed with a natural rhythm that took her breath away. Of course, most athletes had good body control, but that didn't mean they could actually dance. She'd seen enough dugout dance-offs to know that most baseball players left their skills on the field. But Gavin? Wow. Where'd he been hiding this?

"Do you regret not having a real w-wedding?" he asked after a moment of quiet swaying.

"We did have a real wedding."

"You know what I mean. A big wedding."

Her gut twisted. This was dangerous territory as far as conversations went. "Not really. Do you?"

"I didn't used to, but now I think I'd like to have the memory of you walking down the aisle in a white dress."

"It's just a dress."

"*This* isn't just a dress." His hand splayed across her back. Her heart raced. The flirting that had bothered her so much last week was giving her warm fluttery feelings tonight, and that was not good. She stared at his shoulder to avoid his eyes.

"What about a honeymoon?" he murmured.

"What about it?" This was definitely venturing into dangerous territory. Thea focused on her steps, her breathing.

"I regret not having one of *those*," Gavin said playfully, rubbing the pad of his thumb suggestively across her low back.

Thea coughed. "Where would you have wanted to go?"

"Someplace warm where you could walk around in a bikini all day."

Laughter bubbled up, unbidden. "I haven't worn a bikini since the girls were born."

"I know. It's a source of great d-disappointment for me."

They danced in silence for a beat, but then he spoke again. "If we'd had a w-wedding, w-would you have had your dad walk you down the aisle?"

Thea swallowed and closed her eyes. She didn't want to think about that bastard right now. Not when she was all tangled up in other confusing emotions. And that kind of question was why she shouldn't have opened the door to the conversation at all.

"Talk to me, Thea," he said against her hair.

"Why does any of this matter?"

"Because you matter."

Thea shook her head. "I don't know," she admitted. "It seems like the kind of a thing a man should have to earn, not just expect to be able to do."

Gavin tugged her closer. "He didn't earn it."

"No. He definitely did not."

They danced in silence for several minutes after that. Thea's body chronicled every way his body brushed and molded against hers. He bent his head and kissed the top of hers.

"Why don't you want to go to the wedding?" he asked quietly.

For some reason, she answered. "Because I can't stand to watch another young, naïve woman get scammed into believing that she's the one who will change him, that she's the one who will make him stay. He won't. He'll leave her, because that's what he does. He leaves."

The ride home was silent.

Not tense silent. Just . . . weird silent. All night, they'd existed in a sated, peaceful void, avoiding the unpleasant, lumbering elephants between them. So much unresolved unpleasantness had been blissfully forgotten for one night.

Gavin pulled into the driveway and killed the engine. Neither of them moved to get out, though.

"I had fun tonight," he said.

Thea didn't want to admit that she had too, so she said nothing. What good would it do to encourage him with false hope? Once they exited the dark haven of the car, the jungle of reality would unleash the trumpeting herds, and no amount of missing and wishing for things to be different would chase them off.

Gavin cleared his throat. "So . . ."

Thea looked over at him. "So?"

"Since this is a date," he started. "Do I get to kiss you in the car before I walk you inside?"

Air seeped from her lungs. "Is that what people do on dates? I've forgotten."

"I remember doing a lot more than that in a car with you," he said, his voice husky.

Thea's cheeks got hot. "You know that's probably the night I got pregnant, right?"

"I always w-wondered." The heavy-lidded way he looked at her suggested he had wondered but didn't particularly care; he just liked the memory and wouldn't mind making a new one.

Which was why the smart thing to do would be to get out of the car now.

But she wasn't feeling very smart. She was just feeling. "Yes," she murmured.

"Yes?" he repeated.

She looked at his lips.

A happy sound rose from Gavin's chest as he claimed her mouth. This wasn't like before. This wasn't like the kiss from the kitchen or the one the night he moved home. This kiss was no explosion of passion, but it was every bit as shattering. Who knew there could be such volatility in such tender pressure? This was a kiss that required a slow breath through her nose and a strong grip on her seat. The kind of kiss that told her she was going to be in trouble if they kept up this charade of dating.

Gavin adjusted the angle of his mouth and brushed her lips once, twice, a third time. Then he pulled back and gazed down at her, a half smile lifting the corner of his mouth.

Gavin rubbed his thumb across her lower lip. "You feel like reading tonight?"

Thea's head nodded up and down on its own.

An hour later, she fell asleep to the soft cadence of his voice and the confused beating of her heart.

CHAPTER SIXTEEN

"Did you kids have fun last night?"

The next morning, Gavin swung the fridge shut to find that Liv had materialized in the kitchen as if she'd teleported. He jumped and swore.

"Yes."

"Bummer," Liv said. "I was hoping to get out of the basement."

Gavin set down the milk for the girls' cereal. Thea was upstairs getting the girls dressed. He hadn't actually seen her yet this morning; he'd only heard her movements. "You know, Liv, this little thing we d-d-do is amusing and all," Gavin grumbled, "but I don't have the patience for you this morning."

"Just watching out for my sister. Didn't I warn you about hurting her?"

Gavin opened a pantry and withdrew the Cheerios. "Did it ever occur to you that this is none of your business?"

"She's my sister."

"And my wife."

"I live here."

"Feel free to move out."

"You first." She snapped her fingers. "Wait. You already tried that once."

"And I don't plan to do it again."

Thea shuffled into the kitchen, and Gavin fumbled the cereal. "Hey," he breathed.

"Morning," Liv chirped.

Thea stopped short, her eyes darting back and forth between them. "What's going on?"

"Nothing," Gavin said.

"Just telling my brother-in-law how much I think of him."

Thea sighed and reached with both hands to twist her hair atop her head. The girls stumbled into the kitchen in matching pink T-shirts and purple leggings. Gavin scooped them both up and poured their cereal.

Thea's shoulders were stiff as she filled a cup of coffee. Had she slept any better than him? Because he'd slept like shit. Crawling out of her bed last night to return to the guest room had taken Herculean strength. He didn't possess it this morning. He had to touch her.

He walked up behind her, slipped his arms around her waist, and nuzzled her cheek.

She turned her face up to his with a surprised, wide-eyed glance. He dropped a kiss on her lips. "Good morning," he murmured.

"Morning," she whispered.

"I had fun last night."

Liv made a gagging noise.

Gavin looked over his shoulder and curled his lip. Liv narrowed her eyes. He bared his teeth. She waggled her fingers and hummed P!nk's "U + UR Hand."

Thea turned around with another sigh. "You two need to get over this."

"She started it."

Thea tilted her head. "I don't even let the girls get away with that excuse."

The twins, who'd been silently poking dribbly spoonfuls of Cheerios into their mouths, must have picked up on the weird tension in the room, because they started griping about who got more cereal. Gavin tore his gaze from Thea and intervened. "You each got the same amount, girls."

"I'm done," Ava said, pushing her bowl away, pouting for no good reason.

"Wait for your sister, and then we'll go get you dressed," Thea said, walking to where the girls sat. She started wiping mouths but paused when her cell phone buzzed in her pocket. She made an annoyed noise but pulled it out.

She froze.

"What's wrong?" Gavin asked.

"It's an email from Vanderbilt."

Liv set down her coffee. "Shit."

"Open it," he said.

With a deep swallow, Thea swiped the screen a couple of times. Gavin held his breath as her eyes skimmed the screen.

A smile broke out on her face as she turned the screen around.

"Holy shit," he breathed. "You got in?"

"I got in." She raised her arms and let out a victory whoop. Liv did a dance around the island as the girls laughed at the hijinks. Gavin wanted to join in the celebratory melee. He wanted to wrap his arms around Thea and congratulate her with a kiss, but he chose restraint.

"That's amazing, Thea," he said from a safe distance. "Congratulations."

"When do you start classes?" Liv asked.

Thea looked at the email again. "January 18."

"We are sooo going to celebrate tonight," Liv said, hugging Thea from behind.

Gavin bristled but fought it down. She and Liv already had plans together tonight to help Liv's friend with the café. He'd save his celebration for another night, when they could be alone.

She looked up, and her cheeks flushed under his gaze. He must not have been very good at hiding his thoughts. "I have to get dressed," she said.

Gavin cleaned up the girls' cereal and helped them down from their chairs. Then he walked to the whiteboard, dug out a dry erase marker, and circled January 18 on the calendar.

"I wouldn't plan too far out, Gavin," Liv said, coming up behind him. "Your calendar ends at Christmas."

Not if he could help it.

Last night had been a turning point for them. He could feel it. She'd revealed some things to him that she'd never told him before. She'd danced with him. Kissed him.

The guys were right. He needed to be patient. But Liv was right too. The calendar was not his friend, and her news about getting into Vanderbilt was a new plot twist he needed to figure out.

It was time to get serious.

Gavin hammered out a text message to the guys. *Emergency meeting tonight. My house.*

. . .

After dropping the girls off at school, Thea ran home to quickly shower and dress. Gavin, thankfully, was gone for his morning training session. She couldn't handle any private conversations with him. Not after the way he'd looked at her this morning. Not after that sweet little kiss and all it implied.

Liv was right. She was caving. From a couple of tender kisses and one thoughtful date and— Thea shook her head. The email from Vanderbilt had arrived at the perfect time. He'd been spinning cobwebs in her brain, but getting notice from Vandy was like a sweep of the clarity broom.

She had too much to do, like drop off the paperwork that had been requested in her acceptance email, register for classes, and stop at the bookstore. A lot of it could have waited until later, but she'd been waiting almost four years to go back to school. She was tired of waiting.

The Vanderbilt campus was a half-hour drive from Franklin. Thea found a metered spot across from the administration building, poured a handful of quarters into it, and went inside. The admissions office was on the third floor. A secretary with cat-eye glasses gave her a quizzical look when Thea handed her the paperwork.

"You know, you can do all this online," the woman said.

Thea shrugged. "I know. But I wanted to come in."

She'd missed this. Missed the vibe of a college campus. Missed the creative rebellion of the arts and theater majors, the bleary-eyed straggle of all-night studiers, the sardonic wit of cocky professors. Thea had never felt more like herself than she had when she was in school.

After visiting the administration building, Thea popped into the on-campus bookstore. On a whim, she bought a couple of Vanderbilt T-shirts for the girls.

Shit. The girls. Thea dug out her phone to check the time. She was going to be late picking them up. Unless Gavin did it.

Thea hesitated but sent him a text to see if he'd get the girls from school, because Thea was going to go straight to Alexis's café. Gavin responded quickly that he would and then asked how things were going on campus. She ignored the question and simply replied that she'd be home by ten.

Thea grabbed a sandwich at an on-campus deli and then returned to her car. The drive to Alexis's café took forty minutes in the afternoon traffic. She pulled into the row of parking spaces behind Alexis's building, where a door had been propped open.

Thea poked her head in. "Hello?"

Hearing nothing, she slipped inside and tried again. Still nothing. The kitchen was full of boxes and piles of bubble wrap, with shiny pots and pans hanging from a row of hooks above a new range.

"Liv? You guys here?" Thea dodged boxes as she walked through the kitchen. A swinging door led to what Thea assumed was the café area beyond. She pushed open the door and . . .

"Surprise!"

Thea squeaked and slapped a hand over her heart. Liv and Alexis stood in the center of the café by the one and only table that wasn't covered with boxes and stacks of dishes waiting to be put away. Instead, it bore a bottle of champagne, three flutes, and a massive card that read *"Congratulations."*

"What is this?" Thea laughed.

"I told you we were going to celebrate!" Liv said. "Surprise!"

Alexis grinned. "Liv told me your good news. That's so awesome. And it's perfect timing, actually."

She and Liv shared a glance.

Thea walked in farther. "Perfect timing for . . ."

"Well," Alexis said, drawing out the word. "I have some super-plain walls that are in desperate need of artwork. I was just thinking that it would be awesome to be able to show some original pieces from a local artist."

Thea stopped and stared. Liv rolled he eyes. "She means you, Thea."

"You want me to hang some of my pieces here?"

"Are you willing? I want to regularly showcase local artists, give them a space where they can sell their work."

Thea almost pinched herself. In the span of one day, she'd been accepted back into art school and been handed a chance to showcase her work. She didn't believe much in signs, but this felt like one.

Thea surveyed the café. "So what do we do first?"

Liv walked closer and shoved a glass of champagne in her hand. "First, we toast."

Thea accepted the champagne.

Liv raised her glass. "To new beginnings."

Thea matched Liv's pose. "New beginnings."

But when the champagne touched her tongue, the bubbly *and* the sentiment left a sour aftertaste.

CHAPTER SEVENTEEN

"Can we get down to business, please?"

Gavin opened a beer and plopped onto the couch with as much dignity as any grown man could muster while wearing a red feather boa and reindeer antlers. Ava, Amelia, and Jo-Jo had demanded the men play dress-up with them before settling down in the girls' bedroom with a movie while the men "worked on the wall." But the choice of *The Little Mermaid* had sparked a debate back downstairs, and now things had gone off the rails.

"She has to literally change from one species to another in order to be with a man," Mack said, waving his hands around to finish drying his nails. Ava made him paint them alternating green and red for Christmas. "What kind of message is that for little girls?"

"It's a *movie*," Del growled, defensive because he had been the one who suggested it.

"Del makes an excellent point that we shouldn't overlook," Malcolm said calmly. The mini jingle bell ornaments dangling from his beard made a festive sound as he spoke. "We shouldn't assume that women and girls don't know the difference between reality and fantasy. We don't fear that men who read murder mysteries and thrillers are going to have a hard time not becoming serial killers, so why should we assume that a girl won't know that she doesn't have to change from a mermaid to human in order to find love just because of a movie?"

"Because that's the only message girls get sometimes," Mack argued. "It's not one movie. It's, like, every fucking movie."

Everyone nodded in silent agreement. The Russian lifted a hip and farted.

"True," Malcolm said. "But we must find a way to produce and enjoy content that celebrates the fierceness of women without, at the same time, belittling a woman's ability to decipher fact from fiction."

"Like romance novels," Gavin grumbled.

Mack covered his heart with his hand. "Our boy is growing up."

"Our boy is growing angry," Gavin said. "It's getting late. We're running out of time."

The Russian stood with a look on his face that said he was running out of time too. "Where is restroom?"

The room erupted in a loud chorus of *noooo*. Mack jumped up and headed for the kitchen. "Don't let him near your bathroom, Gav Man," Mack said, opening the fridge like he owned the place. "You'll never get the smell out. The man grows toxic waste in his colon."

"I have digestive problem," the Russian said.

"Use the bathroom in the basement," Gavin grumbled. "And you, get the fuck out of my fridge."

Mack emerged with a take-out container. He peeled off the top using the tips of his fingers to avoid smudging the nail polish. "What is this?"

"I don't know."

"Can I eat it?"

Gavin shrugged. "Yes, whatever. Can we get started, please?"

Each guy had arrived with a bag full of books for him and unceremoniously dumped them out on the floor. Gavin picked up the first one he saw—a dark cover featuring a shirtless man holding a gun. "What the hell is this?"

"Romantic suspense," Del said.

"Romantic suspense?" he repeated skeptically.

"Yeah, you know." Mack held up a fist and spoke dramatically to the ceiling. "Is this guy *ever* going to get laid? Story of your life, dude, amirite?"

Gavin threw the book back on the pile. "I'm being serious," he grumped. "We made a lot of progress last night, but she got weird this morning when she found out she got into Vanderbilt."

"Tell us what happened," Malcolm said.

Gavin summarized the key moments of their date and the morning.

"You're in the dreaded middle of your story, man," Del said. "It's going to feel like one step forward, two steps back for a while, just like in the book. Remember when Irena finally opens up to Benedict about her sister, how they wanted to escape to America?"

Gavin nodded.

"Well, that left her feeling vulnerable and even a little pissed off when he left."

Gavin covered his ears. "Spoilers! I haven't read any further than that."

"The fact that Thea opened up to you a little about her dad is a good sign, but that kind of progress is also scary for her," Malcolm said. "You made her talk about things that hurt. The G-spot is most tender before it starts to sing."

"I will pay each of you a million dollars to stop saying G-spot," Gavin snapped.

"The point is, you chipped away at her walls last night. That's going to leave her feeling exposed, vulnerable."

"Yeah, well, so do I," Gavin admitted quietly.

The room stilled.

"Keep going, man," Mack said. "This is the good stuff."

Malcolm leaned back. "Gavin, we spend a lot of time talking about what she's afraid of, her resistance. What are *you* afraid of?"

"Losing her."

"Bullshit," Del said.

Gavin whipped his gaze to Del's. "Excuse me?"

"That's surface-level bullshit," Del said. "Of course, you're afraid of losing her. That goes without saying. But if you think all you have to do is win her back to be happy, you're wrong. You might as well quit now."

"I don't—" His mouth froze for a moment. "Can you just stop speaking in riddles and fucking tell me something!"

"What Del is trying to say," Malcolm said, "is that she can't be the only one revealing scary things. Have you opened up to her? Really opened up to her?"

"I don't . . . I d-don't know." His armpits began to sweat.

"Then start with opening up to us," Del said. "What is the

one thing you think you'd never, ever be able to do? What scares you more than anything? What don't *you* want to talk about?"

The guys stared pointedly.

No. He couldn't tell them. Not that.

He shook his head.

Malcolm sighed with atypical frustration for the Zen master of book club. "Gavin, we can't help you if you're not willing to help yourself."

"You don't understand. It's personal."

Del grunted and stood. "I can't waste any more time on you if you're not going to—"

"She faked it."

Holy shit. Holy fucking shit. He'd said it out loud. He braced for the laughter, for the jokes, the sky to fall.

But it didn't happen. He looked up and found nothing but sympathetic faces.

"She faked . . . orgasms?" Mack asked.

"No, genius. The moon landing."

"Wow, man. That sucks," Del said. "I'm sorry."

"She faked it all the time?" Malcolm asked. "Or just sometimes?"

"All the time." Bitterness stung his tongue. "As far as I know, I've given my wife exactly one real orgasm our entire marriage."

Mack swore under his breath. "Shit, man. I'm sorry. All the fucking jokes about sex . . . I didn't know. I'm a fucking prick."

The apology was surprisingly heartfelt. "There's no way you could have known."

Del coughed discreetly. "So, I'm assuming that you figured out she was faking it because . . . ?"

His neck got hot. "Because one night she didn't fake it, and it was obvious."

"I don't understand," Mack said. "She kicked you out because you gave her an orgasm finally?"

Gavin bristled at the word *finally*. "No. She kicked me out because I didn't react well to learning the truth."

"Meaning?" Del prompted.

"Meaning I moved into the guest room and stopped talking to her."

The room finally erupted like he knew it eventually would. Every man jumped to his feet. Del began to pace, punching his fist into his other hand. Malcolm stroked his jingly beard and starting chanting like a monk. Mack shoveled angry forkfuls of brown noodles into his mouth, alternating between eating and pointing a silent, angry finger in Gavin's general direction.

"You dumb fuck!" Del finally said.

"I know I didn't handle it well," Gavin said, defending himself instinctively. "I tried to apologize when I went to the house after she asked for the divorce."

"Gavin, you have a lot more to apologize for than that," Malcolm said. "Women don't fake orgasms unless they're faking other things too."

Christ. Back to the fucking riddles. "Just . . . just tell me wh-what to do."

"You need to stop focusing all your attention on the fact that she faked it and start asking yourself why the fuck you didn't notice."

Malcolm's words landed with a thud in his gut.

"Yeah," Mack said, wiping his forearm across his grease-covered lips. "And why you didn't have the fucking balls to talk to her when you learned the truth."

"And then you need to open a vein," Del said. "She might have been dishonest about the orgasms, but how honest have you been with her? You can turn this around, but not if you don't take the same kind of emotional risk that you're asking of her."

"She's moving on without you, man," Malcolm said. "She has plans. Goals. She's starting school again, and she doesn't need you. Not unless you give her a reason to trust that you—"

A sudden yellow glow through the front curtains stunned them all into silence. Then a collective *oh, shit* sent them scrambling.

"I thought you said she'd be gone until ten," Del barked.

"That's what she said!" Gavin looked at the floor. "The books. Hide the fucking books."

Gavin and Mack dropped to the floor and started grabbing and piling paperbacks.

The headlights went dark outside. "Under the couch," Gavin hissed.

"My nails are still wet," Mack whined.

Gavin glared and started shoving books under the couch. Thea's footsteps sounded on the porch.

"Put some behind the cushions," Del hissed.

The Russian farted and held his hand to his stomach. "I need bathroom again." He ran to the basement.

The door swung open. Gavin threw the last several books under a blanket and knocked Mack down to sit on them.

Thea walked in, followed quickly by Liv, and every man froze.

Gavin cleared his throat. "Hi. Hey."

Thea's eyes darted around the room. "Um . . . ?"

Gavin remembered their costumes. "Oh, uh, the girls w-w-wanted to play dress up."

"I see." She looked around again. "And where are the girls now?"

"Asleep upstairs."

"I see."

Mack looked over the back of the couch and blew on his nails. "Hey, Thea. Congratulations about school."

Liv moved into the room and immediately spotted the take-out container. "Who ate my Chinese food?"

Gavin pointed at Mack.

Who had gone strangely still. He stared at Liv with wide eyes. Like, wide eyes. "Hi," he said stupidly. "I'm, I'm Braden."

Liv shot him a glare that could have ignited a brush fire, and then she stomped toward the kitchen. In her wake, she left an unnatural, disbelieving silence, like the kind after a streaker runs naked across the outfield.

A woman had just walked away from Braden-Fucking-Mack.

"Never thought I'd see that," Malcolm said in his calm baritone.

"I feel like we just witnessed Jesus appear in a piece of toast," Del said.

Liv opened the fridge. "Oh my God! Did you guys eat my left-over pizza too?"

She stomped toward the basement.

"Liv, you might want to wait—"

The slam of the door cut off Gavin's warning, but no more

than ten seconds later, Liv let out a yell. Her footsteps pounded on the steps as she raced back upstairs.

The door flew open. She barreled out, gagging, and bellowed, "I. Hate. Men!"

Gavin pointed to the front door. "Time to go, boys."

CHAPTER EIGHTEEN

Gavin didn't exhale for twenty minutes, not until the guys had scattered, the women retired to their respective rooms, and he finally had time to retrieve the hidden books. He put them in two shopping bags and shoved them in the guest room closet. Then he sank to the mattress to dig the heels of his hands into his eyes.

That was a close one.

The sounds of Thea's nighttime routine drew him to her door. The splash of water in the sink as she washed her face. The quiet scratch of toothbrush against teeth. The slide of a drawer as she pulled out her pajamas.

Open a vein, Del had said as he walked out the door, a sleeping Jo-Jo on his shoulder.

Gavin knocked.

"Come in," Thea answered a moment later.

She stood at her dresser, pulling out pajamas. His heart thudded with want and nerves.

"How, um, how was today?" he asked, lingering in the doorway.

"You mean at Vanderbilt or at the café?"

"Both."

She gave a shrug. "Fine."

There it was. She was pulling back again. *Take an emotional risk*. "I was thinking of turning on the fireplace outside. D-do you want to come out with me?"

Thea glanced at the bed and then back at him. "Um . . ."

"We could read out there."

"O-okay," she finally said.

Gavin went out first to turn the fire on. Then he set out a blanket on the patio couch, opened two beers, and waited for his wife. She came out a few minutes later in his sweatshirt, a pair of leggings, and fuzzy socks. She'd piled her hair on her head. In her hands, she held their book.

"Hey," he said, struck dumb at the sight of her.

She stopped a few feet away from him. "Hey."

"The fire isn't hot yet, but I brought out a blanket."

"OK." Her eyes darted to the couch, lingered there a moment, and then returned to his eyes. The expression in her gaze sent a shockwave straight to his impatient parts.

She looked at him with longing. Blatant and unmistakable. Her chest rose and fell with labored breath. Her gaze dropped to stare at his mouth. His body went hot and hard. Painfully hard.

He cleared his throat and he could barely get a word out. "You're killing me, Thea."

She blinked. "What?"

"You either have to stop looking at me like that or kiss me, but you have to be the one to d-do it, because I d-don't want to ruin this."

Her eyes widened, but then she faked a laugh and shook her head. "Don't be ridiculous."

Gavin hid his disappointment and waited for Thea to sit first. Then he lowered to the couch next to her. Automatically, as if they'd done it a hundred times before, he turned so his back was against the arm of the couch so she could lean back against his chest. Thea pulled the blanket over their legs. Gavin wrapped his arm around her torso and tucked her against him. "This okay?"

She made an mm-hmm noise and rested the back of her head against his shoulder. They stared silently at the fire for a moment, adjusting to whatever this was, whatever had started last night.

"I hear you thinking," he said.

She answered with silence. Gavin held back his sigh. It wouldn't do any good to get annoyed with her. He tried a different tactic. "We should've done this more often before," he said quietly.

"There never seemed to be time."

Open a vein. "There was, though. I could have made the time."

Her breath caught.

"I put baseball first. I know that now. I missed everything. The girls' first steps. Their first words. The trip to the emergency room when they were sick. I justified it all because my career was important, but I would give it all up right now if it meant saving us."

Thea slowly sat up and turned to look at him, probably to gauge whether he was being honest or not.

She gave no indication either way, but he wasn't prepared for what she said next. "Remember when you asked me how my mom was taking it that my dad is getting remarried?"

"Yeah."

"The truth is, I don't know. I haven't talked to her since before Easter."

He had no idea where she was going with this, but it felt important. "Why?"

"She'd gloat if she knew that you and I were having trouble."

He stiffened. "Gloat?"

"When I got pregnant, she accused me of doing it on purpose. To, you know."

Holy shit. "Trap me into marriage?"

"Yes." It was one word, but it held a dictionary's weight in hurt.

"Jesus, Thea." Fiction and reality suddenly collided.

"She told me that I was definitely her daughter." A sad laugh escaped. "Because she got pregnant with me on purpose."

"She told you that?"

"I had always sort of suspected it, at least that I was not planned. My dad's nickname for me was—" She stopped again. Gavin squeezed her gently with his arm until she started again. "He used to call me *Shotgun*."

Gavin's hand clenched the arm of the couch.

"I always thought when I was little that it was because I was kind of a little pistol as a kid. Then I learned that it had a specific meaning."

"How old were you when you figured that out?"

"Nine."

Gavin cracked a molar. "Thea, you have to let me call that sonuvabitch." Or better yet, let him drive all the way to the asshole's house and slam his fist in the man's face.

"He's not worth it."

234

"You are."

She studied his face again, looking for signs of deceit.

"What your mom said—is that why you avoided me after you found out you were pregnant? Because you were afraid *I'd* think you were trying to trap me?"

"Partly," she said and shrugged. "And partly because I was just plain scared. I was young. We were young."

Gavin slid his hand into her hair and cupped the back of her head. For once, he didn't have to ask *What would Lord Benedict do?* to know what to say. "You getting pregnant was the best thing that ever happened to me. And not just because I can't imagine my life without the girls, but because I can't imagine my life without you."

A battle played out on her face, and he knew exactly the war that was waging inside her. A pathetic desire to believe him versus the cynical realities life had taught her. Words were beautiful. Didn't mean they could be trusted. She was scared to cross this broken bridge, because she knew what was on the other end. Uncertainty and passion and joy—the kind that goes away. The kind that hurts.

Love isn't enough.

"Thea, if anyone trapped anyone, it was me. I trapped you."

Thea's lips parted again on a small breath. "What?"

"I proposed wh-when you were scared. When you were vulnerable. I should have just made sure you knew I was in it for the long haul and let you adjust to the news before I brought up marriage."

A sarcastic eyebrow rose above her right eye. "I could have said no. I wasn't helpless."

"But you didn't know what you were getting into. I knew

what it would be like being married to a Major League baseball player, but you didn't. You never had the time to get used to it, to adjust to this."

Time stalled, and he noted every movement of her muscles. The way her jaw tightened as she swallowed. The way her eyes traced a path to his lips. The way she sucked in the corner of her bottom lip between her teeth.

And finally, thank God, *finally*, the way she reached out with one tentative hand and pressed it to his chest.

She raised her face to his. Her expression was every bit as raw as last night, but also different. Last night she'd been overwhelmed. Tonight, she looked at him with longing. Desire.

He dipped his head and pressed his lips to hers.

Thea leaned into him, mouth open and willing. He wrapped both arms around her and hauled her onto his lap. The rush of blood pounding in her veins drowned everything but the sound of her trembling breaths.

This was why she'd been hesitant to come out here with him. Why she'd needed space earlier in the day. This was what made him dangerous. She had no willpower in his arms, not after the beautiful things he'd just said.

Oh, why had they stopped kissing like this? *When* had they stopped? And why couldn't she stop now? Every second it went on, it became harder to maintain the barriers she'd built between them, but who was she kidding? They'd been knocked into fine particles of useless dust the instant he removed that blindfold and she realized he'd taken her to buy art supplies for their date. She could barely remember why she needed the barriers in the first place when little zings of pleasure ping-ponged from one body part to the next.

"God, Thea," he moaned, kissing a line down her jaw to her throat. She tilted her head and gave him access. His hand drifted up her waist into her shirt until his thumb brushed the underside of her breast. "Can I touch you?"

Thea shuddered with a yes. His fingers pushed aside the lace of her bra and caressed the hard tip of her nipple. She couldn't stifle her reaction. She wrenched her lips from his and let her head fall backward with a groan. His lips found a new home on the sensitive pulse in her throat, while his fingers working magic against her swollen, aching breast. He flicked, rolled, tugged on the hard point of her nipple. All the while, his tongue plunged in and out of her mouth with an erotic rhythm.

Thea sat up and pulled off her sweatshirt. Gently, but with a sense of urgency, Gavin slipped a finger beneath each bra strap and tugged them down over her shoulders. Her breasts popped free of their binding, and she reached around to undo the clasp. There was a rush of cold and then a flash of heat as his hands covered her flesh.

She moaned and covered his hands with hers. His mouth claimed hers, his tongue plundered her mouth as his hands kneaded, his fingers twisted and flicked her hardened nipples.

Butter suddenly barked and leaped up to chase something in the yard.

Thea jumped, the interruption like a slap of common sense. She slipped off his lap and held her arm across her breasts. "Oh my God. What are we doing?"

Gavin shifted uncomfortably. "Making out."

"We haven't made out like that in a long time." Thea tried to catch her breath as she pulled her sweatshirt back on.

"Maybe we should," Gavin rasped between breaths. He rolled his head to stare down at her, and the look in his eyes was as terrifying as it was heartwarming.

"I should go to bed," she said.

"I'll come with you."

"No." Thea shook her head and stood. "I—I need some time."

Gavin stood and blocked her path. "Look at me."

She did, but reluctantly. His eyes bore into hers, asking questions that couldn't be conveyed in words. "If we're going too fast for you, we can take things slower. You set the pace, Thea. I promise. I won't push you."

At her silence, he lowered his forehead to hers. "Talk to me, Thea. Please."

"I'm scared, Gavin." The words were out of her mouth before she could think about the consequences of such truth.

But he answered with a truth of his own. "So am I."

Courting the Countess

$\mathcal{O}$h, she could get lost for days in here, Irena thought as she took in the towering shelves of the library. If only she could. Benedict had been gone ten days. Ten days without a word from him or anyone else about what was happening at Ebberfield.

And the only thing more infuriating than his inadequate explanations was her own dismay at his long absence.

Irena had taken to exploring the library at night to keep from going mad.

"Looking for something?"

With a startled gasp, Irena whirled in the dark. Across the room, Benedict lounged like a lazy cat on a small couch. He raised his hand in a casual greeting that spoke of familiarity between them. His stocking-clad feet hung over the arm, and his shoulders filled out the cushion beneath him. He'd removed his jacket and cravat, leaving the skin of his throat exposed to her gaze.

"You're home," she said as calmly as one could with a racing heart.

"I am," he said, his voice low and tired.

"I didn't hear you arrive." *And why the bloody hell didn't you tell me?*

"I did not wish to wake you."

Irena curled her bare toes into the rug. "What are you doing in here?"

"Perhaps the same thing you are."

"You're looking for books about the engineering of ancient Roman chariots?"

"Thankfully, no."

"Then what are you doing?"

"Avoiding the temptation of the unlocked door separating our bedchambers."

"No. Not the same thing at all, then."

His hand flopped inelegantly against his chest. "You wound me, my dear."

A smile tugged at her lips despite her best effort to maintain a well-deserved state of self-righteous indignation. "I didn't even know you were home, Benedict."

"And now that you do, what shall we do with our stolen time in the dark?" A teasing lilt had crept into his speech, but there was also a dark edge to his words, as if he were angry with her. But what right did he have to be angry? He was the one who had disappeared for days.

"I suggest we look for my book."

With a graceful, fluid motion, Benedict straightened and rose from the settee. "Of course. Because what else do husbands and wives do in the dark?"

Irena ignored the jab.

Benedict slid the library ladder along the railing that circled the room until he stopped at a section that looked like the sort where someone might hide books no one wanted. Which usually meant they were the kind Irena most wanted to read. He climbed the ladder several rungs and turned with one hand outstretched.

"Candle?"

Irena handed it to him and waited patiently as he cocked his head to read the spines. After a moment, he plucked a book from the shelf. He handed back the candle and then descended the ladder. Turning, he pressed a thin book into her. "Will this do?"

She blinked in surprise at the title. "*Engineering in Ancient Rome*. I suppose this is exactly what I am looking for."

"Excellent. Then I shall light us a fire, and you can read to me until I fall into a deep slumber and forget the past ten days."

Her spine stiffened. "Forget the past ten days?" she snapped. "You disappear without a word after commanding me to stay, and you think I'm going to just read you to sleep?"

Benedict dragged his hands down his weary face. "Irena, please."

"It's late, my lord. You are clearly exhausted. Perhaps we should return to our rooms."

Benedict reached out and grasped her elbow. "I have no

desire to spend another night alone in my empty chambers, Irena. Not tonight. Please. I just need to hear your voice for a while."

His quiet pleading broke her resolve. "What happened at Ebberfield, Benedict? How is Rosendale?"

Benedict swallowed deeply but said nothing.

Irena removed herself from his grip. "My lord, you have asked me repeatedly to trust you. Yet time and again you refuse to trust me. Until you do, there can be no starting over with us."

Clutching the book to her chest, Irena turned toward the door. She made it fewer than ten steps before he spoke again.

"He's gone. He held on for days, but his injuries were too severe. There was nothing to be done."

Irena turned around. In the low light of the candle, Benedict's features chased a shadow that had nothing to do with the flickering flame.

"Oh, Benedict. I'm sorry." Irena walked back to where he stood. "You were close to him?"

"I've known him all my life."

She silently begged him to say more, and for a disappointing moment, she thought he wouldn't. But the moment passed. "He raised me," he said.

"What do you mean?"

Benedict strode to the fireplace and fixed his eyes upon the flames. "He was more a father to me than my real father."

"Why?"

He shrugged. "I was my father's heir. That's all that mattered. I once went two full years without seeing him. He didn't even recognize me after all that time."

Irena let out a breath of air. "Oh, Benedict."

He turned around. "Rosendale didn't have children. He and his wife couldn't. Their home became mine." A ghost of a smile appeared on his face as if picturing them. "He took me everywhere. Everything I know about running the estate I learned from him. And Elizabeth, his wife, always greeted us at the end of the day with a sweet pastry or a bowl of stew."

"Your mother didn't wonder where you were all that time?"

"My mother didn't live there most of the time. She spent the season in London and summered at our Scottish estate. I only saw her at holidays."

"Benedict, that's horrid." She approached him. "Your parents abandoned you," she said, stopping inches from him. "It's unforgivable."

"I was better off without them. Life was rather unpleasant when they were in the same house."

"Why? I realize members of the peerage rarely marry for love, but most at least settle into a tolerable companionship. Even my parents enjoyed that much."

"Perhaps my parents were less companionable than most." He said it with a smile, but the tightness of his jaw told her he wasn't as cavalier about it as he wanted her to believe.

Irena lifted her hand, hesitated for a second, and then rested her palm against his cheek. The stubble of his day's growth was scratchy beneath her fingers, but his skin was warm and soft. With a quiet groan, Benedict closed his eyes and pressed his face into her touch, like a flower turning to the sun.

"I missed you so much, Irena," he said.

"I missed you too," she admitted.

With a groan, he lowered his forehead to hers. "I am at your mercy, Irena. From the moment I first saw you, I have been half a man because the other half belongs to you. End my agony, love. I beg you. Kiss me. Let me hold you. *Please.*"

She would no sooner deny him the comfort he needed than she would deny a starving man food. She pressed her lips to his. Softly at first, but then with more pressure. He groaned again and quickly took charge. He pulled the book from her fingers and dropped it. Then he lowered her to the floor. His lips moved across her heated skin, teasing and taunting a hot trail from her jaw to her throat to the rise and fall of her rounded breasts. His hand slid up her side, gathering and dragging fabric to reveal her legs, then farther still until his fingers brushed the underside of her breast.

The need to be touched sent her arching into him with a fervent plea on her lips, but a plea for what, she knew not.

"My love," he murmured. "May I touch you?"

"Yes," she moaned. "Yes."

CHAPTER NINETEEN

"How's it coming, Thea?"

Thea dropped her paintbrush and whipped around, face red. "What?"

It was nine days later, and they were at Alexis's café. Thea was painting the restaurant's logo onto the raw brick wall behind the bakery counter. And not for free, either. She was getting paid for this gig. Her first real paid job as an artist.

Liv clunked the large vase she was carrying onto the nearest table and crossed her arms. "Okay, that's it. What the hell is up with you?"

"What do you mean?"

"You're distracted, edgy. You've been avoiding me for a week, and you've barely said a word since we got here. It's like you're itching in your own skin or something."

"I'm fine," she lied. Thea *had* been avoiding Liv. There was no denying it. But this was why. Her sister could always see right through her, and she was tied up in enough knots already without her sister's sarcasm. Something significant had happened between her and Gavin the night by the fire, and things had been different between them ever since. They had come closer and closer every night to crossing the final bridge, but they always stopped.

But tomorrow night was the team Christmas party. The night when she would be spending a night alone in a hotel with him. And both of them knew what that meant.

Oh, the irony. Liv used to be the only person she trusted with the truth. Now she was back to faking it. For Liv.

Liv suddenly laughed behind her. Not a funny, ha-ha laugh, but an OMG cackle, as if she'd suddenly figured out the punch line to a joke she heard hours ago. "Holy shit," she said with a snort.

Thea looked over her shoulder. "What?"

"I can't believe it. I missed the signs, but holy shit." Liv laughed again.

"Are you going to let me in on this little epiphany?"

"Yep." Liv said and grinned, crossing her arms. "You're *horny*."

A hot flush raced up Thea's neck. "Shut up."

The door to the kitchens swung open and Alexis emerged. A cat named Beef Cake followed at her heels. "Who's horny?"

"Oh my God, no one." Thea returned to her mural.

"Admit it. You are. I know he makes nightly visits to your bedchamber—" She said that last one with a horrible British accent. "It's starting to get to you. And if *you're* this horny, think about the state he must be in. Serves him right. He's probably primal at this point. I bet the sheets in the guest room are as stiff as he is."

"Ew, Liv!" Thea choked.

Liv started dancing a little jig. "You're horny. You're horny. Admit it, you're horny."

Thea jammed her paintbrush into the jar and whipped around. "Fine. Yes, I'm horny. But why shouldn't I be? Have you seen my husband? It's like living with a walking firemen's calendar. The shirtless ones. Every day it's a different month—shirtless with the dog, shirtless with the kids, shirtless working on the wall, shirtless reading."

Alexis shook her head. "Wow, I have no idea what is going on."

Liv crossed her arms and raised an eyebrow. "Yes, your husband has a nice body."

"Nice? *Nice?* His trainer has him doing some new core work, and you know those little V things guys have just above their hips?" Thea ran a finger up and down each side of her pelvic bones.

"Uh—"

"I mean, Gavin has always had them, but now he *really* has them. And then there's the beard! And oh my God, Liv, do you know what he did tonight as I was leaving? He leaned. You know what I'm talking about, right? The man lean? He put his hands on either side of me and *leaned* to kiss me. He's trying to kill me!"

Liv's cackle sounded like a dying rooster. "So sleep with him already. Use him for his body and then throw him out."

Alexis cleared her throat. "Um, who exactly are we talking about again?"

Liv and Thea spoke over each other.

"My husband."

"Her husband."

Alexis cocked her head. "You need permission from your sister to have sex with your husband?"

They spoke over each other again.

"No," Thea growled.

"Yes." Liv laughed.

Beef Cake meowed.

"Gavin and I have been . . . having trouble," Thea explained, cheeks hot.

"Having trouble?" Liv snarked. "Is that how you're describing it now?" Liv looked at Alexis. "She was ready to divorce him as of three weeks ago, but he sweet-talked her into letting him move home for a second chance."

"He's trying to fix our marriage." There it was. She was defending him. The world had turned on its axis.

Liv's laughter faded. "Wait. Are you—are you actually thinking about taking him back?"

Thea returned to her painting.

"Thea, you can't be serious."

Thea bit back a snarky response and settled for, "Why not?"

"Because you're doing exactly what he wanted you to do. He has known all along how to get to you. This is what he does. He's a professional athlete."

Thea whipped around again. "What the hell does that have to do with anything?"

"It means he's a natural competitor, and you are nothing but a game to him."

"Gee, thanks."

Liv pointed a finger for emphasis. "Do *not* let him win."

Alexis stepped between them like a referee. "OK, how about

I break open a bottle of wine and we can talk about this like sisters and friends—"

"I am not going to stand by and let him hurt you again," Liv interrupted.

Thea felt cold and hot and furious all at once. "Liv, I love you, but you seem to have a really low opinion of my ability to decide for myself what is best for me."

"Your track record isn't great."

Alexis spoke quietly. "Liv, I say this as one of your best friends. You are not being very fair to your sister right now. Things get complicated in relationships. Things can change when you least expect it. Can't you support her during this?"

Liv's face fell with a betrayal that hit Thea straight in the heart. "No. I can't." Liv grabbed her coat from the chair where she'd tossed it earlier. "Maybe Mom will support you. You are officially her daughter."

Irena and Benedict were getting. It. On.

Gavin decided to catch up on some reading after putting the girls to bed, but holy shit. He had no idea a major sex scene was coming up. And not just any sex scene. This was fucking filthy. Did people actually do that shit back then?

Of course, we did, Lord Jelly Finger responded. *Do you really think white, Western civilization invented cunnilingus in the twentieth century?*

Whatever. All Gavin knew was that it finally happened.

He got a goddamned Book Boner.

He shifted uncomfortably on the couch and reread the scene.

Benedict had his face up her skirts. Irena was panting. Moaning. Benedict worked two fingers inside her. In and out. In time with his tongue.

Sweet Jesus . . . he was definitely going to do that to Thea if he ever got the chance, and damn. The instant he replaced the image of Irena with the image of Thea, it was too much.

"Listen to me, my love," Benedict whispered in her ear. *"When we're together like this, you are in charge. When we are together like this, I surrender to your pleasure alone."*

Gavin gave in and rubbed his hand down the front of his throbbing—

The front door suddenly flew open. Gavin jumped like a teenage boy caught looking at porn on his laptop. The book tumbled in the air, and he managed to grab it and shove it behind the couch cushion just before Thea rushed in.

"Hi," he squeaked. "Whoa, what the . . ."

Thea whipped off her T-shirt, straddled his lap, and kissed him like there was buried treasure in his throat. He held on and enjoyed the attack until he almost suffocated. "Honey," he panted, pulling back. "Not that I am in any w-w-way opposed to this, but w-w-what's happening?"

Thea stood up. "Lie on your back."

Gavin fell flat on the couch, his legs hanging at an angle toward the floor. Thea stood before him and undid her bra. His eyes followed as she flung it across the room before he brought his gaze back to her breasts. But he was quickly distracted by the sight of her paint-spattered fingers on her button, then lowering her zipper. He forgot to breathe as she slipped pants and underwear down her hips. At the sight of her nakedness, he moaned and prayed to whatever gods were listening that this wasn't a dream or some kind of Book Boner psychosis. It could be a thing. He'd have to ask the guys.

But this was no dream. Thea, naked now, bent forward and yanked at the button of his jeans. He stopped her. "Wh-what are we doing, Thea?"

"I thought it was obvious."

"I need you to say the w-words."

"What words?" She licked a rim around his belly button. His hips bucked instinctively.

"Tell me you want this," he somehow managed to say. "Tell me you're ready for this."

Thea reached inside his jeans and wrapped her fingers around his cock. "I'm ready, Gavin."

His voice nearly broke. "Thank God."

He'd never undressed so fast in his life. Thea once again pushed his chest and told him to lie down. He did, reaching for her at the same time.

Thea straddled his lap and slid back and forth until he thought he'd lose his mind with need. Finally, sweet God, finally, she lifted her torso, reached between them, and guided him to her slick entrance. And then, inch by aching inch, she sank down on him.

Ah, fuck. Fuck. Gavin's head rolled back against the cushion. Their groans mingled and blended as he stretched her, filled her. He looked up at her to find her head tipped back, eyes closed.

"Look at me," he said.

She opened her eyes and gazed down at him.

"You are in charge," he said. Sweet heaven, he had no idea he'd be able to use those words so soon after reading them. "When we are together like this, I-I'm surrendered, I surrender to your pleasure."

Her eyes blinked rapidly. "What?"

"All you have to do is tell me where to touch you. How to touch you."

Thea guided his hand to their joined bodies. "I need . . ."

"What? Tell me what you need."

"I need you to touch me here when you're inside me."

Gavin pressed the pad of his thumb against her swollen clit. He could do this. He'd learned a few things in the past few minutes from Lord Licks-A-Lot. "Like this?"

Thea nodded, panting too hard to speak. She gripped his shoulders, fingers digging into him to the point of pain. She rocked her hips, rode him. He circled her with his thumb while his other hand dug into her hip.

She moved faster. He thrust up into her. She whimpered and moaned.

Holy shit. Was this really going to happen?

"Gavin," she panted. "God, yes . . ."

"That's it, baby. Come on."

"Oh my God . . ."

"That's right, Thea. You can do this."

She tossed her head back and grabbed her own breasts, and holy shit, he was going to ruin this if he didn't slow his own desire.

"You can do it, baby—"

She smacked a hand over his mouth. "Will you stop cheering me on like we're at batting practice?"

"Sorry," he mumbled. Her hand slipped to his shoulder again. "Sorry, baby. I just want to encourage you. God, you're so fucking hot."

"Stop talking." Thea threw her head back again. She returned to her rhythm, fast and hard. But something was different. Thea planted her hands on Gavin's shoulders.

"Honey . . ."

"Maybe . . . maybe we should change position."

In that instant, Gavin realized the best perk about being a professional athlete was having the brute strength to seamlessly roll his wife onto her back without once breaking their stride. She hooked her legs around his waist. He thrusted into her until sweat soaked his brow, his back.

"Gavin," she said, her hands falling to her sides. Her voice had a resigned defeat to it.

No. No, no, no. Gavin hunched to capture one of her nipples in his mouth.

"Gavin, stop. It's not . . . it's not going to happen."

Gavin stalled, still inside her. "Baby, you were so close. Tell me what to do."

"I'm sorry."

The tremor in her voice brought him up on his arms. Tears glistened in her eyes, and everything inside him froze. "I'm sorry, Gavin. I don't know what happened. I don't know what's wrong."

"Baby, don't. It's OK." Gavin withdrew from her body with a grunt. God, that hurt. "We w-went too fast. That's all. We should have taken things more slowly."

"We've been taking things slowly all week!" Thea pushed away from him and stood up.

Gavin dry washed his face and silently recited every curse word Lord Dirty Mouth could think of. Qualling shard-borne canker blossom!

He forced his voice to remain calm. "Just talk to me, Thea. Tell me what I'm doing wrong."

"I don't know." Thea yanked her shirt over her head and searched for her jeans.

"Just *talk to me*."

Thea pulled her jeans on. "I don't know what to say! I don't know what's wrong! You can't just snap your fingers and say, *Come, baby*, and make it happen. God, what is it with men? You think that just because you have a hard-on, we women are supposed to just roll over and start moaning like a porn star for you."

Steady, mate. Don't say something you cannot take back.

The beastly, humiliated side of Gavin punched Lord Magic Dick in the face. Gavin shot to his feet. "Except that you did, Thea. Every time. I thought I was the king of the fucking sheets thanks to your acting skills." He dragged his hands over his hair. "God, Thea. Was it just with me? Am I the only man you've never been able to orgasm with?"

"How dare you bring up other men! I had exactly two boyfriends before you, and for your information—not that it is any of your business—yes, I did sometimes orgasm with them."

Her admission seemed to steel his breath. "Why didn't you just *tell me*?"

"Why didn't you know?"

"Because I'm not a mind reader. W-we have to talk openly and honestly about these things."

"We haven't talked openly and honestly about anything in a long time, Gavin."

Gavin searched for his clothes and yanked them on. "You make it sound like things were horrible between us, Thea. They weren't."

"Is that the highest standard you aim for? *Not horrible*?

Would you really prefer to go back to the way we were before that night?"

"I'd rather that than this."

Her face fell. "That's what scares me, Gavin. There are a lot of ways to fake it. I'm just the only one willing to own up to it."

"What the hell does that mean?"

"It means that sometimes I think you wished you never found out that I was faking it."

"That isn't true."

"Dammit, Gavin. Be honest with me!"

Gavin clenched his fists. "You want honesty? Fine. Yes, god-dammit. I wish I'd never found out that my wife had treated our entire marriage like one long pity fuck!"

Oh, you coddle-woppled worm fart. That was too far, mate. I can't save you on that one.

"Pity fuck?" Thea reared back as if he'd slapped her. "I don't know who that's more insulting to, Gavin, you or me, but my body is not a charity. I don't fuck anyone unless I want to. Even my husband."

Regret was a sour taste in his mouth. "That's not—that's not what I meant, Thea."

Thea shook her head and spoke with a sadness that gutted him. "You broke my heart, Gavin."

Gavin's chest caved in on itself. He crossed the room and gripped her shoulders. "Let me fix it."

"I can't go back to where we were, Gavin. To who I was. I can't."

"I don't w-w want that, either. I want to move forward."

She hugged herself. "I don't know if I believe you."

Gavin spun and stormed to the console table by the door. He grabbed his keys and his wallet and then shoved his feet into his shoes.

"Where are you going?" Thea asked breathlessly.

"I need to clear my head."

"You're leaving?"

He threw open the door and stomped out.

CHAPTER TWENTY

Gavin drove straight to the community rec field. He was going to break into the goddamn park and hit some balls until his hands bled and the pain of the cuts overpowered the bleeding, gaping wound in his chest.

He pointed his car to the batting cage at the front of the diamond and left his headlights on. From his trunk, he pulled out his duffel bag with his bat and the dozen or so baseballs that were always rattling around in there.

With a strong toss, he heaved the duffel bag over the top of the fence. Then, with a running start, he made easy work of climbing the fence until he dropped to the other side. If he got caught, fuck it. What were they going to do? Write him a ticket? Arrest him? Jail would be a blessing.

Gavin dug out the first ball and his bat. He tossed the ball in the air and swung. The bat connected with a satisfying *whack* and sent the ball flying into the net at the other end.

Another followed. And then a third. Gavin shoved up his

sleeves. *You broke my heart, Gavin.* A fourth ball joined its brothers at the end of the batting cage.

I don't know if I believe you. He hit the fifth ball so hard that it bounced back immediately and nearly took out his kneecap. Just to get back at it, he hit it again and told it to fuck off.

That felt so good that he did it again with ball number six. By ball seven, he stopped cursing and started talking directly to Thea.

"You broke my heart too," he grumbled. Then whack. The ball flew into the net. "You're not the only one."

Ball eight went flying. "You threw me out!"

Ball nine hit the net. "Do you know how that feels?"

Ball ten nearly broke at the seams. "What the hell was I supposed to do?"

A pompous British accent answered in the dark. *You were supposed to fight for her.*

Ball eleven nearly punched a hole in the cage. "She asked me to leave!"

She was testing you.

"That's bullshit." Ball twelve damn near broke his bat.

Why did you move into the guest room?

Gavin stomped to the net and started throwing balls back.

Avoiding the question, I see.

"I don't answer to you, Lord Chest Hair." He picked up his bat again.

You wanted to punish her.

"She lied to me for three years," Gavin growled, whacking another ball.

But that's not what you were punishing her for.

Whack. Another ball.

You blamed her for ripping the rosy veil off your marriage.

"Bullshit."

For forcing you to deal with something you didn't want to deal with.

"Fuck off."

Because you were afraid of the truth.

"Fuck. YOU."

Gavin abandoned the bat and began whipping balls to the other end of the cage until there were none left to throw, nothing left to hit. Panting, sweating, he bent and braced his hands on his knees.

Thea was right. Lord Tight Pants was right. The entire fucking book club was right.

He *was* faking it. He'd been faking it for months before that night. Pretending everything was okay between them when it clearly wasn't because it was easier than facing the truth—that they were growing apart, that he was losing her. And he was *still* pretending, thinking he could win her back with a book and a romantic kiss and date nights, that he could fix things without actually addressing what was broken, because that was easy.

Because that required nothing of him.

No soul searching. No examinations of his own behavior. No *bloody* inconvenient epiphanies like the one that was making his stomach churn right now.

She's starting school again, and she doesn't need you. Not unless you give her a reason to trust . . .

Gavin grabbed the balls and stuffed them back in his bag. He was covered in dirt and sweat, and there was a rip in one elbow of his shirt. His tires spun in the gravel parking lot as he peeled out. The house was dark when he pulled back into the driveway. No porch light. No blue glow from the TV. No yellow warmth illuminating the bedroom curtain. Gavin leapt over the stairs onto the porch with a loud thud and threw open the door.

Gavin took the stairs two at a time. Her door was shut. If it was locked, he'd know he was truly fucked. He grasped the handle. Leaned his forehead against the wood.

Please don't be locked.

The knob turned beneath his fingers.

Thank fucking God.

The room was pitch black, but he could make out two forms on the bed. One had a giant, fluffy tail and was way too comfortable on Gavin's side of the bed. The other, hidden beneath the thick comforter, rolled over quickly at the intrusion.

"I—I'm home," he said dumbly.

"Fine," was her quiet response.

Gavin snapped his fingers at Butter, who moved to the foot of the bed with a put-upon sigh. *Yeah, yeah. You at least get to sleep in the same bed with her.* Thea sat up straight, a protest ready on her lips.

"I want to tell you something," he said, cutting her off.

"Gavin, I'm tired of this. I can't do this."

He rounded the bed to her side and lowered to his knees. "Wh-when I was in high school, I had a crush on this girl. She w-was pretty and popular. I finally got the courage to ask her out, and she laughed at me. Made fun of my stutter right to my face."

"Gavin, I'm sorry, but—"

"It gets worse. About a w-w-week later, a list started going around school. Top Ten Guys Most in Need of a . . ." He stopped to swallow against the bile of remembered humiliation. "A pity fuck. I was listed number one. She was the girl behind it."

Thea rubbed her temples.

"Thea, I've never been confident about sex. I was . . . I was a late bloomer. I didn't lose my virginity until college. And there's always been—" He sucked in a shaky breath. "I've always had a fear that I was the one who was most in love in this marriage."

"Gavin," she breathed, eyes softening.

"I've always feared that you wouldn't have married me, that I wouldn't have been able to keep you, if you hadn't gotten pregnant."

Her hands fisted in his shirt. "How can you think that?"

"So, yes, there is a part of me that w-wishes I didn't know you'd been faking it with me, because then I could keep pretending we were fine. That I wasn't losing you."

A tear leaked down her cheek.

"I was pretending that we could just move forward like nothing happened, but that's not fair to you. Or to me, either, I guess."

Thea swung her legs off the bed and tugged him closer. Which was as good an encouragement as any. He was officially going for broke. Gavin dropped his forehead to her knees. "I'm at your mercy, Thea. From the moment I first saw you, I have been half a man, because you've always held the other half of me."

"Gavin . . ." His name came out scratchy, as if she was suddenly finding it as difficult to breathe as he was.

Gavin raised his gaze to hers. "End my agony, Thea. I beg you."

His heart bounced like a grounder at second base as he waited for her to move. Indecision and longing ebbed and flowed between them with each mingled pant of their breaths. Inch by aching inch, she lowered her mouth toward his. Her breathing became erratic as her fingers encircled his straining biceps.

Gavin rose and pushed her gently onto the bed. Thea sank into her pillow, opened her mouth wide, and something released in his chest. A rush of oxygen and elation flooded his veins, a heady cocktail of relief and lust.

He hadn't kissed his wife like this in so long, and he wasn't talking about the passionate kisses he planted on her the past couple of weeks. He hadn't kissed her this way in longer than he could remember. It was lazy and hot, with the comfort of familiarity but the thrill of newness. Her hands were in his hair. Her leg on his hip. Her breasts pressed against his chest. Even their wild kisses earlier tonight hadn't come close to this simple intimacy. He poured apology and promises into every nudge and dip of his mouth, and he tasted the first hint of acceptance in return.

His body burned to shed their clothes and bury himself deep inside her. But he knew neither of them were ready. Their marriage wasn't ready. They were on the verge of something new between them. Something better than before. He wasn't going to risk it just to serve the needs of his body.

Especially since he still wasn't sure he could serve the needs of hers. And any failure now would set them back to a place he never wanted to return. Not when he knew there were moments like this ahead of them.

And as the oxygen rushed from his lungs, something that felt like gratitude swept in to expand them. Yes, *gratitude*. For this moment. For this second chance. For this woman.

She'd owned half his heart for so long that the full, frenzied pounding of it was as foreign a sensation as the completeness of life that he only felt with her, had *only* ever felt with her. Thea made a noise, a soothing murmur as if she understood, as if she were feeling it all too.

She glided her hand along his jaw and parted her lips against his throat, her breath to his pulse. They moved. They touched. They spoke only through feathered lips to fevered skin.

It was, Gavin realized with a shuddered inhale, the most important moment of his life.

Gavin lifted his face enough to look in her eyes. Her chest shuddered with an inhale.

"Talk to me," he whispered.

She smiled through tears. "Will you stay and read?"

CHAPTER TWENTY-ONE

Thea woke up naked.

They hadn't made love—or tried to—again, but Gavin spent the night in her bed, and they'd made the unspoken agreement that clothing was optional.

Gavin made a sleepy sound behind her. "I can hear you thinking." His arm tightened and tugged her closer. "Sleep OK?"

"Mmm."

"Tell me wh-wh-what you're thinking about," Gavin said, burrowing his face deeper into the crook of her neck and murmuring against her ear.

Oh, you know. Nothing much. Just sex.

Hot sex.

Sloppy sex.

Scrape my fingernails down your back sex.

I can't believe it's not an orgasm sex.

Ugh.

He teased her earlobe with his lips. "Know wh-what I'm thinking about?"

"Sex?" she blurted.

His bark of laughter jiggled her boobs. "That goes without saying." He slid his hand up her body and captured her hand with his. "But I was actually going to say bacon."

Thea turned her head to look over her shoulder. "Is that a euphemism?"

"You have no idea." Gavin rose up on an elbow and gazed down at her in that sexy, tired way of his. "Morning."

Thea rolled onto her back so she could see him better. "Good morning."

"Want me to make the pancakes?"

Oh, yeah. It was Saturday.

"Sure. Not yet, though. It's early. The girls aren't even up yet."

He raised an eyebrow. "What shall we do with our stolen time in the d-dark?"

She laughed, and it became a shriek when he whipped the comforter over both their heads, hiding them in a dark cocoon. They stilled at the same time. Soaked in the moment. Catalogued all the places where the hard parts of him pressed against the soft parts of her.

Thea captured his bottom lip in both of hers and tugged.

That's all it took. Gavin made a noise low in his throat and slanted his mouth over hers. He pressed her into the mattress as his lips nibbled and massaged, cherished and explored. He kissed her like they had all the time in the world, but when she slid one of her legs up along his, dragging her toes across his calf, something changed. *He* changed. He curled his free hand along the curve of her jaw and changed the angle of his kiss, taking it deeper, harder, his tongue sweeping inside her mouth.

Thea wrapped her arms around him. Her fingers explored the finely honed muscles of his torso, every ripple, every ridge, every swell of sinew. Her exploration seemed to fuel his fire, because a groan came from deep in his chest and he shifted his hips to grind into the parts of her that now throbbed with need. She wanted to crawl inside his skin. She wanted to kiss every inch of him.

She just *wanted*.

Wanted to feel his sweaty weight on top of her. Wanted to pump her hips beneath him. Wanted to moan and writhe and gasp.

She wanted his hands on her skin, his lips on her breasts. She wanted to feel him hard and long and thick thrusting deep inside her. She wanted to find that place again where heat and sparks and tornados lived. And then she wanted to curl against his side, trail her fingers down his damp chest, and place hot, sloppy kisses on his stomach.

She wanted.

She wanted *him*.

"Gavin," she rasped. "Can I ask you something?"

He licked a spot beneath her ear. She sucked in a gasp. Oh, she liked that. She fought for air. "How did you know that night?"

"Know what?" He sucked on her earlobe.

"That I had an orgasm."

"At first, it was the noises you made." He sucked on the tender place where her pulse pounded in her throat. "I'd never heard you make a noise like that, like a wh-whine or a whimper."

Thea shifted beneath him. The growing pressure between her legs sought the hard length between his.

"And you started moving against me." Gavin tilted his hips into her. Thea gripped his shoulders.

"You started saying my name," he rasped, his breath hot against her neck. "Over and over. Until you couldn't actually say it."

Thea moaned and ground into him again.

"You became frantic," he panted, sliding his erection against her cleft. She gasped and rocked back and forth against his length.

"And then your whole body tensed." His fingers dug into her hips. "You called my name, and inside you. Christ, Thea, inside you . . ."

His hands slipped between them and found the source of her ache. His fingers began to explore. She groaned and threw her head back.

"I could feel it, Thea. Your orgasm." He slipped two fingers inside her, and she cried out.

"Your muscles squeezed around me and, God . . ." Gavin dropped his head against her shoulder and pumped his fingers in a steady rhythm. "It was the most amazing thing I've ever felt, baby. And when I came, I've never come like that before."

Thea covered his mouth with hers. They tongue-kissed like teenagers as she rode his hand. She rocked her hips, seeking that feeling, that pleasure.

He let out a moan. "I've been in agony since that night. I w-want to make you feel that way again. I want you, Thea. So bad."

The bang of a tiny fist on the bedroom door made her eyes fly open. "Shit!"

"You've got to be kidding me," Gavin groaned.

"Mommy!" It was Amelia.

"Just a minute, sweetie." Thea pushed Gavin off her and grabbed the nearest item of clothing—a long T-shirt draped over the foot of the bed. Gavin rolled over with a dramatic flop. As Thea yanked her shirt over her head, Gavin threw an arm over his eyes.

"Just a sec, honey, I'm coming."

"Not anymore, you're not," Gavin grumbled. Thea threw the covers over his lap as she rose to unlock the door.

Amelia shuffled in, dragging her blanket in one hand. Ava followed, clutching her duck.

"Daddy's in here?" Amelia asked, her steps picking up.

"Yep. Come here and snuggle us." The girls walked to Gavin's side of the bed and waited for him to lift them up. They both laid down on top of the covers in the space between their parents.

"Daddy's back doesn't hurt anymore?" Ava asked. That was the reason they'd given for him sleeping in the guest room.

Thea dodged the question. "You're up early," she whispered, pressing a kiss to Amelia's cheek. "Why don't you go back to sleep for a while?"

The girls both closed their eyes. Thea rolled onto her side to spoon Amelia, and Gavin did the same with Ava. Above their daughters' bodies, they locked eyes, and what she saw in Gavin's made her throat thicken and her heart race.

The world turned on its axis again.

At ten o'clock that morning, Thea was cleaning up the kitchen when she got a text from Liv, who hadn't come home last night.

She was staying at Alexis's house for a few days and wouldn't be able to watch the girls tonight.

Even just a few days ago, Thea would have immediately called her and tried to smooth things over. Not today. Not this time. Liv was behaving like a spoiled child.

Gavin hugged her from behind, a cup of coffee in one hand. "Liv?" he asked.

"She's not going to watch the girls tonight."

"She'll get over it. We'll figure something out for tonight."

Thea turned in his arms, rose on tiptoe, and kissed him. Gavin made a noise low in his throat, set down his coffee, and hauled her tightly in his arms.

"We'll figure out something for tonight," he rasped. "If I have to spend twenty grand to fly my parents here, we will stay in that hotel."

She lifted her mouth to kiss him again, but he held back with a wicked grin. "You know that thing I did with my hand this morning?"

"Yes," she breathed.

"Next time I'm going to use my mouth."

CHAPTER TWENTY-TWO

They didn't have to spend twenty grand to fly his parents down.

Del and Nessa offered to let the twins stay at their house with Jo-Jo and a babysitter and then spend the night there. They'd apparently decided not to stay in the hotel because Nessa was still battling morning sickness.

"How long do we have to stay?" Thea asked as they pulled into the parking ramp of the ballpark, where the party was held. She tugged her pashmina around her shoulders.

"If you want to head straight to the hotel, I'm sure I can be persuaded," Gavin said.

They'd been doing that all day. By unspoken agreement, *the hotel* had been the catch-all for what was actually going to happen there. As if saying the words out loud would jinx it all, like the superstition that you couldn't say the words "no-hitter" when it became clear that a pitcher was headed for one.

Tonight, they would have sex again.

The question was: Would Thea be able to orgasm? And what would happen if she didn't?

"I suppose we should make an appearance," Thea joked.

Translation: *I'm so nervous that I won't even jump on the chance to avoid another run-in with my best friend, Rachel.*

"We should probably stay through the awards," Gavin said. Translation: *I'm nervous too.*

"So leave after that?" Translation: *So, I have two hours to get over my nerves?*

Gavin killed the engine and looked at her in the dark. "Deal," he said. Translation: *I have two hours to get over my nerves.*

Gavin gripped her hand as they exited the elevator on the top floor of the administrative wing of the ballpark, where every year the facility and banquet staffs transformed the soaring, spacious lobby into a Christmas ballroom. Gavin led her through a maze of tall cocktail tables to where Del and Nessa waited for them. Most of the players they passed waved or fist-bumped Gavin as they walked by, but their wives and girlfriends couldn't have been more obvious in their dismissal of Thea. Their eyes shifted away from hers, their smiles brittle. Which wasn't all that unusual, but tonight it seemed more pronounced.

She found out why as soon as she and Nessa sat down while the men went to grab drinks.

"Rachel and Jake had a massive fight," Nessa said, looking like a runway model in her floor-length, beaded gold gown. "I don't know if it's true or not, but he apparently told her tonight he wants to stay in a hotel for a while."

Thea felt a surprising flash of empathy for Rachel. "Are they here tonight?"

"Yeah, but it's pretty clear something is going on."

"She blames me, doesn't she?" Thea said, finally catching up. "My bad mojo at Thanksgiving?"

Nessa winced. "I did hear something like that."

Great.

When the men returned with drinks, Nessa and Thea dropped the conversation. Del held his beer up in Gavin's direction. "To beautiful wives."

"I will definitely drink to that." Gavin leaned forward and clinked his bottle against Del's before taking a drink.

Then he bent close to Thea's ear. "To the *most* beautiful wife in the room," he whispered, lightly tapping his bottle against her glass. He kissed her before letting her drink.

"I'm feeling a little ignored over here," Del joked. "What about you, Ness?"

Thea looked up. Nessa's smile was sentimental, Del's naughty. Gavin swiped his lips across her temple. This was going to be a long night.

Other tables began to fill up with couples over the next half hour, but theirs remained conspicuously empty. Even Yan and his wife, Soledad, chose to sit on the other side of the room, which stung. How could people be so superstitious? Did they really think she had anything to do with Jake and Rachel possibly breaking up? Thea drank her champagne quickly and let Gavin get her another.

A few minutes before dinner, two of the coaches and their wives finally took mercy on them and asked if the seats were taken. Apparently, the superstition didn't extend to the coaching staff.

By the time dinner was over and the awards ceremony started, Thea had consumed three glasses of champagne and realized with a quiet giggle that at least she was no longer stressing about having an orgasm later.

The awards were for a combination of serious accomplishments and silly traditions. Most Epic Playoff Beard. Worst Bull Pen Dance. Del jokingly refused to accept the award for Worst Dugout Tantrum for a botched attempt to steal second early in the season. But each award took them closer to the inevitable moment when Gavin's grand slam would be recognized, and with every minute, she tensed in anticipation.

If they didn't make a big deal out of it, she'd be fine. But there was no way they'd rush through that one. It was the biggest play of the year. They'd probably show a video of the entire thing, which would be the first time she'd watched it since the night it happened. She hadn't allowed herself to watch any replays because the memories were too raw. The night of his greatest career accomplishment had been the night of her greatest humiliation and hurt. The fact that both could exist in the same space and time was a cruel twist of fate, and she would have to relive it in front of all these people.

If Gavin shared her anxiety, he didn't let on. He kept a hand on her or an arm around her at all times, glancing at her every few minutes with that dizzying smile or a wink.

"This next one is a no-brainer," the marketing guy finally said. "Best Long Ball goes to . . ."

The room erupted in an almost choreographed chant of *grand slam, grand slam, grand slam*. A now-iconic photo of Gavin leaping into his teammates' arms at home plate appeared on the giant screen. The room erupted in applause. The video switched to slow motion as he rounded third base toward home. Midway down the stretch, he whipped his batting helmet in the air, an exuberant action that spawned a thousand *Has Gavin Scott's helmet landed yet?* tweets the next day. His waiting teammates hauled him into a throbbing, leaping, screaming huddle. They jostled him. Hugged him. Knocked him to the ground and hauled him back up. Ripped the jersey clear from his body, revealing a black performance undershirt that clung to every ripple of muscle in his stomach, chest, and shoulders. *That* photo sparked a thousand *I want to have Gavin Scott's baby* tweets.

Gavin strode to the stage to accept the unofficial award amid back-pounding hugs and bursts of laughter. When he returned to the table, he bent and kissed her loudly but didn't sit. The marketing guy said it was time for the last one, a new award that the guys themselves decided was long overdue.

"Legends, please stand."

Every player and coach stood. Thea glanced at Nessa, who shrugged as if she were as confused as Thea.

"We all know that the real heroes of this team are the partners at home who somehow put up with us," the guy said into the mic.

Thea's heart stopped. What was this?

"You stand by us through the wins and losses. Through the stress of contract talks and trade deadlines. You make this crazy dream of ours possible, and we don't do enough to let you know how much we appreciate it."

Thea swallowed hard. Her heart thudded against her rib cage.

"Legends," the man said. "Show your appreciation."

Catcalls and wolf whistles followed. All around them, players and coaches pulled their wives and girlfriends to their feet and into their arms for surprise, passionate kisses. A flash of uncertainty crossed Gavin's face as he held out his hand. Thea folded her fingers in his and stood on unsteady heels.

"This is why I wanted you to come tonight," he said quietly, sliding his arm around her waist to draw her close.

Thea tilted her face up to his, and what followed was the kind of movie-quality, time-stood-still moment when the rest of the room faded away and there was nothing but Gavin's eyes and smile and hands. God, his hands. Big and calloused from years of hard work. His fingers on her back trailed a lazy path up and down her exposed skin. A shiver raced through her, the hot kind.

His fingers wrapped loosely around the back of her neck as he bent his head. His lips hovered above hers as if he wanted to give her a chance to back away because his body language told her this wasn't going to be like all the other kisses he'd dropped on her tonight. Those had been the warm-up. The batting practice to the big show. This kiss was going to be the real deal.

He teased her with a nip at her bottom lip that sent tremors through her entire body.

"Gavin," she whispered, pleaded, letting the champagne make all the decisions.

With a smile, her husband slanted his mouth fully over hers. Finally. Completely.

A floaty feeling took over, dizzy and light, but it wasn't the champagne. It was him. The scent of him, the taste of him, the strength of his lips. It was the way he pulled back only so he could plunge deeper, again and again and again. It was the heady excitement of kissing in a room full of people who had ceased to exist within their private cocoon. It was the tender yet possessive way he cradled her head with his fingers. Thea cupped his softly bearded cheeks and pulled her lips away. Their rapid, ragged breaths mingled and blended into a single pant and then a shared puff of surprised laughter. Sounds came back slowly to her. The clink of glasses. The murmur of couples whose embraces had already ended. The click of high heels on the tiled floor. The romantic strains of a slow song by the band.

Gavin nudged her face up to look in her eyes. "I d-don't know about you, but I'm ready to get out of here."

Game time. Thea nodded. "Let me run to the bathroom first."

Thea grabbed her clutch purse from the floor and gave him a grateful smile when he gripped her elbow to help her stand again.

"Be right back," she said.

The bathroom was down a long hallway and around the corner. As she left the ballroom, the sound of the band faded until all she could hear was the rapid beat of her own heart.

Which didn't, however, drown out the voices around the corner.

She stopped and held in a groan. Rachel and her coven were apparently sitting in the waiting area between the offices and the bathrooms. Which left Thea with two options: go down one floor to use another bathroom, or walk past them with a wave and otherwise ignore them. Dammit! She didn't want to take the time to go all the way to another floor. And what the hell? Why should she have to? Just because Rachel had managed to turn most of the other women against her didn't mean she had any less right to be there. She and Gavin were still married.

With a deep breath for courage, Thea took a step around the corner.

But Rachel's next words brought her once again to a halt.

"I can't believe they had the balls to show up tonight," Rachel said, her words slurred just enough to reflect the steady flow of alcohol she'd consumed.

"It's so selfish," said Mia Lewis, fiancée of outfielder Kevin Krieg. "I'm sorry, but they are officially bad luck."

Thea's stomach twisted into a painful cramp. There could be no doubt that they were talking about her and Gavin.

Rachel snorted. "Did you see them kissing?"

"I thought it was sweet," said another voice. Maybe Mary Phillips? The wife of Brad Phillips, the backup catcher, had always been nice to her. What was she doing with them?

"It was gross," Rachel sneered. "Like, God. Get a fucking room."

"Everyone else was kissing," Mary said.

"Yeah, but it's *them,*" Rachel said. "I bet they were both virgins when they met."

"That is so mean," Mia said, laughing.

"Can you imagine being married to him?" Rachel asked.

Thea's hand curled into a fist against her stomach.

"Have you ever tried to have a conversation with him? I bet he even stutters in bed."

Rage. Hot and red. It flushed Thea's skin and dimmed her eyesight. A vision flashed through her mind of launching herself at Rachel, knocking her to the ground, and pummeling her in the face. Instead, she stomped around the corner and revealed herself. "How dare you!"

The three women whipped their heads around and had the decency to at least momentarily look guilty for being caught.

Thea surged forward. "Who the hell do you think you are?"

Mary blanched and stepped forward. "Thea, we didn't— We weren't talking about you guys."

Rachel rolled her eyes. "I don't think she's going to buy that."

Fury rolled through her like a thunderstorm. "You can say

whatever the hell you want about me. But do not *ever* disrespect my husband. Gavin has more dignity, integrity, and guts than every man on this team combined, and more than the three of you could ever dream of."

Mary swallowed hard. "I'm sorry. I'm . . . I'm going to go back to the party." She raced past Thea with cheeks blazing.

Rachel rolled her eyes. "Look, if you expect me to apologize, you're going to be waiting a long time."

"I don't expect it, and frankly I don't care. But if I ever hear you disparage my husband again—"

"You'll what?" Rachel stood, taking advantage of every inch of her tall, lithe form. "You'll be mad? You'll go tell your husband? This isn't high school, sweetie."

Thea barked out a laugh. Talk about the pot calling the kettle black. Rachel wobbled drunkenly on her heels again. "How much have you had to drink, Rachel?"

"None of your fucking business."

As she said it, though, she wobbled again and nearly wiped out. Thea gripped Rachel's arm and steadied her. Rachel yanked her arm away. "Don't touch me."

Thea wouldn't be surprised if she pretended to spray herself to kill the cooties.

Mia grabbed Rachel's arm. "Let's just go."

Rachel yanked away. "No. Why shouldn't she know the truth?"

Mia's eyes darted sideways to a spot behind Thea. "Rachel, come on."

"Know the truth about what?" Thea snapped. "That you blame me for your own problems?"

Rachel lurched forward. "Jake and I would be fine if we'd

made it to the World Series! And the only reason we didn't is because your husband choked in that last game!"

"Okay, what you're doing right now is called projection, and
it's sad."

"I had plans!" she shrieked. "You think I want to live in this
hillbilly city forever? Your husband stole the ring right off Jake's
finger and all the endorsement deals that should have come with it!"

Thea sputtered like a rusty tractor engine after a long winter
in the barn. But when she finally got into gear, her rage propelled
her forward with a kick. "*My* husband? Let's talk about your
husband and that two-run homer he allowed in the third inning!
Or how about that double that gave the Cubs the lead?"

Rachel reared back, looking surprised. "Well if your husband
had done *anything* at the plate in game seven—"

"There wouldn't even have been a game seven if not for what
my husband did in game six!"

It was exactly the opening Rachel had been waiting for. Her
lips pursed, and one perfect eyebrow arched in derision. "And if
you were any kind of baseball wife, you would've been at game
seven."

"What the hell is going on?" The booming voice of her
husband brought Thea around in a whirl. Gavin stood a few feet
away, face stormy.

Rachel snorted out a laugh. "Aw, here he is. The big strong
man to the rescue."

Except the big, strong man wasn't alone. Rachel's husband, or
maybe soon-to-be ex-husband, rounded the corner with what appeared to be half the team behind him. That same flash of empathy rose again, and Thea considered for a moment just walking
away.

But that's what she used to do.

She was done walking away from the fight.

Thea stepped closer to Rachel, so close the woman had to take a wavering step back. "You want to know what kind of baseball wife I am? I'm the kind of baseball wife who had to give birth alone because her husband was gone. I'm the kind of baseball wife who had to spend twenty-four hours in the emergency room with twins *by herself* because they had a stomach flu during the season. I'm the kind of baseball wife who still isn't sure the difference between a no-hitter and a perfect game, and you know what? It doesn't matter. Because I didn't marry baseball. I married Gavin, a man with more integrity than you could ever dream of having."

Rachel actually looked a bit afraid now, and she took another retreating step on her own, her back hitting the corridor wall. Thea stepped forward one more time. "And I'm the kind of baseball wife who put her own goddamn dreams on hold for three years so I could support my husband's career and try to fit in with the likes of you, but that is a mistake I am finally fixing. And the only reason you actually hate me is because you don't have the guts to do the same. You'd rather lash out, blame other people. But no one broke up you and Jake but you."

She spun on her heel but then stopped and came back for one last comment. "And for your information, yes, Gavin stutters in bed. And it's fucking beautiful."

And then, without even looking at Gavin or the rest of the team, Thea lifted her head and stalked away.

CHAPTER TWENTY-THREE

Gavin caught up with Thea at the elevator. She'd retrieved her scarf and her purse.

"Thea—"

She held up a hand. "Don't. She had it coming."

The elevator arrived, and he followed her in. She was still breathing hard from the argument, and her words reverberated in the charged air between them. *Yes, Gavin stutters in bed. And it's fucking beautiful.*

He should be humiliated. Furious. But he wasn't. He was hard as a fucking rock.

Thea met his eyes and he felt a shock wave all the way to his groin. She was as turned on as he was. They peeled away from their corners at the same time and collided like two mating animals on a crash course with nature's primal calling. Gavin stumbled, and together they fell against the wall.

"You're not faking it tonight," he growled into her mouth. "You hear me? You're not faking it ever again."

He'd never driven so fast through the city. The hotel was only a mile away, but it felt like the far side of the Earth. He screeched to a stop at the entrance and tossed the keys to the valet. The kid could keep the car for all he cared.

Gavin grabbed their bags from the back seat. Thea waited for him on the sidewalk, eyes dark and hooded with desire.

His wife has having an orgasm tonight if it killed him.

Checking in took no more than five minutes, but it felt like an hour. In the elevator, they collided again with hands and lips, stumbling out when the doors opened on the top floor. He'd booked a suite because he could, and because tonight was special.

His hand shook as he shoved the key card into the slot.

It beeped red.

Gavin growled and tried again. Finally, the light turned green. He shoved open the door, threw their bags inside, and turned around to reach for his wife.

They hit the wall again, grinding into each other. "Turn around," he ordered.

His fingers shook again as he lowered the zipper to her black dress. If he weren't so desperate, he'd take his time. Undress her slowly and kiss every inch of exposed skin, but that would have to wait for another time.

The dress pooled at her feet, and she kicked it aside as she turned around. She stood before him in nothing but stiletto heels and a thong. Gavin made a noise that was barely human as he wrapped an arm around her waist and dragged her close. She kissed him with an unguarded passion that had been missing for so long. *She* had been missing for so long. This feisty woman he'd fallen in love with. And God, he'd missed her.

Between their bodies, Gavin slid his hand down her stomach,

and she arched with a moan. When he reached her wet curls and parted her with his finger, she cried out and lifted her hips into his touch. God, if he could make her come just like this, standing here as she rode his hand.

"Gavin," she said, gripping his head. "Make love to me."

Gavin palmed her ass and hoisted her in his arms. Her legs went around his waist, the heels digging into his ass. She was so keeping those on.

He stumbled toward the bed and lowered her to the mattress. His hands whipped off his shirt and fumbled with the zipper of his pants, which were already about to burst. Thea shimmied out of her thong, leaving her bare but for those shoes.

Gavin groaned and fell to his knees at the edge of the bed. Time to put the book lessons to good use.

"Gavin, what are you doing" Thea whispered. "I want you."

"Let me love you like this first," he said, thanking God that Lord Sex Machine knew the right things to say.

Gavin slid his hands under her ass and leaned forward until his lips touched the seam of her desire. "Oh my God," Thea panted, her fingers fisting the comforter.

Gavin blew on her heated skin and was rewarded with another gasp, another arch of her back. When he parted her with his tongue, her guttural groan nearly made him explode right there.

He licked until she squirmed, alternating between gentle flicks of his tongue and sucking on her swollen nub. Her moans made him wild, but he pulled back to let her breathe. Something he learned from Lord Happy Tongue. Let her adjust to the sensations before going deeper. Use words, not just body.

He blew gently on her heated skin again. "I love the w-way you taste," he said, licking slowly up and down.

He'd never thought to tell her that before until the book. She reacted as he hoped. She hooked a leg over his shoulder. "You do?" she whimpered.

"I could kiss you and feast on you all day, Thea," he growled.

Her hips lifted, seeking his mouth again. This time when he lowered his lips to her clit, he worked two fingers inside her. Pumped them in and out in time with his tongue.

Thea bucked. Her hips pumped against his face. Her hands were in his hair.

He increased the pace to match hers.

Her thighs began to tremble.

Her moans became whimpers.

Her pleasure built until she was writhing. *Writhing.* And it was the hottest fucking thing he'd ever seen. A wave of tenderness washed over him as potent as the lust surging through his veins. She was his wife. The love of his life. And for three years, he had failed to make her feel this way. To make her feel safe enough to be open to feeling this way. He had failed her so many ways, so many times. He wasn't failing her again.

"Gav . . ." She couldn't say his name. She was so close.

"Yes. Yes, oh, God."

Her fingers dug into his scalp, and she wrenched her head back with a cry. Her body shook. Her intimate muscles clenched and pulsed around his fingers. Her hips lifted into his face for one last grind against his mouth.

And then she went limp. Her throat cry faded into a soft grunt, another whimper, another *oh, God.*

Holy shit. He'd done it.

He'd made his wife come.

Holy shit.

She came.

From Gavin's hands and mouth alone. Thea's legs went lax on his shoulders as she came back to her senses. "Gavin," she whispered.

He kissed a path up her stomach. "Talk to me," he said, voice shaking.

"I want you inside me."

He didn't bother shedding the rest of his clothes. Gavin shoved his pants and briefs down and leaned over her. The urgent press of his erection against her still-throbbing vagina sent her hips off the bed in search of the pleasure again.

"Tell me what you want," he said. "Say the w-words. Say exactly wh-what you want me to do to you."

"I want you inside me," she said again.

"Tell me more," he panted, pressing just the tip of himself inside her.

She lifted her mouth to his ear. "I want you to make me come again."

Gavin thrust inside her. Fully. Deeply. He buried his erection inside her body, sending a cry of bliss from her mouth.

Thea wrapped her legs around his waist. "I want you fuck me, Gavin," she groaned, and holy shit, that was the hottest fucking thing his wife had ever said.

She clung to him. "I want you hard and fast."

He obeyed. He rose on his elbows and set a pace that made her forget how to speak after that. His biceps bulged and strained on either side of her head. Sweat dripped from his body to hers.

She came so suddenly that he wasn't prepared for it, could do nothing but hold still as she dug her fingernails into his back, until he could hold on no longer and he followed her over the cliff, thrusting one last time with a shudder, a grunt, and the hoarse whisper of her name.

Her muscles turned to noodles, and she went limp beneath him, her hands slipping from his sweat-slicked back to the comforter beneath them. Gavin fell heavy on top of her, every last ounce of strength in his body vacated with his release. Twice. He'd made his wife come *twice*. He could win the World Series five times in a row, and it wouldn't feel as good as that.

"Gavin," she said, turning to press her lips to the side of his head. "Guess what?"

He mumbled a response, his face pressed to the bed.

"I didn't fake it."

Gavin lifted his face and kissed her. "Guess what?" he murmured when he pulled away.

"Mmm?"

"Neither did I."

Thea laughed. Gavin rolled over on the bed and pulled her with him until her naked body lay draped across his bare chest. He wrapped an arm around her waist to hold her secure and then curled the other up around her head, holding her there, cradling her.

His stomach rumbled. Thea ran her fingers down his abdomen. "Hungry?"

"Always," he said.

"You want room service?"

"Are you on the menu?"

Thea laughed again. "I'll get the menu."

His arms tightened around her. "I'll get it. You stay in bed and do not take those shoes off."

"Oh, you like the shoes?"

He rolled them again in one strong move until she was once again beneath his body. He peeled himself off her with a line of kisses down her throat, her chest—stopping to pluck at each nipple with his lips—and farther still to her belly button.

Then he stood with a groan. "Be right back."

After he left, Thea rose and dug into her bag for his jersey. She pulled it on over her naked body and—

"Jesus Christ, are you trying to kill me?"

She bit her lip and turned around. "You like this?"

"Better than any lingerie on the planet."

She tugged at the hem of the shirt. "Really?"

"You want to see what's happening in my pants right now?"

"Yes," she said, breathless as an erotic thrill shot through her. Where had this confident, dirty-talking man come from?

Gavin dropped the menu and stalked to where she stood. Grabbing her hand, he tugged and settled it over the growing bulge.

"I d-didn't even know it was humanly possible to get hard again this fast, Thea."

She licked her lips. "Then we definitely shouldn't waste it."

"Definitely not." He hooked an arm around her waist, dragged her backward toward the bed, and freed his erection.

He sat, pulling her with him until she straddled his lap. With a single thrust, he was inside her again. At the intense pleasure, something took hold of them both, something primal, fierce, unrestrained. Thea burned with a fire she'd never felt before.

His hands slid down to palm her butt cheeks, squeezing and kneading and holding them steady as she used her knees on the bed to lift and lower in an erotic rhythm. She gripped his shoulders, dug her fingers into his skin, and rocked against the hard length of him. His thick, calloused fingers brushed the underside of her breasts and then higher still until her pebbled nipples strained beneath his hurried exploration.

When she looked down, her hands on his shoulders, he met her gaze with a hungry, possessive fire.

"You're so fucking beautiful," he rasped. Then he tore open her jersey, sending buttons flying, and leaned forward. He took one hard nipple into his mouth. Thea let out a cry and tilted her head back, her hands threading in his hair to hold him there. He lavished each breast with attention, sucking and licking until the pressure between her thighs became unbearable.

Thea lowered back down on his erection. He wrapped his arms around her and they clung to each other, moving and groaning. Thea widened her legs to go deeper, to thrust against the hard walls of his stomach.

The deep, guttural sounds he made filled her with an erotic satisfaction that she never knew she possessed.

"Fuck, Thea," he groaned, grinding against her. His hands dug into her ass. And then he spanked her.

Holy shit.

Thea froze and looked down at him. "Did you just spank me?"

"Uh, did, um, did you like it?"

"I think so. Maybe, maybe you should do it again to be sure."

Gavin said something that sounded like *holy muddy-mottled wagtail*, which was weird, but she would have to figure it out later, because his hand spanked her again.

"Oh, God, yes." He did it again. "Yes, I like it."

Her body exploded in color and sensation, and as she rode it out, he joined her until he fell back against the bed with a surprised look on his face.

She laughed as she gazed down at him. "I've come three times, and you haven't even taken your pants off."

"Honey," he panted. "We're just getting started. I have three years to make up for."

CHAPTER TWENTY-FOUR

He made up for it.

Once more in bed.

Once on the floor in the outer room after finally ordering room service.

At three o'clock, when she woke up from an exhausted slumber to the feel of his hands on her breasts.

At six o'clock, when she woke him with her hand on his morning surprise.

After that one, they slept like the dead.

When she woke up next, she found him staring at her from his pillow, a tender look in his eyes and a sweet smile on his lips. He reached over and brushed the hair from her face. "Morning," he whispered.

"Hi." She yawned. "What time is it?"

"A little after ten."

She mmm'd in disappointment. "We have to check out soon."

"I know." He tucked a strand of hair behind her ear. "I was

thinking that maybe after we pick up the girls, we could stop and get our Christmas tree."

"We could decorate and make hot cocoa."

"Let the girls watch a movie."

She kissed him softly. His forehead rested on hers. "I'm afraid to leave this bed."

Warmth spread through her chest. She hated to leave this bed too, but she looked forward to what came next. "Our bed at home is better."

He covered her mouth and kissed her senseless. A little while later, she snuggled, warm and sated, into the crook of his arm. "Let's go home, Gavin."

Courting the Countess

*I*rena was right. Balls were a horrid, stuffy affair. And not just for all the reasons she disliked them, but because society's rules for some bizarre reason prohibited a husband and wife from dancing with each other more than once.

Benedict wanted her in his arms. Now. Always. Everything had changed since the night he finally opened up to her. Her innocent touch and hesitant kiss had lit a fire, and though he would have been willing to wait longer, she consummated their marriage at long last. Making love to his wife was so transcendent an experience that he resented the very appearance of the sun every morning.

"Latford." A hearty, heavy hand slapped him on the back.

Benedict turned away from watching his wife to find his friend, the Viscount Melvin.

"Didn't expect to see you here," Melvin said.

"Why?"

"Your last appearance among the *ton* left quite an impression."

Benedict didn't want to think about that. He'd thrown his wife to the wolves and naively thought she was strong enough to fight them off with sheer will alone.

"I daresay you're making an entirely new impression tonight," Melvin mused.

"Why's that?" His eyes strayed once again to Irena.

"It has not gone unnoticed that you have all the appearances of a man completely besotted with his wife."

"I am." A strange giddiness that felt entirely unmanly but completely freeing lifted his chest. "I am a happily married man, my friend."

"And I am glad to hear it. Just be careful, Latford. Not everyone is forgiving." He nodded toward the group of women where his wife had been standing.

Just in time to see Irena dash away.

Benedict followed in the direction he'd seen his wife disappear. To the outside world, she would have appeared fine. But he knew her better, and something was wrong. It was in the tight line of her lips, the way she clutched her hands to her stomach, the quick steps in slippers she despised.

He found her in the library.

Of course.

He closed the heavy door behind him. The click of the latch was the only sound in the room save a soft, uneven breath.

"Irena?"

He found her sitting on a straight-backed chair facing the massive hearth on the other side of the room. She looked small against the imposing velvet piece. But not just in stature. She looked defeated. "Are you unwell?"

He crouched before her and covered her hands with his. They were ice cold. As was her gaze.

"Irena, what is it?"

"What could possibly make a man and wife despise each other to the point that they abandon their own child just to avoid being in the same house?"

A twinge of alarm shot through him. Benedict sat back on his haunches. "What are you talking about?"

"You said your parents were particularly unhappy people, but that never seemed an adequate explanation."

"Why are we talking about this?" A cold alarm swept through him. "What did those women say to you?"

"Don't put this on them. Tell me the truth."

Benedict rose slowly. "I have no idea what we're talking about." But he did. And he was a fool for thinking he could keep this from her, for believing it wouldn't reach her ears eventually.

Her eyes followed him as he stood. "The *ton* never forgets a scandal. Haven't you learned that by now, my lord?"

The use of his title created a churning sensation in his stomach. "Irena, listen to me—"

"Tell me the truth."

"What happened with my mother and father has nothing to do with us."

An ugly scoff emerged from her delicate lips. "It has everything to do with us. Say it. Say the words. Tell me what happened."

"She trapped him."

CHAPTER TWENTY-FIVE

"Yay! Aunt Livvie's here!"

The Thursday after the team party, Thea saw her sister's Jeep pull into the driveway at the same time that Amelia shouted. Liv hadn't returned a single call or text since the night of their fight.

"Did she tell you she was coming over?" Gavin asked. He had just set his suitcase by the front door and had to leave soon for a photo shoot in New York. He would only be gone for the weekend, but Thea dreaded his absence. She never wanted him to leave again. Baseball season was going to be hell.

"No," Thea said, watching her sister through the kitchen window.

Gavin stood beside her with his hand on her back. "Do you want me to take the girls somewhere so you two can talk?"

She smiled up at him. "No. Thank you, but no. She probably just wants to get some of her things." Secretly, though, Thea hoped Liv had simply gotten over her snit, grown tired of sleeping on her friend's couch, and was ready to come home. And it was her home. Even Gavin had missed her.

Thea opened the front door and let Butter out. He paused to lift a leg on a bush and then ran to Liv. Thea met her on the porch.

"Hey."

"Hey," Liv said. "I came to get my stuff."

"Liv, you don't have to do that."

Her sister ignored her and disappeared into the house. Thea followed her to the basement. Liv opened her dresser and began yanking out clothes.

"I wish you'd stay," Thea said, coming up behind her.

Liv shoved a stack of T-shirts in a duffel bag.

"Where's your husband?"

"Upstairs. He wants you to stay too."

Liv wadded up a sweater and shoved it in her duffel bag. "I take it he's out of the guest room?"

"Liv, can you stop that for a minute?"

"I have to work this afternoon, so no."

"Yes, he's out of the guest room. Which means you are more than welcome to move back in there for as long as you want."

Liv zipped the bag and stood up. "You guys need some time together without me getting in the way."

"You're not in the way. The girls want you here. I want you here."

"Look," Liv said, facing her for the first time. "I know how this works, okay? You and Gavin are this bright, shiny thing again. The OTP. I'll just be in the way."

"Is that what this is about? You're worried I won't have time for you if Gavin and I are back together?"

Liv snorted, the sound more sad than sarcastic. "Don't worry. I'd never make you choose. I've never come out on the winning end of that choice in my life."

The big sister in her wanted to drag Liv into a protective hug against the ugly pain revealed in that single sentence. But they weren't children anymore. "This isn't the same thing. I'm not our parents, and I'm not rejecting you by taking Gavin back."

Liv rolled her eyes, a classic Liv deflection move that she'd been pulling since childhood. "God, please. A few days of good sex, and she's a therapist."

Thea had to breathe in and out several times not to react. Instead, she tried another tactic. "So where are you going? Back to the farmhouse?" Before Liv moved in, she'd lived in a garage apartment on a co-op farm outside the city.

Liv hoisted the strap of her duffel bag over her shoulder. "Don't know yet. I'm hanging out at Alexis's place for now."

"I still have work to do on the mural, so I'm sure I'll see you at the café," Thea tried.

Liv lugged her things toward the stairs but stopped at the bottom. "Thea, I take no joy in what I'm about to say. I hope you know that."

Oh, boy. Thea crossed her arms.

"Men who like to win will do whatever they have to to get what they want."

Thea let out a frustrated noise and shook her head. "Gavin has a lot of faults, but this Machiavellian picture you paint of him isn't true."

"Then go look at what he's hiding in the guest room closet."

A twinge of alarm raced through her. That was an oddly specific thing to say. "What are you talking about?"

Liv stormed up the stairs. Thea followed, anger and alarm fueling every step. "Liv, you can't just say something like that and leave."

Liv's duffel thumped, thumped, thumped up the stairs as she dragged it behind her. "Liv!" Thea snapped.

Her sister ignored her.

Gavin appeared at the top of the stairs. "Everything okay?"

Liv told him to move, and he did.

The wheels of Liv's duffel bag were loud against the hardwood floor and caught the attention of the girls. Amelia ran over to her but stopped with a skid. "Where are you going?"

Liv dropped her duffel, crouched down, and opened her arms to both girls. She kept her voice light and funny, and Thea knew she was doing it for their benefit. "I am going on an adventure!" she said. "I'm off to ride elephants and search for unicorns and—"

"And rhinos!" Amelia giggled.

"And wild hedgehogs," Liv said. But then her voice faded.

Thea watched as Liv kissed each cheek and stood. "Actually, girls, I'm just going to live somewhere else. Because now that Daddy's baseball is all done for a while, you guys don't need me anymore."

Ava hugged her legs. "No! We need you, Aunt Livvie."

Gavin approached. "Liv, you don't have to go."

He picked up her duffel bag. Liv yanked it away.

"Let her go, Gavin," Thea said softly. Once her sister had made up her mind, there was no changing it.

Liv grabbed her things and walked out the door without so much as a wave goodbye.

It's not like she was going anywhere. She worked in Nashville, would still live in Nashville. But Thea felt her departure like the snap of a tether.

And she heard her words like a song stuck on repeat in her head.

"Gavin?" she asked.

He looked down, the tone of her voice bringing a pinch to his brow. "What?"

"What's in the guest room closet?"

Courting the Countess

Say the words, Benedict. Tell me what happened."

"She trapped him."

Irena's bottom lip wavered before she caught it with her teeth. "Well that explains a lot, doesn't it?"

Benedict dragged his hands over his hair. "No, it doesn't. I know what you're thinking, but don't. Their relationship has nothing to do with—" He cut himself off, immediately disproving his own denial.

"With your immediate assumption that I was guilty?" she charged. "With your fervent willingness to believe the worst of me?"

"Our situation was, *is*, completely different."

"Then ask yourself something. Why is it that you presume

she trapped him? Was your father not in attendance during their dalliance?"

"Of course, but—"

"Were you not in attendance during our dalliance?"

"Of course! But—"

"But what? It's always the woman's fault, never the man's?"

"I—"

"You've spent your entire life believing one version of the truth, that your father was the victim. Have you ever looked at things from your mother's point of view? Have you ever considered that she was the one who ended up trapped that day?"

His mother, trapped? Something cold snaked across his skin and raised the hair on his arms. He pictured his mother over the years, regal and icy. But had she really been that aloof, or had it simply covered a sadness he'd never considered?

Irena held herself rigid before him, but her hands shook at her sides. "I hate what she did to you, Benedict, the way she abandoned you. There is no excuse for it. But I also ache for her. She had to spend her entire life inside a cold, cruel marriage with a heartless man who hated the very sight of her, despite the fact that he once desired her enough to convince her to throw away the dictates of society, to risk her reputation, and to huddle in dark corners with him."

His stomach began to eat itself.

"She had to endure his disdain the way she once enjoyed his affections. What were his intentions toward her during those escapades if not to marry her?"

"I don't know," he admitted, voice hoarse with shame and dread, not only for what he'd never considered before but for new revelations that were surely to come next.

"Yet he hated her when that was the outcome," Irena continued. "And she is the one you blame."

Desperation pushed him forward. "I was wrong about you and your intentions and have admitted as much. When Lord Melvin told me the truth about how we got caught—"

"That's the point, Benedict!" she yelled, her elevated voice so uncharacteristic that his skin jumped atop his bones. "You needed to hear it from someone else to believe I was innocent of deceit! Just like you needed to hear it from me that perhaps your mother was not the schemer you've always believed."

Irena shook her head. "Have you ever considered for one moment that when my mother walked in on us, I was just as trapped as your mother?"

Trapped? By becoming married to an earl? No, it had not occurred to him. Why would it? He'd been raised from birth to believe he was one step short of being a god, that a woman would do anything to marry him. That she would, in fact, lie or cheat to secure his hand and his title.

But Irena's words had the effect of a blindfold being torn from his eyes, and the world looked different from this vantage point, from *her* vantage point.

He'd been an active participant in their rendezvous. He'd initiated them, for God's sake. But she alone carried society's cross of shame. She alone suffered the wrath of the *ton*. She alone had been branded a schemer.

Reality was far different.

Their dalliances hadn't been his secret.

They'd been *hers*.

Dear God, he'd been her dirty little secret. Her whirl-wind rebellion against a society she despised. He was an earl, and being forced to marry him had ruined her bloody life. He'd forced her into ball gowns and waltzes. He'd tossed her into a viper's pit of gossip and scorn, foolishly believing his title alone would be enough to rescue her.

A strange, hysterical laugh burst from his chest, the kind that made him double over and brace his hands upon his knees.

"Look at me, my lord."

Benedict sucked in a breath and stood. The stony expression that greeted him did not ease his sense of dread.

"I'm leaving," she said.

CHAPTER TWENTY-SIX

Gavin sprouted a line of sweat on his forehead like he was facing down a Cy Young winner.

"Thea, listen."

"Oh my God," Thea groaned. "What is it? What are you hiding in the closet?"

"Something that w-will require some explanation, but if you'll just let me—"

Thea had stopped listening. She was headed for the stairs.

Okay. Calm. Think. Gavin dug his phone from his pocket and called up the group text of the guys. "Code red. Books discovered. Need help."

He checked on the girls, told them to stay put on the couch, and took off after her. "Thea," he called, hoping the panic in his voice was not as noticeable as it sounded to his ears. He walked into the guest room just in time to see Thea drag out one bag of books and sit on the floor.

She looked up, brows furrowed. "Books?"

Gavin shrugged. "Yeah. Um, books."

"This is what Liv was talking about."

"I guess so?"

Thea reached into the bag and pulled out two Regencies. Her face scrunched up as she studied the covers. "These are romance novels."

"Uh, yeah. Yeah."

"These are yours?"

"Uh-huh." Gavin was afraid to let his guard down, but so far this wasn't bad. She'd only seen the covers. She wasn't looking inside. Still, if Liv had warned her about them, then Liv must have looked inside one of the books and could have seen the notes. And the underlined passages. And the highlighted dirty parts.

Shit.

Thea picked up another book, and his heart ran for the warning track. *The Sexually Satisfied Countess* stared up at her.

His phone buzzed.

"Do you . . ." She fought back a laugh. "Do you actually like these?"

"There's nothing w-wrong with romance novels. They, they provide commentary on modern, um, modern relationships and feminism and . . . and stuff."

Thea snorted. "Gavin, I know. I love romance."

"You do?"

"My e-reader is full of them. I just . . . since when are you a fan?"

His phone buzzed again two more times in rapid succession. Shit. "Um, honey. Just, um, hang on a second."

He turned and ducked out of the room. He had three text messages from the guys.

Stay calm. That was from Del.

Ask if she wants to act out the dirty parts. Mack, of course.

Above all else, do not lie. Malcolm.

Okay. He was going to tell her about the book club. He just needed to get her away from the books before she opened one or found some of the notes. Because that would be way too humiliating.

"Daddy?" Ava's voice called up from the bottom of the stairs.

Gavin swallowed a groan. "What, sweetie?"

"I'm hungry."

Gavin silently screamed a thousand curse words. *Puke-stocking whey face!* "Um, OK, honey. Can you wait a second?"

"Gavin."

Thea said his name. Quietly. Ominously. He turned and walked back in.

She held *Courting the Countess* in her hand, open, his notes and underlined passages plain to see.

Thea looked up. "Which one of us has been faking it?"

Thea watched Gavin's face for any sign that this was a joke or a mistake or, or, or some kind of twisted prank left by Liv. Anything to convince her this wasn't what it looked like.

His voice was tight. "Thea, listen."

"All those amazing things you said to me . . ."

"They're not my words, but—"

She stood on shaky legs. "I've been half a man. End my agony. I'm at your mercy." The last part came out a groan. He'd seduced her with those words. Earned her trust with those words. Was Liv right? Had this just been some kind of game to him? Winning her back by any means necessary just because he could?

Gavin rushed forward from the doorway. "They're my feelings, Thea. That's what matters."

"You seduced me with someone else's words!"

"Just a few lines from a book, Thea. That's it. Just to help me talk to you wh-when I couldn't."

"They weren't just a few lines from a book. They were beautiful and made me think that things were different, that we could be different." She backed up until her legs hit the bed. "How much else?"

Gavin scrubbed his hands over his hair.

"Do I have to read all these books to find out how much of the past month has been a total fabrication?"

"None of it w-was! The past month with you has been the most important of my life."

"You made it up!"

"No, I didn't. I was d-d-desperate. I didn't know wh-what to do to get you to give me a chance, and Del and the guys said they could help, and—"

Her stomach bottomed out. "Del knows about this?" Her legs gave way as puzzle pieces began to fit into place. They formed a picture of total humiliation. She sank to the mattress. "Mack. And Malcolm? The night they were here playing dress up? That was this?"

"It's a book club." Gavin dropped to his knees in front of her. "W-we read romance novels to improve our relationships."

"You pretended to be someone else!"

"No. This is me. And I am a better person than I was before. Not because of the books, but because the books helped me see things differently. *Please*, honey."

She was going to be sick. Thea stood. "I need to think. I need to clear my head." She dodged him as he rose from the floor. "I need to figure out—"

"Figure out what?" he snapped. "Whether you love me?"

Thea whipped around. The beseeching pinch of his eyes had been replaced by the hard glint of resignation. "That is not what this is about," she said.

"Isn't it?" Gavin took two steps toward her and looked down at her upturned face. "I love you."

A painful thud originated in her chest and quickly spread through her body.

"I love you, Thea. I've tried to find other w-ways to tell you because you didn't want to hear the exact words, but maybe the problem is you just don't want to hear them at all."

A breathlessness took hold of her voice. Her thinking. "You're trying to confuse things, equate things that aren't connected. I am not going to have that conversation right now."

"That conversation is everything!" Gavin gripped her shoulders. "Tell me you love me."

A sob choked her throat.

"Why can't you say it, Thea? After everything we've been through. Do you love me or not?"

"I . . . I don't trust you."

Gavin made a garbled noise and grabbed his hair as he turned away from her. After a moment, he faced her again, a resigned slump to his shoulders. "What do you want, Thea?"

"I want honesty."

"You lied to me for three years. Don't talk to me about honesty."

"That's not fair." It was a weak response. A desperate response. An *I have no other defense* response.

"Maybe it's time you started being honest with yourself."

"I have been honest with myself. That's why I finally asked you to leave! Why I'm going back to school."

"That's surface-level bullshit, Thea." He laughed, shook his head, and pointed. "And those are not my words. It's what Del said to me when I refused to do what needed to be done. But I have now. I've done everything I can. But I can't be the only one doing the work."

He sidestepped her and walked out. His soft footsteps faded down the hallway toward their bedroom.

Fear and pettiness rose and grabbed the mic. Thea stomped after him. "You're going to walk away from this? Why am I not surprised?"

She stopped and caught her breath when she saw him toss his suitcase on the bed.

"You already packed," she said.

"For New York."

"What are you doing?" she whispered.

"The one thing that scares me the most," he said, walking to his dresser. "The thing I swore I'd never be able to do, w-which means it's the thing I absolutely have to do."

He pulled a stack of clothes from the top drawer and carried them back to the bed. "I'm leaving you."

"Of course you are," Thea snapped, but the venom of her voice was just a cover for the way her heart was breaking. "Because that's what you do. You leave."

Gavin didn't take the bait. He calmly zipped his suitcase and hefted it off the bed. "No, I don't. That's your father. And I am not your father."

"Gavin . . ." The beseeching tone was hers now.

He paused in the doorway but wouldn't look at her. "Backstory is everything, Thea. Dig into yours. Maybe then we'll have a chance."

CHAPTER TWENTY-SEVEN

A half hour after Gavin left, Thea returned to her old lying ways. She told the girls that Daddy had to go to New York for a photo shoot and would be back in time for Christmas.

Then she brewed a cup of coffee she didn't want, pushed down the emotions she didn't want to feel, and pretended everything was fine.

It all went to shit when she heard a key in the door. Heart racing, Thea leapt from the couch and raced into the hallway. "Gavin—"

Liv stood in the entryway. "It's me."

The girls, who'd been coloring on the floor in the living room, raced toward her like they always did. The raw sting of betrayal, guilt, and old-fashioned heartbreak brought a sharp whip to Thea's voice. "Did you forget something?"

Liv extracted herself from the girls. "No."

"So, you're here to rub it in? Say *I told you so?*"

"No. I'm here because Gavin texted me and said you might need me."

Thea's entire body jolted. She squashed the reaction and turned toward the kitchen. "I don't."

"Thea, I'm sorry," Liv said, following.

"For what?" Thea mindlessly walked to the coffeepot just to have something to do.

"This is my fault."

"Nope. Not your fault."

"Look," Liv said, moving forward. "Maybe I was wrong. Texting me was a pretty decent thing to do."

Thea scoffed. "Now you think he's decent? You've spent the past two months convincing me he was an irredeemable asshole."

"I'm sorry." Liv's voice and expression were sincere, and they had the effect of dousing the petty rage controlling Thea's words. "Is he coming back?"

"I-I don't know."

Liv rushed forward. "I'm sorry, Thea. I was just so afraid of, of losing you the way I lose everyone else. I'm sorry, Thea. I'm so sorry."

Thea hugged her sister. "It's not your fault."

Liv slung an arm around Thea's shoulders, and Thea let her. "Want to eat ice cream and watch *Golden Girls*?"

No, not really, but Thea said yes anyway. Because the thing she wanted to do even less was sit alone and listen for the sound of his car returning and realize that she finally understood another one of Gran Gran's sayings.

A lonely marriage is the worst kind of lonely there is.

Thea felt as alone now as she'd ever felt in her life.

. . .

Gavin spent a long, dark night on one of the couches in Mack's basement because it seemed fitting to have this whole thing end the same place it began.

Well, and because no one else would let him stay. Del and Yan both said he needed to face this one alone, Malcolm had other plans, and there was no way he was going to the Russian's house. Who knew what digestive horrors awaited there?

Mack had let him in, handed him a bottle of whiskey and a blanket, and told him he'd cut off his balls if Gavin threw up anywhere but in the toilet.

Now he was awake, the bottle of whiskey unopened and untouched on the coffee table, and a pair of eyes he didn't recognize were staring openly as if he were an exhibit in a zoo.

"Are you sick?" The little girl had dark pigtails and clutched a pink stuffed rabbit. "Uncle Mack says you're sick."

Gavin cleared his throat. It felt like sandpaper. How was it possible to have a hangover without alcohol? "Uncle Mack?"

"Yeah, he's my uncle."

"And you are?"

"Lucy."

"Nice to meet you."

Lucy put her hand on his forehead. "You don't have a fever. Your breath is kind of stinky, though."

Despite the clanging in his head and the empty cavern where his heart used to be, Gavin managed to crack a smile. "I'm sure it is."

"Uncle Mack told me to give you this." She pulled a green apple from the pocket of her sweatshirt.

Gavin puffed out a laugh. "Where is Uncle Mack?"

"Upstairs with my mommy and daddy and my sisters."

The clanging in his head became a jackhammer as a stream of sunlight broke through the blinds to the French doors that led to the backyard and pool. "Well," Gavin said, sitting. "Thank you for my apple. Would you ask Uncle Mack to come downstairs?"

"Okay!" Lucy skipped away, leaving Gavin with a spiking panic that he'd been too rash yesterday. That he should have turned around and gone back the instant he left. That he should have just begged for forgiveness. But he couldn't do that. Not anymore.

Thudded footsteps on the stairs announced Mack. He rounded the corner and smirked. "You alive?"

"I didn't drink anything."

Mack raised an eyebrow. "Wow. You have changed."

Gavin dry washed his face. "I didn't know you have a niece."

"I have several. My brother's kids."

"Didn't know you have a brother, either."

"There's a lot you don't know about me."

Gavin acknowledged that with a nod. "Thanks for letting me stay."

"When does your plane leave?"

Right. New York. As if he cared about any of that right now. "Couple of hours."

Mack dropped into a game chair and leaned forward, elbows on his knees. "Leaving was a bold move, Gav."

"Del didn't seem to think so."

"Well, you did sort of violate the number one rule."

"Don't talk about book club?"

Mack looked sideways. "OK, the number two rule."

"Don't let the Russian shit in your bathroom?"

THE BROMANCE BOOK CLUB

"You weren't supposed to re-create the book, smart-ass. We told you that."

Gavin stared at the apple in his hand. "However this turns out, I w-w-want you to know that I appreciate everything you and the guys have done."

He was a different man than he'd been before book club. He recognized his own faults and shortcomings. He was more confident in expressing himself. And, yeah, he was a better lover.

But it still wasn't enough. Love isn't enough.

"What's your next move?" Mack asked, standing.

"I have to catch a plane. After that, I have no idea."

The ball was in Thea's court. All he could do was wait.

CHAPTER TWENTY-EIGHT

Thea awoke in the guest bed. Her neck was stiff from the awkward position she'd slept in because she'd fallen asleep reading. All night she dreamed in Regency England, but the people were real.

And when she woke, so was the shame.

"You want coffee?"

Thea glanced over her shoulder. Liv stood in the doorway. "Sure."

Liv wandered in and sat down on the bed. "What are you doing in here?"

Thea stood and walked to the window. "You know what I did all night?"

"Smashed the wall?"

Thea managed a laugh. "No. I thought about Mom."

"You've spent your entire life believing one version of the truth . . . Have you ever looked at things from your mother's point of view?"

Liv reared back. "Why?"

Because backstory is everything. "Just trying to think about things from her perspective."

"Yeah, I'm not sure she deserves that."

"Maybe not, but automatically hating her for the decisions she made hasn't exactly worked for me. Or for you. Has it?"

Liv stood. "Don't go kicking over logs if you're not prepared for what comes crawling out."

Thea laughed. "Gran Gran." Liv and Thea had heard that phrase perhaps more than any other. A philosophy for life that Thea had completely misunderstood. The point wasn't to fear the ugly crawly things. The point was to be strong enough to face them.

"I'm a coward, Liv."

Her sister did her usual *what nonsense are you spouting* smirk. "You? A coward? You're the strongest person I know."

"No. I'm not. Gavin was right about me. I'm a coward."

"Don't, Thea."

"I have to. Do you know what caused our breakup?"

Liv blinked, wary.

"I was faking it in bed. He found out, and he was hurt. He handled it badly, but so did I. I wasn't fair to him—"

"You've been more than fair."

"Have I really, though? I faked everything with him, and it's not because of anything he did. It's because I'm broken, Liv. I'm scared to open up to him, really open up to him. And now he's gone. Again."

He was right. Backstory was everything. The faked orgasms. The unwillingness to say she loved him. Her reaction to the books, to believe the worst about him. They were all part of the same twisted knot of issues that she'd never dealt with. Her parents had left her unable to trust. And it was costing her the man she loved.

She loved him. So much.

He hadn't left her.

She'd pushed him away.

Thea turned around and embraced her sister. "Thank you for being here."

Liv squeezed. "Yeah, yeah. You and me, always."

Thea pulled back and smoothed her hair off her forehead. "Liv, I know I've relied on you a lot, but do you think you could stay here this weekend with the girls?"

Liv grinned. "Are you going to New York to see Gavin?"

"No. I'm going to Dad's wedding."

Gavin barely made his flight on time. Del, Yan, and the other Legends players who were part of the photo shoot were already in their seats in first class when he dragged his bag and his ass on board. As he shoved his luggage and coat into the overhead bin, Del watched with one of his silently seething death glares that were so intimidating on the field.

Gavin glared back and sank into the open seat next to him. Then he closed his eyes, tilted his head back, and hoped Del got the message that he was in no mood for another round of *you fucking idiot.*

"You fucking idiot."

"I d-d-did what I had to, Del."

"How could you think leaving her was a good idea?"

Gavin opened his eyes and glowered. "I didn't think it was

a good idea. It fucking sucks. I'm dying here. Bleeding out of my chest—"

Gavin's phone buzzed, and he scrambled to dig it out of his jeans pocket. *Please be Thea. Please be Thea.*

It was Liv. *Mother-fobbing bugbear!*

"Answer it, idiot," Del said.

He swiped the screen. Liv didn't bother with hello. "I just thought you should know that she's going to need you."

Gavin sat up straight, heart pounding as he imagined the worst. "What happened? Is it one of the girls?"

"She's on her way to Atlanta."

He searched the fog of his brain for the significance of that. Then, "She's going to the wedding?"

"I don't know what the hell is going on, but she tore out of here like it was the most important thing in the world to her."

"Backstory."

"What?"

"She's doing it. She's digging into it."

"Am I supposed to know what any of that means?"

"Thank you for telling me, Liv. You have no idea how important this is."

She paused and softened her voice. "Just make sure she's OK."

Liv hung up. Gavin sat in motionless indecision for a split second before he shot to his feet. He whacked his head on the overhead bin and swore out loud. "Urchin-snouted codpiece!"

Rubbing his head, he ducked out of his row. A flight attendant told him he needed to take his seat because the outer door was about to close.

Del leaned over. "Dude, what are you doing?"

"I have to get off the plane." He opened the bin and grabbed his shit.

The flight attendant approached, hands raised. "Sir, I really need you to sit."

"I can't. You have to let me off. I have to . . . I have an emergency."

"I have to get off too." Del suddenly stood.

Followed by Yan. "*Yo también.*"

"Gentleman, please—"

"Listen, we have an emergency here," Del barked.

"Is someone ill?"

People were staring now. Another flight attendant was making her way up the aisle.

Del grabbed Gavin's arm and grinned. "Grand gesture time?"

"Oh, yeah." Gavin turned back to the flight attendant and conjured his sternest game face. "Let me off this plane. I have to go marry my wife."

CHAPTER TWENTY-NINE

A line of vintage Rolls-Royces parked in front of the soaring stone cathedral was the best indication that Thea was in the right place. Her father never did anything halfway. Well, except marriage. Her father had been half-assing marriage forever. But the weddings? He spared no expense for those.

Thea had driven the entire four hours to Atlanta this morning. She started and stopped to call Gavin no less than a dozen times on the way. She didn't even know if he would answer, and even if he did, she wasn't actually ready to talk to him.

By some miracle, she arrived early enough that she landed a prime parking spot on the opposite side of the church that would let her flee in a hurry, if necessary. The bad news was, now she had to sit there with just her thoughts for way too long.

Thea closed her eyes and leaned her head against the seat. God, what was she doing there? Of all the stupid, impulsive things to do. What was this going to accomplish? It wasn't fair to confront her father on his wedding day, and she had no desire to ruin his fiancée's big day. Poor woman had enough hurt coming her way eventually, anyway.

But she'd come all this way, and she needed to get through this. Because Gavin was right. She'd been running and hiding from her own backstory for too long, and her father played a starring role in it.

Thea jumped at the sound of a knock on her window. Her eyes flew open to find—oh, crap. Her father peered in at her. In his charcoal gray tuxedo and with his salt-and-pepper hair, he looked more like the father of the bride than the groom.

Thea lowered the window, which seemed to amuse him. "You ever going to come in, or are you going to watch the whole wedding from out here?"

"How'd you know I was here?"

He pointed to an upper level of the church. "Window."

"You recognized me from all the way over there?"

"I recognize my daughter, yes."

The word *daughter* stung like a sharp needle. She knew this man so little that even calling him *Dad* made her squirm. But he could just blurt out "my daughter"?

"I didn't think you were coming," he said.

"Don't worry, I won't eat anything."

"Don't be mulish, Thea. The wedding planner is already working to seat you with Jessica's parents."

"With her parents?" Thea reared back. "Oh, no. That's not, please don't. That's like, way too up front."

Her father straightened and tipped his chin toward the passenger seat. "Can I get in?"

"Don't you have groom things to do?"

"I've done this a few times. I know what my job is."

"That probably sounds funny to you, but it's actually pretty gross."

He gestured to the seat again. "May I?"

Thea hit the unlock button and watched him walk around the front of her car. Someone must have called his name, because he lifted his hand in greeting before continuing to the passenger door.

Silence screamed as he slid in. Sitting in a car with someone was one of those everyday acts of familiarity that could either be unremarkably mundane or incredibly awkward. This was awkward. The comfort that most people felt around their dads didn't exist for Thea. The man next to her had never tucked her in at night, never kissed scrapes and boo-boos, had never lifted her high into bed and snuggled her while she slept. She'd never crawled into his lap for comfort, never made pancakes with him. He was a stranger. Like a distant uncle who you saw every five years at family reunions and whose only point of conversation was to say over and over again how tall you'd gotten.

Yet, somehow, this stranger's behavior had left enough emotional scars that Thea was going to lose the man she loved. A man who loved her enough that he read, underlined, and quoted romance novels to win her back.

The scars of this stranger in her car now had made her so distrustful that she couldn't see Gavin's efforts for what they were—a beautiful, heartfelt, *honest* statement of his feelings.

"Gavin and the girls aren't with you?" Dan finally asked.

"No. Just me."

"Liv?"

"Sorry."

"Well, I'm glad you came. What changed your mind?"

"I'm kicking over some logs."

The corner of his mouth ticked up. "And are you prepared for what's going to crawl out?"

Thea stared out the windshield. "I don't know why I'm here, actually. I'm pretty sure it's a mistake."

"Only if you leave without saying it."

"Saying what?" She wrapped her hands around the steering wheel.

"Whatever it is you think you need to say to clear out those logs."

"I don't have anything to say. I think I just wanted to see."

He tilted his head. "See?"

Thea met her father's gaze directly for the first time in years. "How you look at me."

His features slipped for the smallest of moments, and a small crack in her chest opened up. Like a fissure spitting steam from the Earth, it threatened to release the noxious gas of years of suppressed *backstory*. And God, did it feel good to relieve some of the pressure.

"I wanted to see if you look at me like Gavin looks at our daughters. Have you ever looked at me like that?"

He let out an impressed hmph. "And you thought you had nothing to say."

Thea shook her head and pressed the button to start her car. "You should go in. You're going to be late for your own wedding, and this has clearly been a mistake. I'm going to get nothing out of you that matters."

He let out another one of those impressed laughs. "I know I was a shitty father, and I know I'm a sad cliché for hoping that it's not too late to make up for that."

"It is," she said, more steam billowing out. "It's too late."

"Then you should be happy to know that I suffer for it. I have to stand back and see the woman you've become, the woman your sister has become, and know I can't be part of it. I see your gorgeous daughters and know I can't be a grandfather to them."

Thea let her hands fall to her lap as her mouth dropped open. "No, that doesn't make me happy to know that. At all. It makes me really sad, because it didn't have to be that way. You chose to stand on the sideline of our lives, to replace us over and over again with someone else."

"I've never tried to replace you, Thea."

The fissure whistled with fresh steam. "You let your second wife sell our house. You let her say that we couldn't live with you. You chose her and every other woman over your daughters. Why?"

"Because you and Liv were better off without me!"

The fissure becoming an eruption. "Is that really what you tell yourself?"

"It's what I told myself then. I was never going to be the kind of man who coached your softball team or, or—"

"Made Saturday morning pancakes?"

"I made money. That's what I did, and I did it well, and that's how I could be a father to you."

"Well, while you were telling yourself that, Liv and I were growing up believing something was wrong with us. Something that made people leave us, would always make people leave us. And now I'm about to lose my husband because I pushed him away out of fear."

Dan looked over sharply. "What's going on with you and Gavin?"

She waved her hands to ward off the question. "I'm not here for fatherly advice, so don't, like, pull a muscle or anything. Just tell me one thing."

Oh, God. She was going to do it. She was going to ask the question that had haunted her her entire life.

"Do you regret . . ." She puffed out a breath. "Me?"

"Never," Dan said, his voice rough and certain. "Never. Not once."

Thea closed her eyes.

"Look at me," her father ordered. And for the second time, she met his gaze directly. "Your mother getting pregnant was the best thing that ever happened to me. I was simply too stupid and selfish to know how to be the father you deserved."

The door to the church opened, and a frantic-looking woman in a red suit emerged, her head darting back and forth.

Dan sighed.

"Is that the wedding planner?"

"Yeah."

"She looks like she's afraid the groom got cold feet. You better go in."

He nodded, lost in thought for a moment. Then he opened his door. "I hope you'll stay," he said. "But I'll understand if you don't."

Thea watched him jog across the street. The wedding planner spotted him and threw her hands in the air.

Dan soothed her, apparently reassured her, because they turned and walked up the stairs to the church. At the doors, he looked back.

And then he walked inside.

Thea wiped her hands across her cheeks. Great. Now her

makeup would be streaked. Which, actually, was as good an excuse as any for leaving.

She looked at her purse on the floor, where she'd irrationally and impulsively shoved *The Annoying Countess* when she left this morning.

Thea pulled the book from her purse and opened it to the place where she'd stopped reading last night.

*B*enedict blinked. Coughed. Tugged on his coat. "I—I will have our coach brought around."

"You mistake me, my lord. I'm going to the country."

No. Dear God, no. "Irena, please."

"I cannot heal a festering wound that you refuse to acknowledge, Benedict, nor will I allow myself to be blamed for it."

"I haven't asked you to do either."

"You may visit when you feel you are ready for an heir, and we can negotiate the terms of—" her voice caught— "of procreation. But I can't do this."

"Irena, please. I love you."

"I thought you'd learned at least that much, my lord. Love isn't enough."

What bullshit. What utter molly-coddled bullshit.

Love is enough.

It's always enough.

Thea got out of the car and jogged in her heels across the

street. She walked in with barely five minutes to spare. A woman in a pink suit gave her a program and a dirty look when she quick-stepped through the vestibule. A string quartet played something soft and romantic as Thea walked in. The groomsmen had already lined up along the altar in matching dark gray tuxedos. She didn't recognize a single man up there, save her father, who stood by the pastor, hands clasped in front and rocking back and forth on the balls of his feet like a nervous, first-time groom.

Thea slid into a seat in the second-to-last pew, earning an annoyed glare from another couple, as the string quartet began to play "Canon in D." Bridesmaids in emerald green dresses slow-walked down the aisle clutching red roses. Then the congregation rose and turned for the big moment—the bride. Her new step-mother.

Thea couldn't see her face well behind her veil, but she looked no older than Thea. Her smile shone through the lace netting that otherwise camouflaged her face. She locked eyes with Dan, who never once looked away as she approached on her father's arm. And when she reached the end of the aisle, Dan took her hand with a look of—holy shit, he was head over heels in love.

This was real for him.

And for Jessica.

And Thea knew it because she knew that look. She knew what it felt like.

Oh, God. What had she been thinking? She should have gone after Gavin, the man who loved her despite the many ways she'd held him at arm's length. Not drive to Atlanta for a man who didn't know how to love her. Thea checked the time on her phone every three minutes, earning annoyed glances from the couple sitting next to her. Yeah, yeah. She had come in late and couldn't wait to get out of there. So what? Didn't they know this was an emergency? Didn't they know she had to go save her marriage?

And she was going to. As soon as the bride kissed the groom, she was going to New York to do the thing she thought she'd never do.

She was going to beg her husband to take her back.

CHAPTER THIRTY

"Why are we running?" Mack yelled.

They were all running.

Mack. Del. Yan. The Russian. Gavin. Running up a crooked sidewalk in Atlanta toward the giant church in the distance.

"Because this is grand gesture," the Russian panted. "You always run for grand gesture."

"And because you parked seven blocks away!" Gavin yelled.

Mack protested something about the GPS on his phone being wrong, but Gavin didn't care. He could see the church, and nothing was going to stop him from getting to his wife. So he ran faster. He'd been running since he got off the plane. He ran through the airport. Ran to his car. They picked up Mack and the Russian on the way and drove as fast as possible.

But it was now after three, and they were late.

So he sprinted. Because if he missed the vows, he missed his chance.

. . .

Finally, after what felt like an hour, the bride and groom faced each other for their vows.

Thea bounced her knee up and down, earning another glare.

Her father went first. He recited every word when prompted, though he probably had the words memorized by now. He vowed to love her. To cherish her. To be her best friend through sickness and health and all that.

Thea checked the time.

The bride quietly began to recite the same stuff as her father.

Love. Honor. Cherish. Sickness. Health. I do. I do.

Jesus, just kiss already!

The crowd clapped as her father dipped his head to kiss his bride, but a massive crash at the back of the church sent bride and groom apart. Every head swiveled, ladies gasped in surprise, and men exclaimed a creative collection of bad words.

But then a voice rose above it all. A loud, panty stammer.

"I d-d-do."

CHAPTER THIRTY-ONE

Okay, so, he maybe should have thought this through.

Two hundred stunned faces stared at Gavin in the doorway. The bride's hand flew to her mouth, and the groom—uh, yikes. Thea's father looked like a storm.

A man from the bride's side leapt to his feet. "What the hell is the meaning of this?" he boomed. "This is my daughter's wedding."

The pounding sound of running and skidding brought the congregation into a collective lean so they could peer behind Gavin.

Mack skidded to a stop next to him. "Shit."

Del bent and panted, hands on knees. "Did we miss the vows?"

Yan and the Russian collapsed against the wall.

"What is going on?" the man up front demanded again. "Who are you people?"

Mack lifted his hand. "Braden Mack."

Gavin tugged down on his suit coat. "Sorry. I'm, uh, I'm looking for Thea."

"Who the hell is Thea?" the man barked.

"My daughter," Dan said, pointing toward a pew in the back. Gavin could've sworn that Dan was smiling now.

Every head followed Dan's point, and that's when he finally saw her. Sitting no more than twenty feet away, mouth agape, chest rising and falling with labored breath. She stood slowly. A thousand emotions danced across her face—surprise, embarrassment, amusement. *Love.*

"Hi," she breathed.

Gavin wiped sweat from his brow. "Hi. Can w-we—" He motioned to the door behind him.

Thea scooted down the pew, bumping into knees, murmuring *sorry, excuse me, sorry* until she made it out. She looked up the aisle at her father. "I'm going to, um . . . I'm going to go now."

"You're staying for the reception, right?" the bride asked.

"Not sure yet?" Thea squeaked.

"I hope you do, because we haven't even met yet."

Heads in the congregation swiveled back and forth during the conversation.

"Right," Thea said. "Nice to meet you. Sorry. I'm going to just go . . ."

Thea walked stiffly on quick steps toward the door. Gavin waved as he backed up. "Sorry for the interruption."

He pulled the door shut as he backed out, turned around, and—

"Damn you, Gavin," Thea said. "*I* was going to do the grand gesture."

Then she grabbed his lapels, yanked him forward, and kissed

him. Oh, how she kissed him. She kissed him with her hands in his hair, her heart on her sleeve.

She kissed him as she spoke. "I was going to go to New York." Kiss.

"I was going to find you." Bigger kiss.

"I was going to walk in and tell you . . ." Deeper kiss.

"I love you."

Gavin cupped her face and pulled back. "Say it again."

"I love you, Gavin. I love you. And I'm so sorry. You were right about me. I was scared and stupid."

"So was I."

"We'll probably be scared and stupid again at some point."

"But we'll get through it," he vowed.

Mack cleared his throat. "Speed this up. They're almost done with their vows."

Right. He wasn't done. Grand gesture wasn't over. Gavin dropped to one knee and took Thea's hand.

"What are you doing?" Thea laughed.

"I didn't get a chance to do this right before, so I'm doing it now. Thea Scott, will you marry me?"

"Right now?"

"Yes. Right now. We're in a church."

Thea laughed as Gavin stood. "Russian," he panted. "Come here."

"His name is Russian?"

"My name is Vlad. Sorry about your bathroom."

"So you guys . . . you're the bromance book club?" Thea said.

Mack nodded slowly, then quickly. "I like that. The Bromance Book Club."

"Just do it," Gavin said.

He took Thea's hands and faced her.

"Repeat after me," Vlad said, unfolding the paper Gavin had given him. "I, Gavin Scott—"

"I, Gavin Scott."

There was applause inside the church.

"Promise you, Thea Scott."

"Promise you, Thea Scott."

Music blared. Shit. Gavin tore the paper from Vlad's hands and repeated it by memory. "Promise you, Thea Scott, to always tell you how I feel. To read to you every night. To cherish your body—"

Mack and Del covered their ears. "Not in front of the children!"

Gavin tugged her close and whispered the rest in her ear. "And to never forget that love—"

"Is enough," Thea breathed.

Gavin kissed her again just as the doors burst open and the new bride and groom—the other new bride and groom—strode out on a wave of applause and "Canon in D."

"Well," Dan said flatly. "I see things are working out."

Gavin looked at his father-in-law, a man he'd just as soon punch in the face than anything else. "Sorry we can't stay, Dan. We have our happy ending to live."

Gavin scooped Thea in his arms. "Ready, my love?"

Thea traced a line down his jaw. "I'm at your mercy, my lord."

EPILOGUE

Christmas Eve

Thea curled into Gavin's side and trailed her fingers lazily up and down his stomach. The lights of the Christmas tree cast their bodies in a soft, yellow glow. Upstairs, the girls were asleep, dreaming of sugarplums and new Nintendo games.

Downstairs, Mom and Dad renewed their vows over and over again.

Gavin's voice was tired as he read to her. They'd read every night since Atlanta. Just a different book.

"*Irena, wait!*"

Benedict raced after his wife. The shocked gasps and stares of the members of the ton *who were so eager to shun her now couldn't tear their eyes away from the drama playing out before them.*

Benedict stalked across the ballroom.

Irena whipped around. "My Lord, don't do this."

"Don't do what? Admit in front of the entire world that I love you?"

More gasps greeted his words.

Benedict stalked toward her, wrapped an arm around her waist, and—

Gavin stopped. "Should he kiss her or ask permission?"

Thea hmm'd. "At this point, I think a sneak-attack kiss is good. This is his grand gesture, and that's the best part."

Gavin kissed her nose. "Agree."

and wrapped an arm around her waist. "I'm here to propose to my wife."

And then he kissed her. In front of everyone. The gossips tittered. The young women swooned. Irena swayed on her feet and into him.

"I love you," he breathed into her mouth. "I married you because I love you. You have changed me as a man. You have made me a better man."

Gavin looked down at Thea. "I can relate to that."

Thea lifted her lips and kissed him. Her lips lingered and nudged his as her hands drifted lower on his body.

Gavin smiled. "Are we d-done reading?"

"Mmm."

Gavin dropped the book and rolled them both over. Thea lifted her legs around his waist and kissed him with as much emotion as she could convey. They were getting so good at talking.

Gavin slanted his mouth against hers, and things went from zero to orgasmic. Need clawed inside her skin—need and desire and jumpy-jumpy girly emotions that made her tremble in his arms.

"I can't get enough of you," Gavin rasped, fingers working the buttons of her jersey. The new one. The old one was ripped. He slid the shirt open to reveal her breasts and lowered his mouth to one nipple and then the other.

Thea reached between them and freed his erection from his shorts, and then, oh God, he was inside her. "I can't get enough of you, either."

Gavin breathed a reverent curse.

He stretched her. Filled her. Loved her.

"Talk to me," Thea whispered. "Tell me what you want."

Gavin rolled them again until she was on top. "I want you to ride me," he groaned.

She rose up and down. Rocking her hips to take him farther each time. They breathed each other in, mouth hovering over mouth, hips tilting and thrusting as one.

"I want you to take your pleasure," he rasped.

Thea bent until nipples brushed the course hair of his chest.

"I want you to love me forever, Thea."

Her orgasm hit suddenly. As it did so often now. As if there existed inside her a deep well of trust that only Gavin could touch.

"I love you," he said, holding her as she rode out the waves of pleasure.

"I love you," she answered, moving again, lifting and lowering until he shuddered with a deep upward thrust, her name a prayer on his lips.

Thea slumped against his chest, face buried in the crook of his neck.

He held her there, fingers woven into her hair. "How d-do you think it will end?" he asked.

"I think Benedict and Irena have earned their happy ever after," she whispered.

"Me too," Gavin said. He kissed her hair. "I think we have too."

Thea felt her throat thicken. They had almost lost this. They had almost lost each other.

She rose on her elbow to gaze down at him. "Know what I think?"

"Tell me."

"I like our happy ending best."

It was a long time before they slept.

Lauren Perry of Perrywinkle Photography

Lyssa Kay Adams read her first romance novel at a very young age when she swiped one from her grandmother's stash. After a long journalism career in which she had to write way too many sad endings, she decided to return to the stories that guaranteed a happy-ever-after. Once described as "funny, adorable, and a wee bit heart-breaking," Lyssa's books feature women who always get the last word, men who aren't afraid to cry, and dogs. Lots of dogs. Lyssa writes full time from her home in Michigan, where she lives with her sportswriter husband, her wickedly funny daughter, and a spoiled Maltese who likes to be rocked to sleep like a baby. When she's not writing, she's cooking or driving her daughter around from one sporting event to the next. Or rocking the dog.

Ready to find
your next great read?

Let us help.

Visit prh.com/nextread